"Evidently we have succeeded," Medina said. "The men have captured the gods."

"Or the baboons have captured the men," said Narden.

Medina shrugged. "Choose your own analogy, Major. Just be careful not to take it too seriously. The Cibarrans have existed longer than we; they've had time to learn more, even to develop more brain . . . it does not make them supernatural," he finished. "I've always suspected that intellect is a necessary but somewhat overrated quality. Baboons have killed men in the past, and now men have made prisoners of half a dozen Cibarrans."

Narden shifted in his chair. The office was a shining bleakness around him, broken only by the regulation portrait of the Imperial Mother and a map of Earth. "Baboons are extinct," Narden pointed out.

"They never learned how to make guns."

THE GODS LAUGHED

POUL ANDERSON

The Gods Laughed

TOR

A TOM DOHERTY ASSOCIATES BOOK

Copyright © 1982 by Poul Anderson

A TOR Book

Published by Tom Doherty Associates, Inc., 8-10 West 36th Street, New York, New York 10018

First TOR printing, November 1982

ISBN: 523-48-550-6

Cover art by Michael Whelan

Printed in the United States of America

Distributed by:
Pinnacle Books, Inc.
1430 Broadway
New York, New York 10018

Table of Contents

The Martyr   7

Nightpiece   35

When Half Gods Go   57

Peek! I See You!   73

Details   117

Captive of the Centaurianess   149

Soldier From the Stars   233

The Word to Space   269

A Little Knowledge   291

Acknowledgements: The stories contained herein were first published and copyrighted as follows:

"The Martyr:" *The Magazine of Fantasy and Science Fiction,* copyright©1960 by Mercury Press, Inc.

"Night Piece:" *The Magazine of Fantasy and Science Fiction,* copyright©1961 by Mercury Press, Inc.

"When Half Gods Go:" *The Magazine of Fantasy and Science Fiction,* copyright©1953 by Mercury Press, Inc.

"Peek! I See You!" *Analog,* copyright©1968 by Conde Nast Publications, Inc.

"Details:" *Worlds of If,* copyright©1956 by Galaxy Publishing Corporation

"Captive of the Centaurianess:" *Isaac Asimov's Science Fiction Adventure Magazine,* copyright©1978 by Davis Publications.

"Soldier From the Stars:" *Fantastic Universe,* copyright©1955 by Great American Publications, Inc.

"The Word to Space:" *The Magazine of Fantasy and Science Fiction,* copyright©1960 by Mercury Press, Inc.

"A Little Knowledge:" *Analog,* copyright©1971 by Conde Nast Publications, Inc.

THE MARTYR

"Evidently we have succeeded," Medina said. "The men have captured the gods."

"Or the baboons have captured the men," said Narden.

Medina shrugged. "Choose your own analogy, Major. Just be careful not to take it too seriously. The Cibarrans have existed longer than we; they've had time to learn more, even to develop more brain . . . perhaps. And what of it?" An expression crossed his flat countenance, but not one that Narden could interpret. He gestured above his desk with a cigar. "It does not make them supernatural," he finished. "I've always suspected that intellect is a necessary but somewhat over-rated quality. As witness the fact that baboons have killed men in the past, and now men have made prisoners of half a dozen Cibarrans."

Narden shifted in his chair. The office was a

shining bleakness around him, broken only by the regulation portrait of the Imperial Mother and a map of Earth which, X light-years away in direction Y, betrayed a milligram of human sentimentalism in the hard alloy of Colonel-General Wan K'ung Medina.

"Baboons are extinct," Narden pointed out.

"They never learned how to make guns," snapped the other man. "We'll be extinct too, some generations hence, if we don't overhaul Cibarra."

"I can't believe that, sir. They've never threatened us or anyone else. Everything we've been able to find out about them, their activities at home, on other planets, it's all been benign, helpful, they've come as teachers and—" Narden's voice trailed clumsily off.

"Yes," gibed Medina. "Spiritual teaching, personal discipline, a kind of super-Buddhism *sans* karma. Plus some information on astronomy, physics, generalized biology. Practical assistance here and there, like making a Ta-Tao High Dam possible on Yosev. But any basic instruction in psi? Any hints how to develop our own latent powers—or even any proof or disproof, once and for all, that our race does have such powers in any reliable degree? If they really gave a hoot and a yelp for us, Major, you know they couldn't watch us break our hearts looking for something they know all about. But never a word. In fifty years of contact, fifty years of watching them do everything from dowsing to telepathic multiple hookups and teleportation across light-years . . . we've never gotten a straight answer to one single question about the subject. The same bland smile and the same verbal side-stepping. Or silence, if we persist. God of Man, but they're good at silence!"

"Maybe we have to find all these things out for ourselves," Narden ventured. "Maybe psi works differently for different species, or simply can't be taught, or—"

"Then why don't they tell us so?" exploded Medina. "All they offer us, if you analyze the pattern, is distraction. Twenty years ago, on Marjan, Elberg was studying the Dunne Effect. He'd gotten some very promising results. He showed them to a Cibarran who chanced to be on the same planet. The Cibarran said something about resonances, demonstrated an unsuspected electric phenomenon . . . well, you know the rest. Elberg spent the remainder of his life working on electron-wave resonance. He came up with some extraordinary things. But all in the field of physics. His original psionic data have gathered dust ever since. I could give you a hundred similar cases. I've collected them for years. It makes a totally consistent pattern. The Cibarrans are not giving out any psionic information whatsoever; and most of the intellectual 'assistance' we get from them turns out to be a red herring pointed away from that trail." His fist struck the desk. "Our independent research has taught us just enough about psionics to show we can't imagine its potentialities. And yet the Cibarrans are trying to keep it from us. Does that sound friendly?"

Narden wet his lips. "Perhaps we can't be trusted, sir. Our behavior in the present instance suggests as much."

Medina thrust out his jaw. "You volunteered, Major. Too late now for jellyfishing."

Narden felt himself redden. He was a young

man, stocky and blond like many citizens of Tau Ceti II, speaking Lingua Terra with their Russki accent. The black and silver uniform of the Imperial Astronaval Service, scientific corps, fitted him crisply; but the awkwardness of the provincial lay beneath. "I volunteered for a possibly dangerous but important mission, sir. That was all I knew."

Medina grinned. "Well?"

After a pause, the general added, "It might cost us our lives, our sanity—even our honor, for the Imperium will have to disown us if we fail and this becomes public. So you'll understand, Major, that shooting a man who drags his feet on the job won't bother me in the least." Harshly; "If we succeed, we stand to gain a million years of progress, overnight. Men have taken bigger chances for less. We're going to learn from those prisoners. Gently if possible, but we'll take them apart cell by cell if we must. Now go talk to them and start your work!"

Baris Narden saluted and marched from the office.

The corridor was even more sterile, a white tunnel where his heels clacked hollowly and a humming came from behind closed doors. Now and then he passed a man, but they didn't speak. There was too much silence. Light-years of silence, thought Narden—beyond these caves, the rock and the iron plains of the rogue planet, glaciers and snowfields that were frozen atmosphere, under the keen glitter of a million stars. Perhaps a dozen men of the hundred-odd manning this base knew its location and its sunless orbit. This was like being dead. He remembered the hills of Novaya Mechta, his father's house under mur-

murous trees, and wondered what had driven him thence. Ambition, he thought wearily; the Imperium and its glamour; most of all, the wish to learn. So now he had his science degree, and his small triumphs in the difficult field of psionic research, and was lately a collaborator in kidnapping, which might lead to torture and murder . . . oh, yes, a career.

The guards at the entrance to the research area let him through without fuss. Medina wasn't interested in passes, countersigns, or other incantations. Beyond lay a complex of laboratories and offices. A door stood open to a room where Mahammed Kerintji worked amid crowded apparatus. Meters flickered before him, and the air was filled with an irregular buzzing that sawed at the nerves.

The small dark man didn't seem bothered. He glanced up as Narden passed, and nodded. "Ah, there, Major."

"All serene, Captain?" asked Narden automatically.

"Quite, and better." Kerintji's eyes glistened. "I am not only keeping our tigers tame, but learning a few new things."

"Oh?" Narden stepped into the room.

"Yes. First and foremost, of course, General Medina's basic idea is triumphantly confirmed. Faint, randomly pulsed currents, induced in their nervous systems by the energies I am beaming in at them, do inhibit their psionic powers. They've not teleported out of here, telekinecticized me outdoors, anything at all." Kerintji chuckled. "Obviously! Or we wouldn't be here. Maybe this entire planet wouldn't be here. The facts do not, however, confirm the general's hypothesis that psionic energies arise in the brain analogously to ordinary encephalographic waves."

"Why not?" Despite himself, Narden felt an upsurge of interest. This all fitted in with his previous laboratory results.

"Look at these meters. They are set in a dowser-type hookup. Energy is required to move the needles against the tension of springs. And the needles are being moved, in a pattern correlated with the randomizer's nerve-currents. Furthermore, the work done against the springs represents too much energy for any living nervous system to carry. The neurones would burn out. Ergo, the randomizer which keeps the Cibarrans helpless does not do so by suppressing their psionic output, but merely prevents them from controlling it. Also ergo, the energy does not come from the nervous system, which is probably just the modulator."

Narden nodded. "My own data have led me to speculate that the body as a whole may be the generator," he said, "though I've never gotten consistent enough readings to be certain."

"We will now," crowed Kerintji. "We can use calorimetry. Measure every erg passing through the Cibarran organism. If output, including psionic work done, is greater than input, we will know that psi involves tapping some outside, probably cosmic force."

"Those are delicate measurements," warned Narden. "I found out how delicate, in my own lab."

"You were using humans, and had to be careful of them. Also, the human output is so miserably feeble and irregular. But look!" Kerintji twisted a dial. One of his meter needles swung wildly across its scale. "I just quadrupled the randomizing energy. The psi output increased fiftyfold. Like sticking a pin in a man and watching him jump. We can *control* this!"

Narden left, a bit sick.

Another pair of guards stood before the prison suite. It was fitted with a spaceship airlock, the outer valve being dogged shut before the inner one could be opened. Narden wondered if it helped anything except the fears of men. The rooms beyond were large and comfortable. And did that help anything except the consciences of men?

Two Cibarrans occupied a sofa. They didn't get up; their civilization had its rich rituals, but almost entirely on the mental plane. Big amber-colored eyes, and the fronded tendrils above, turned to Narden. He felt afresh, sharply, how beautiful they were. Bipedal mammals, long legs giving a sheer two meters of height, three-clawed feet, slender humanoid hands, wide chest and shoulders, large oval heads with faces not so much flat as delicately sculptured short gray fur over the whole body, thin iridescent kilt and cloak . . . words, without relationship to the feline grace before him.

One of them spoke, in calm, resonant Lingua Terra: "I call myself Alanai at this moment. My companion is Elth."

"Baris Narden." The man shifted from foot to foot. The tiniest of smiles curved Alanai's mouth.

"Please be seated," said Elth. "Would you like refreshment? I am told we can ring for food as required."

Narden found a chair and perched on its edge. "No, thanks." *I may not break bread with you.* "Are you well?"

"As well as can be expected." Alanai's grimace was a work of art. Narden remembered the theory of some xenologists, that Cibarran "telepathy" was in part a matter of gestures and expressions. It was plausible, in a race where each individual evolved a private spoken language to express nuances uniquely his own, and learned those of all his friends. But it would not account for the proven fact that Cibarrans, without apparatus, could travel and communicate across light-years.

"I hope"—Narden dragged the words out—"I hope conditions are not unduly inconvenient."

"The nervous-energy scrambling? Yes and no," said Elth. "We can block off physical pain and prevent lesions. But the deprivation— Imagine being deafened and blinded."

His tone remained gentle.

"I'm afraid it's necessary," Narden mumbled.

"So that we can't escape, or summon help, or otherwise thwart your plans? Granted." Alanai reached out to a crystal-topped coffee table on which stood a chess set. He began to play against himself. It was a swift and even match. Brain-jumbler or not, the Cibarrans retained a mastery of their own minds and bodies such as humans had hardly dreamed about.

"I am curious as to how you engineered the kidnapping," said Elth, not unmaliciously. "I have considered numerous possibilities."

"Well—" Narden hesitated. *The hell with Medina*. "We knew your planet was sending a mission to New Mars. The world we call New Mars, I mean. One of the native tribes had asked your help, via interstellar traders, the usual grapevine, to rationalize and make beautiful its own culture. We've seen a lot of planets where you've done a similar job, and didn't expect you could resist such an appeal, even if it was way out of your normal territory. Our psychotechnicians had spent years putting the chiefs of that tribe up to it."

Elth actually laughed.

Narden plunged on, as if pursued. "What little we've been able to discover about psi indicated certain limitations which could be exploited. You can probably communicate across the universe—"

"There are ancient races in other galaxies," Alanai agreed.

A third Cibarran appeared in the doorway. "There is one entire intelligent galaxy," he said, very low. "We are children at its feet."

"Don't you think we might also want to—" Narden checked himself. "Distance can't block a telepathic message, but noise can. If you aren't actually tuned in on someone who is parsecs away, you'll receive only the babble of billions and trillions of living minds on planets throughout space—and block it out of your own perceptions. So we didn't expect you would get any hint of our plot. After all, New Mars is out in his arm of the galaxy, and Cibarra lies twenty thousand light-years toward the center.

"When your delegation arrived, it was invited to visit the Imperial *charge d'affaires*. He knew nothing; it was routine courtesy. The kidnappers were waiting at his house, unbeknownst to him. They were raw recruits from colonial planets where the languages and cultures are different from Earth's. Our researchers had suggested that you couldn't readily read the mind of someone whose socio-linguistic background was new to you. His conceptual universe would be too different. You'd at least need to study him a short while, classify his way of thinking, before you could put yourselves in rapport. So . . . these men knocked you out with stun beams, whisked you onto a spaceship, and kept you unconscious all the way to this base."

Elth laughed again. "Clever!"

"Don't compliment me," said Narden hastily. "I had nothing to do with it."

"You spoke as if you did," said Alanai.

"Did I?" Narden searched a flustered memory. "Yes. Yes, I did say 'we,' didn't I? Must have been thinking in . . . in collective terms. I was only co-opted at the last minute, after the capture. This isn't being done for selfish reasons, you know."

"Why, then?" asked Alanai, but softly, as if he already knew the answer. And the other Cibarrans grew as still as he.

"Not for ransom, as you may have thought, or—anything but the need of our people," stumbled Narden. "It's been fifty years now . . . since Imperial ships, exploring toward galactic center . . . encountered your race on some of the planets there. We've had sporadic contact, from time to time, since then. Just enough to understand the situation. Your home world is much older than ours—"

"It was," corrected Alanai. "The Lost was a planet of an early Population Two star, hence poor in metals. We lingered ages in a neolithic technology, which may have encouraged our peculiar mental form of development. Physical science was carried out with ceramics, plastics, acid-filled conductors, as pure research only. The final hottening of our sun forced us to leave our home. That was many thousands of years ago; and yet we too, in a way, have known the Lost, and mourned it with our fathers—"

Elth laid a warning hand on his wrist. Alanai seemed to wake from a dream. *"Oa, Anna,"* he murmured.

"Yes," said Narden. "I know all that. I know too how you have chanced to meet them. But only in the smallest ways."

"You could not assimilate physical knowledge at a much greater rate than you are already producing it," said one of the other Cibarrans. Four of them now stood in the door. Narden squared his shoulders and said:

"Perhaps. There are no hard feelings about that. We're quite able to learn whatever we wish in physics. We have no reason to believe you're very far ahead of us in any branch of it, either. You may well lag behind in certain aspects which never interested your civilization, such as robotics. In a finite universe, physics is limited anyway. What embitters us is your withholding the next stage of basic knowledge—your active hindering of us, now and then, in our own search."

Elth said, the barest edge of harshness in his tone, "You captured us hoping to make us teach you about that aspect of reality you call psionics. Or, if we refuse to instruct you—and we do—you will seek to gather data by studying us."

Narden swallowed. "Yes."

Alanai said without haughtiness (and did tears blur his eyes?), "Cibarran philosophers were exploring these concepts before Earth had condensed from cosmic dust. Do you really believe we are reticent because of selfishness?"

"No," said Narden doggedly. "But my people . . . we aren't the kind who accept meekly that father knows best. We've always made our own way. Against beasts and glaciers and ourselves and the physical universe. Now, against gods, if we must.''

Elth shook his head, in a slow regretful motion. "I am as finite as you are," he said. "More, in some ways. I do not believe I could find the courage to live, if I were—" He bit off his words, suddenly alarmed.

"We've got to do this," said Narden. He stood up. "Forgive us."

"There is nothing to forgive," said Alanai. "You cannot help it. You are young and raw and greedy for life. Oh," he whispered, "how you hunger for life!"

"And yet you leave us to stagnate, half animal, when we might also be sending our minds across all space?" Narden looked into the grave strange faces. He knotted his fists together and said, "For your own sakes, help me. I don't want to rip out what you know!"

"For your own sake," said Alanai, "we shall fight back. Every step of the way."

At another date Narden remembered the words. He sighed. "It's been one long struggle."

Medina settled himself more firmly in his chair. "They haven't made any physical resistance," he declared.

"This is not a physical problem," Kerintji reminded him.

Medina had the practicality to leave his scientists alone; but he had finally demanded an informal accounting, which Narden had to admit was reasonable. Elsewhere in artificial caverns, engineers worked with the machines that kept men alive, soldiers drilled and loafed and wished

they were home, technicians pondered the inter-
pretation of measurements and statistical sum-
maries. Here in the central office, Narden felt
immensely apart from it all, somehow more akin
to the prisoners.

Isn't every man? he told himself. *Isn't the
Cibarran silence keeping our whole race locked in
our own skulls?* But he knew, tiredly, that his
indignation was only words. One of the slogans
men invented, to justify their latest cruelty and
most fashionable idiocy.

*If we could see across the universe, and into the
heart, as they do on Cibarra, we wouldn't need
slogans,* Narden thought. The idea straightened
his back a little. He looked across the big desk and
said:

"Since they don't co-operate, we've so far used
them as mere generators of psionic forces. We
were held up for days when they worked out some
method to damp their own output. I think we have,
now, an inkling of how that was done—an interference phenomenon within the nervous system itself, probably painful as hell. But it frustrated us
at the time."

"How did you lick it?" Medina inquired.

"Put one of them under anesthesia," Kerintji
said. "We got no response again, to nervous
stimuli. More organized response, in fact, than
when consciousness was present to throw out
random bursts of energy with deliberate intent to
confuse our readings. So we kept him anesthetized
for a week. After that, the others quit their damp-
ing."

Narden remembered how Alanai had lain
amidst the indignity of intravenous tubes, and
how the machine's nerve-pulses had convulsed his

body until he must be strapped down. He remembered how thin the Cibarran was at last, when they let him waken and returned him to the prison suite. And yet he had looked on them without bitterness. It seemed to Narden, thinking back, that the yellow eyes held pity.

"Never mind the details now," said Medina. "Have you reached any conclusions?"

"In four weeks?" scoffed Kerintji.

"Yes, yes, I know it'll take decades to work out a coherent psi theory. But you must at least have some working hypotheses."

"And some clear conclusions," Narden told him, speaking fast to hold at arm's length the image of Alanai.

"Well?" Thick fingers drummed the desk top.

"First, we've established certain things about the energy involved in these processes. It's never very great, by mechanical standards. But at peak stimulation, it does go far over the total possible output of the physical organism. That proves it must come from elsewhere. The psionic adept, to borrow the common term, puts in a small amount of energy himself; in fact, he radiates constantly in the psionic spectrum at a definite minimum level. But for purposes like doing work on material objects—teleportation, telekinesis—and presumably for all other purposes, he's more analogous to an electronic tube than to a generator. He borrows and modulates the psionic energy already there."

"What do you mean by 'psionic spectrum' and 'psionic energy'?" demanded Medina.

Kerintji shrugged. "A convenient label for a certain class of phenomena. It is not in itself electromagnetic, thermal, or gravitational; and yet it's convertible to those physical forms. For instance, it was proven some years ago by a researcher on Earth that poltergeists do work by altering local gravitational parameters."

"Then physical energy must also be convertible to psionic," Medina said.

Narden nodded, with an increase in his already considerable respect for the general's mind. "Yes, sir. The mechanism which makes the two-way conversion appears to be the living organism itself. Most species, including man, are very weak converters, with almost no control. The Cibarrans are extraordinarily powerful, sensitive, and complex converters. They can do anything they want to, repeatedly, with psionic forces; whereas even the greatest human adepts can do only a few simple things sporadically."

"I gather you knew as much before you ever got here," Medina complained. "What have you learned in *this* project?"

"What do you expect in four weeks?" said Narden, irritated as Kerintji had been. "I think we've done rather well. Having a strong, reliable psionic source at my disposal, I've been able to confirm a few tentative conclusions I'd reached previously. Besides establishing that the individual does not provide all his own psi energy, I've shown that its transmission is at least partly by waves. I've created interference phenomena, you see, as registered by detectors appropriately placed."

Medina pursed his lips. "Are you certain of that, Major? I thought psionic propagation was instantaneous."

"And waves require a finite velocity. True. But I've no idea what the speed of a psionic wave is.

Far beyond that of light, certainly. Maybe it only requires a few seconds to go around the universe. After all, the Cibarrans admit being in communication with distant galaxies."

"But the inverse square law—"

"Somehow, they evade it. Perhaps psionic forces operate continuously, no quantum jumps, and have an exceedingly low noise level. Even so, simple broadcast transmission across interstellar distances is obviously impossible. You yourself, sir, realize the Cibarrans couldn't 'listen in' on all the minds in a sphere light-years across; and then there's also attenuation to overcome. There has to be some kind of tuning or beaming effect. How it works, I don't know."

Kerintji perked up. "Wait a bit, Major," he said. "You were speculating about that too, the other day."

"Sheer speculation," said Narden uncomfortably.

"Let's hear it anyhow," said Medina.

"Well, if you insist. Considering that space is of finite extent, however large, and that psi transmission is by waves, however unlike classical electromagnetics ... it should theoretically be possible to establish a, uh, a standing wave on a cosmic scale. In effect, a vast total amount of psionic energy would pervade all space in an orderly pattern. Its source would be the basic psionic radiation of all life, everywhere in the cosmos. An adept could draw as much of this energy as he needed—and could handle—at any one time, and use it. Living organisms would always be putting more back, so the total would remain nearly constant. In fact, it would increase, because radiated energy isn't lost with the death of the radiator, and new life is always getting born. This adds a rather fantastic clause to the second law of thermodynamics. Physical energy becomes more and more unavailable, as entropy increases, but psionic energy becomes more and more available. Almost as if the universe were slowly evolving from an inanimate, purely physical state, to an ultimate . . . well . . . pure spirit."

Medina snorted. "I'll believe that when I see it!"

"I told you it was speculation," said Narden. "I don't take it seriously myself."

"But it would explain all the facts," interrupted Kerintji eagerly. "The mind modulates this standing wave, do you see. Oh, infinitesimally, of course, compared with the enormous natural amplitude; but the modulation is there. It can ride the standing wave with a phase of velocity of the total. It can be directed and tuned."

"There are even weirder implications," said Narden, a little impatiently. "For one thing, this would mean that the mind isn't a mere epiphenomenon of the brain. The modulations of the cosmic wave may be as important to the mind's existence as the physical modifications of neurones and synapses. But don't you see, General, we can't go yondering off like that. We have to work step by step, grab one fact at a time. Fifty years from now it may be possible to talk about mind versus body, and make sense. Right now, it's a waste of man-hours that should be spent measuring the constants of propagation."

"Or getting those damned Cibarrans to co-operate," grumbled Kerintji.

Medina nodded. "Yes, I understand. Actually, gentlemen, I brought you here to discuss practical problems. I only wanted to necessary background first."

He stared at the map of Earth for a while. Then, swiftly, as if his words were a bayonet: "I expected something like this. Planned on it. But there was always a chance the Cibarrans would give up, or that you would make some breakthrough. I suppose both chances still exist. But they look smaller every day, don't they? So this will have to be done the hard way. Years. Our entire lifetimes, perhaps. Not even any home leaves, for any of us, I'm afraid. Because the other Cibarrans will wonder what's happened to their mission, and go looking through the galaxy . . . telepathic. . . ." He took a cigar from the box on his desk, stuck it in his mouth and puffed savagely to light it. "I'll do what I can to make conditions tolerable. We'll enlarge the caverns, build parks and other recreation facilities. Eventually we may even be able to bring in some prospective wives for our personnel. But"—wryly—"I'm afraid we're prisoners too."

Narden entered the suite and closed its inner valve. The six Cibarrans were gathered in the living room. He was shocked to note how gaunt they all were, how their pelts had grown dull. Alanai was almost a skeleton, only his eyes alive. Narden thought: *Being locked up this way, and probed, and watched, and always feeling the energy chaos in their nerve cells, which deafens and blinds their inmost selves, is destroying them. They're going to end my own captivity by dying.*

The ridiculous flutter of hope disappeared. *No. We have bio-chemists on our staff, who understand their metabolisms too well. Vitamins, hormones, enzymes, bioelectrics will bar that road too.*

Elth said quietly, "There is grief in you, Baris."

Narden halted. When he stood, and they sat on the floor or stretched on the couches, his head was above theirs. "I've conferred with General Medina," he said.

One who sometimes called himself Ionar and sometimes Dwanin, but mostly used a trill of music for his name, stirred. "Your determination was reaffirmed," he said.

Their understanding of the human mind no longer astonished Narden. He had learned to allow for the fact that they usually knew in advance, from sheer logic, what he would try next. "We'll continue as long as we must," he told them. "Do you know what that means?"

"Until we are all dead." Alanai's words were barely audible.

"Or rescued," said Elth. "Even unhelped by our own telepathy, our friends will suspect what has happened."

"This is too big a galaxy to ransack," Narden said. "Everyone who knows anything about the project is right here. Why are you holding out? Do you think I enjoy what's being done to you?"

"I beg." Alanai raised one strengthless hand. "Do not hurt yourself so. Your own pain is the worst one we have to endure."

"You can end it all, and go free, any time you wish," Narden replied. "We're not afraid of reprisals from your planet; that isn't in your nature. We'll make any reparation we can. But if you really care about us— Can't you see what it's beginning to do to my race, what it will do more and more as the years go by . . . this living in the shadow of beings who're like gods? Who own powers that make our sciences look like a child playing in the mud? If we can't have a share, even a small share, in the things and discoveries that matter, what's the use of our existing at all?"

Ionar groaned aloud. "Don't," he said. "Have we not watched this happen before, again and again, in the long history of our race? Let us help you in the only way we can. Let us show your people how to make the cultural adjustment and be content with what they have and what they are."

Something stirred in Narden, lifted his bent head and crackled through his voice. "Let you domesticate us, you mean? No, before God! We're men, not those miserable dog-peoples we've found on too many planets where you've been!"

Elth leaned forward. "But see here," he argued, "how do you know psionics would be of any value to you? Do you envy the Osirian his ability to breathe hydrogen, or the Vegan his immunity to ultraviolet radiation?"

"Those aren't lacks which handicap us," Narden snapped. "We can send a remote-control robot anywhere one of those races can go. But how can we even know what we *are* until—"

The idea flashed through him, wildest of chance shots, but he hurried on without daring to stop:

"—our minds have also ridden the standing wave around the universe?"

It grew totally quiet in the room. So quiet that for an instant Narden thought he had been deafened, and knew a little of the horror that his randomizers were working in the Cibarrans, and wondered at a spirit which could endure it and not even need to forgive. But his feeling vanished in the upward leap of a flame.

By Man and Man's God, I've hit a mark! They

*can't hide their own shock. They believed they
could keep me plodding indefinitely, and hoped
something would turn up meanwhile to save them.
Now ... my friends, it is already too late for you!*

Elth spoke, and his lips were the only thing
which moved in all that gray band of beings. "So
you have hypothesized it? I did not believe any
human had quite that much intuitive ability."

"And I'm going to work along those lines."
Narden tried to keep his voice from shaking. His
pulse roared in his ears. "Even so vague and
general an idea puts me fifty years ahead. I'll
know what to try, what to look for. The theoreti-
cians can develop the concept mathematically.
The biologists can work on the exact method of psi
generation. Eventually there'll be an artificial
generator, a mutant animal perhaps, for making
controlled experiments. There's no way short of
war for Cibarra to stop us!" It was anticlimax, but
he dropped his tone again and added, "Why don't
you help us, then, instead of hindering?"

None of them had really listened. Eyes began to
seek eyes. A few words murmured in an unknown
language. Alanai gestured. Elth sprang to him.
Alanai got up, slowly and painfully, leaning on the
other. He passed from the room. The rest followed.

Somehow it was a procession.

Narden gaped a moment, sprang forward and
caught the arm of Ionar, who was at the end of the
line. "Where are you going?" he cried. "What's all
this about?"

Now the amber eyes looked down on him. "We
had discussed this contingency," said the
Cibarran. "We delayed, because physical life is
sweet and none of us had explored its limits yet.
But you leave us no choice."

With sudden unexpected strength, he broke loose and glided out through the doorway. Narden stood staring. He heard a murmur of their voices; perhaps they sang, he couldn't be sure.

Kerintji screamed through an intercom: "Get in there, you idiot! Stop them! They're killing him!"

Narden remembered in shock that every room here had a spy lens. He cracked his paralysis and ran. The main valve opened behind him and a pair of soldiers burst in.

Alanai was already dead. Elth and another Cibarran had broken his neck with a single skillful twist. They laid the body down and turned calmly to face the Imperial guns.

"Don't move," Narden heard himself shrill, and as if far away.

"Separate them," chattered Kerintji through the intercom. "Chain them up. Keep a suicide watch—"

"Whatever you wish," said Elth. "We have completed it."

He stooped and with a slow, tender gesture closed the eyes of Alanai. Yet Narden thought his tone had not entirely hidden an eagerness, like a child on birthday morning.

"They didn't do it for no reason," Medina puffed till smoke hid his face. "They sacrificed the weakened one, who'd be easiest to kill. Didn't even try to eliminate any others. What touched off their action?"

"My guess about the nature of psionic transmission wasn't too far off," Narden said. "They didn't dare let me continue my work."

"But we still have five of them, and the body of the sixth." Medina glanced at Kerintji. "No luck with re-animation, eh?"

"No, sir." The little man shook his head. "Our medics used emergency techniques immediately: opened the skull and applied direct nutrition and stimulation to the brain, as well as the usual visceral procedures. They put in a spiral jack, by-passing the damaged section of cord. By that time, any human would have been conscious again. You would at least expect the organs to respond individually. But no, the Cibarran stayed dead. I mean dead. A piece of meat. Microscopic tissue sections were examined, and even the less organized cells, such as the liver, were inert."

"Well," Medina said, "I guess we can't expect critters from another planet to die after our own patterns."

"But they ought to, sir," Kerintji protested. "They breathe oxygen, metabolize carbohydrates and amino acids, just like us. Their cells have nuclei, genes, chromosomes. Oh, there are peculiarities, of course, such as a very fine net-work of filaments in every cell, whose purpose we don't understand at all. But they should not be *that* different!"

Medina ground out his cigar, stared at it, and fumbled after another. "We'll find out," he said. "Maybe. You're such a good guesser, Major Narden, suppose you tell us why they did this."

"I don't know," said Narden slowly. "I don't seem able to think about it."

"For Mother's sake! Control that damned con-science of yours! We're doing this for man, the whole race, all our descendants, from now till the end of forever."

Narden remembered Alanai again, as if across ages of time. *"You cannot help it. You are young*

*and raw and greedy for life. Oh, how you hunger
for life!"* But his brain felt stiff and strange. He sat
unmoving.

Kerintji said, tense in the lips, "I can guess,
General. And if I am right, we had best evacuate
the whole project elsewhere. At the instant he
died, when he didn't really need his nervous
system any longer, Alanai could have burned it out
by transmitting a telepathic call loud enough to be
heard at Cibarra through the interference of our
inhibitor and all the usual noise. A shout to bring
them here—"

"Yes."

When the word was spoken, Medina laid down
his cigar and sat like a yellow meal sack, all the
life drained from his face. Narden and Kerintji
must turn around in their chairs to see. Kerintji's
hand dropped to his belt and a pistol leaped up. A
force that tore the skin off his fingers yanked
away the gun. It clattered across the floor.

Narden thought, somewhere at the back of his
awareness, that he had always been expecting this
moment. He looked up and up the tall gray form,
to the amber gaze which could not be troubled to
hold anger at him. The head was enclosed in a cage
of wires and the air about it shimmered. He decided vaguely that it must protect against the randomizing energies. Doubtless only the necessity of
constructing such helmets had delayed the rescue
these few hours.

"I congratulate you upon your deduction," said
the voice which was music even in man's
language. "You need not be alarmed for your own
safety. Your victims will now depart, of course,
and we shall take precautions against a repetition
of episodes such as this, but that concerns only

ourselves. It is not our way to interfere with the freedom of others, it would be damaging to our own ethos, but we shall publicly appeal to the Imperium to desist from this research, as being too dangerous; and I think, in the course of time, that men will heed."

Narden rose. He took a step toward the Cibarran, and was halted by an unseen wall. He raised his hands. "But it is my work!" he cried aloud.

The impersonal eyes could not have pierced his skull; but the Cibarran asked gently, "Was there not a house in the forest, on a planet called Novaya Mechta?"

Another shape flashed into the office, Elth. He was helmetless—the randomizer must now be silenced—and his tendrils shivered with joy. "I have come to say goodbye, Baris."

Medina covered his face. "Damn you, damn you."

"We learned something," Kerintji snarled. "A few of us, in spite of all you can do, will keep learning. One day it won't be enough for you to commit murder and get help. There will be no help for you anywhere."

Narden stood silent once again. He had no idea if some little part of him, a rudimentary molecule which might in a million years of evolution become a true psionic organ, had caught one of the great thoughts now swirling and singing around him. It might have been subconscious logic, even. "No," he said.

"What?" Kerintji blinked. And now the Cibarrans grew still.

"Your burnout theory," Narden said. It felt like a stranger talking. "They hope we'll think that was how Alanai got the word to them. But it's another false trail. Communication is by patterns, not by

chaotic bursts of energy. How could he have
organized his nervous system enough, especially
when he was dying? The randomizer was in
operation all that while. No . . . remember what I
also theorized . . . that the pattern which is the
mind could be imposed on the cosmic wave, as
well as on the neurone complex? He died to make
the transfer complete. To liberate his mind, so to
speak, from the confused body. He didn't send a
shout to Cibarra. He went there himself, as a wave
pattern!"

Medina looked up. "You don't mean he's still
alive?" he choked.

"In a way." Narden's words tumbled over each
other. He himself, his consciousness, did not know
whither they led. "In a very real way, yes. But not
identically with his life while the body functioned.
He hasn't got physical parts or senses any longer,
you see. But of course, he must have gained new
psionic abilities which more than compensate. He
could speak mind to mind with living Cibarrans,
tell them the facts—and then, maybe, go on to the
next phase of his existence, like a butterfly leaving
the cocoon—"

He turned to the watching Cibarrans and
shouted, "That's what you've been trying so hard
to keep us from finding out, that death isn't the
end! But why? You claim to be interested in our
happiness. You couldn't have told us anything more
wonderful than that we have immortal souls!"

The stranger vanished. Elth remained a second
more. Narden realized it was a surrender: the answer given now because it would be discovered anyway, unless these humans joined in hiding the fact.
When he spoke, it was with surgical compassion.

"You don't," he said.

Although highly appreciative of the honor, I can't help feeling that asking me to pick my favorite among my own stories is like inquiring whether I like Maine lobster, Moselle wine, or Dutch cigars best. Such things may all be found at the dinner table, but aren't really commensurable. In the same way, the works of a writer who tries his hand at a variety of motifs and approaches, both in and out of science fiction, can't fall into a single file of preference for him. The choice is further confused by all the subjective factors involved, the degree of his personal interest in a theme, private associations which may lend an extra flavor to some particular item, perhaps merely the good or bad mood he was in when he wrote it.

Still, an author obviously prefers *some* stories to some others, whatever may be his reasons for doing so. I've stuck my neck out by choosing *Night Piece* for this collection. It's quite unlike anything else I've done. But that's precisely why I'm fond of it. The basic idea of the story, the problem which arises as a consequence of that assumption, and the resolution of the problem, could have been handled in a straightforward narrative fashion. That didn't seem very challenging, though, nor very rewarding in this case, where the significant action takes place entirely within a man's mind. I have no pretensions to being a Kafka or a Capek, but it did seem to me it would be interesting to use, or attempt to use, some of their techniques. By going at the job sideways, perhaps I could suggest what it would actually feel like to be caught in a situation such as was being postulated.

Therefore *Night Piece* is at least three concurrent stories, two of them symbolic. I'm not likely to do anything of this sort very often—some of those archetypes scared the hell out of me—but I hope that I succeeded in getting across a small part of that which I was trying to get across.

However, my success or failure is for you, the reader, to judge.

POUL ANDERSON

NIGHT PIECE

He had not gone far from the laboratory when he heard the footsteps. Even then he could sense they were not human, but he stopped and turned about with a fluttering hope that they might be, after all.

It was late on Wednesday night. His assistants had quit at five, leaving him to phone his wife that she had better not wait up, then fry some hash over a Bunsen burner and return to the instrument that was beginning to function. He had often done so, and afterward walked the mile to a bus stop where he could get a ride directly home. His wife worried about him, but he told her this was a peaceful industrial section, himself nearly the last living man after dark, in no danger of robbery or murder. The walk relaxed him, filled his lungs with cool air and cleared his brain of potential dreams.

Tonight, when the symptoms began, sheer habit

had made him lock the door and start out afoot. The steps behind made him wonder if he should have called a taxi. Not that wheels could outpace the thing, but there might have been some comfort in the driver's stolid presence. *To be sure*, he thought, *if it is a holdup man—*

The hope died as he looked backward. The sidewalk stretched gray and hard and lifeless, under widely spaced lamps: first a gaunt pole, a globe of glare on top, a dingy yellow puddle of light below; then a thickening murkiness, becoming night itself, until the next globe stood forth, scattering sickly-colored illumination into emptiness. The street ran black of hue, like a river which moved in some secret fashion. Along the other edge of the sidewalk rose brick walls, where an occasional doorway or window made a blocked-off hole. Everything went in straight lines that converged toward an infinity hidden by the dark.

All the pavement was quite bare. A thin breeze sent a scrap of paper tumbling and clicking past his feet. Otherwise he heard nothing, not even the follower.

He tried to slow his heartbeat. *It can't hurt me*, he told himself, knowing he lied. For a while he stood immobile, not so much unwilling to turn his back on the footsteps (for they could be anywhere; more accurately, they were nowhere) as unwilling to hear them again.

"But I can't stay here all night," he said. The whisper made a relieving counterpoint to his pulse. He felt sweat run from his armpits and down his ribs, tickling. "It'll only take a different form. I'd better get home, at least."

He had not known he possessed enough courage to resume walking.

The footsteps picked up. They weren't loud, which was just as well, for they seemed less human each second he listened. There was a slithering quality to them: not wet but dry, a scaly dryness that went sliding over dirty concrete. He didn't even know how many feet there were. More than two, surely. Perhaps so many that they weren't feet at all, but one supple length. And the head rose, weaving about in curves that rippled and rustled—becoming less sinuous as the hood swelled until the sidewise figure eight upon it stood forth plain; a thin little tongue flickered as if frantic, but there was an immortal patience in the eyes, which were lidless.

"Of course this is ridiculous," he told himself. "Giving pictorial form to that which is, by definition, beyond any form whatsoever—" His voice came out small. The rustling stopped. For a moment he heard only the clack of his own shoes and the millrace blood in his body. He hoped, crazily through all the gibberish in his head.

Faustus is the name, good sir, not Frankenstein but Faustus in the Faustian sense if you please and means fortunate in the Latin but one may wonder if the Latin was not constructed with a hitherto unsuspected sense of irony, e.g., my wife awaits me, she may not have gone to bed yet and lamplight would fall on her hair but my shoes are too tight and too loud.

That it might have abandoned him. Or rather, the scientific brain cells corrected, that he had somehow slipped back from the state of awareness of these things. *Because,* he thought, *I deny that rationality is dead in the cosmos, and even that my experiments with the ESP amplifier opened hell gate. Rather, they sensitized me to an unsuspected class of phenomena, one for which human evolution has not prepared me because humankind never encountered it before. (Except, perhaps, in the thinnest and swiftest accidental glimpses, revelation, nightmare, and madness.) I am the early student of X-rays, the alchemist heating liquid mercury, the half-ape burned by fire, the mouse strayed onto a battlefield. I shall be destroyed if I cannot escape, but the universe will still live, her and me and them and a certain willow on a hilltop which fills with sunset light each summer evening. I pray that this be true.*

Then the scales uncoiled and went scrabbling toward him, louder now, and he caught a hot cedary odor. But the night breeze was cold in his hair. He cried out, once, and began to run.

The street lamps reached ahead of him, on to an unseen infinity, like stars in space. No, lonelier than that. Each lamp was an island universe, spinning up there a million years from the next neighbor. Surely, in all that darkness, a man might find some hiding place! He was out of condition. Soon he was breathing through a wide-open, dried-out mouth. His lungs were twin fires and he felt his eyeballs bulge from pressure. His shoes grew so heavy that he thought he ran with two planets on his feet.

Through thunder and breakings he heard the rustle, closer still, and his shoes going slap-slap-slap on bare pavement, under the purulent street lamps. Up ahead were two of them, whose globes looked close together from where he was, and the shadows they cast made a dark shaft between that reached straight upward to an infinity from which stars fountained in horrible fire. He had not imagined there could be so grim a sight. He had no breath left, but his brain screamed for him.

Somewhere there must be darkness. A tunnel to hide in, to close off and seal. There must be warmth and the sound of waters. And darkness again. If he was caught, let it at least not happen in the light. But he begged the tunnel would hide him.

The current up which he waded was strong. It slid heavily and sensuously about him, pushing on breast and belly, loins and thighs. He was totally blind now, but that was good, he was far from the world-spewing globes. The water's noise echoed from the tunnel walls, ringing and booming. Now and then a wave splashed against them, a loud clear sound followed by a thin shower of drops, like laughter. His feet slipped, he flailed about with his arms, touched the warm curved odorous wall of the tunnel and shoved himself back upright. He had a sense of wading uphill, and the current strengthened with each step he achieved. A *hyperbola*, he thought in upsurging weariness. *I'll never reach the end. That's at infinity.*

After centuries he heard the pumps that drove the waters, pumps as big as the world, throbbing in the dark. He stopped, afraid to go on, afraid the rotors would seize him and grind him and squirt him from a cylinder.

But when the hooded swimmer struck him and he went under, he must shriek.

Too late now! The waters took him, stopped his voice, cataracted down his throat and churned in his guts. A momentary gulp of air smelled like cedar. The swimmer closed its jaws. He heard his skin tear under the fangs, and the pisons began to tingle down the skein of his nerves. The head marked with a sideways figure eight shook him as a dog shakes a rat. Nevertheless he planted feet on the tunnel floor, gripped the monstrous barrel of a body, and threw his last energies against it. Back and forth they swayed, the tunnel trembled under their violence, they smashed into its walls. The pumps began to skip beats, the walls began to crack and dissolve, the waters rushed forth across the world. But still he was gripped.

He shook off the hand, leaned his face against blessed scratchy brick and tried to vomit. But nothing happened. The policeman took him by the arm again, but more gently. "What's the matter?"

A lamp near the alley mouth dribbled in just enough light to show the large blue shape with the star on the breast. "What's wrong?" insisted the policeman. "I thought you was drunk, but you don't smell like it. Sick?"

"Yes." He controlled himself, suppressed the last belly spasm and turned around to face the policeman. The other voice came faintly to him, with a curious heterodyned whine, a rise and fall like speech heard through high fever. "End of the world, you know."

"Huh?"

For a moment he considered asking the policeman's help. The fellow looked so substantial and blue. His big jowly face was not unkind. But of course the policeman could not help. *He can take me home, if I so request. Or put me in jail, if I act oddly enough. Or call a doctor if I fall boneless at his feet. But what's the use? There is no cure for being in an ocean.*

He glanced at his watch. Only a few minutes had passed since he left the laboratory. At that time he had wanted companionship, a human face to look at if not to take along on his flight. Now he had his wish, and there was no comfort. The policeman was as remote as the lamp. A part of him could talk to the policeman, just as another part could direct heart and lungs and glands in their work. But the essential *I* had departed this world. The I was not even human any longer. No man could help him find his way back.

"I'm sorry," he said. "I get a bit stupid," His reasoning faculties worked very fast. "During these attacks, I mean."

"What attacks?"

"Diabetes. You know, diabetics get fainting spells. I didn't quite pass out this time, but I got rather woozy. I'll be okay, though."

"Oh." The policeman's ignorance of medicine proved as great as hoped. "I see. Want I should call you a cab?"

"No thanks, officer. Not necessary. I'm on my way to the bus stop. Honest, I'll be fine."

"Well, I better come along with you," said the policeman.

They walked side by side, unspeaking. Presently they emerged on an avenue that had restaurants and theaters as well as darkened shops. Light glittered, blinked, quivered in red and yellow and cold blue, cars went slithering past, men and somewhat fewer women drifted along the sidewalks. The air was full of noise, feet, tires, think it'll rain tomorrow close the deal for paper, mister? A neon sign across from the bus stop made *Idle Hour* Bar & Grill, blink, *Idle Hour* blink *Idle Hour* blink *Idle Hour* blink.

"Here you are," said the policeman. "You sure you'll be okay?"

"Quite sure. Thank you, officer." To please the policeman and make him go away, he sat down on the bench.

"Well, good luck to you." The big blue man walked off and was lost in the drift.

A woman sat at the other end of the bench. In a tired and middle-aged fashion she looked a little bit like his sister. He noticed her casting glances in his direction and wondered why. Probably curious to know the reason he came here escorted, but afraid to ask lest he think she was trying to get picked up. It didn't matter. She was hollow anyway. They all were, himself included. They were infinitesimal skins of distorted space enclosing nothing whatever, not even space. The lights were hollow and the noise was hollow. All fullness was ocean.

He felt much at peace. Now that he was no longer pursued . . . well, why should he be? It had happened to completion. And then after the tunnel broke, the waters had covered everything. They reached vast and gray, warm and still, with a faint taste of salt like tears. In the translucent greenish gray where he lay, easily rocking, there was no place for pursuit, for anything except everything.

Time flowed in the ocean, but a slow soft kind of time. First the light strengthened, sourceless, eventually revealing the eternal overcast, which was cool nacre. Sometimes a lower stratum would form, mare's tails whipped on a sharp wind or blue-black masses rearing up with lightning in their heads. But when that happened, he could sink undersurface, where the water was forever still and greenish. . . . Finally the light faded. The nights were altogether dark. He liked them best, for then he could lie and feel the tides pass through him. A tide was more than a rolling of his body; it was a deep secret thrill, somehow each

atom of him was touched by the force as it passed
and a tingle scarcely sensed would go down all
molecular lengths. By day he enjoyed the tides too,
but not so much, for then other life forms were
about. He had only the dimmest awareness of
these, but they did pass by, sometimes brushing
him or considering him with patient lidless eyes.

"Excuse me, sir, do you know if this bus goes to
Seventh Street?"

It startled him a little that his body should start.
Surely there was no sense to the chilly prickles of
sweat that burst out all over him. "No," he said.
His voice came out so harsh that the woman edged
even further away. Somehow that was an
additional flick across his soft skin. He twisted,
trying to escape; he grew plates of bone so that
they must leave him in peace.

"No," he said. "I don't believe it does. I get off
before then myself—I've never ridden as far as
Seventh Street—so I'm not sure. But I don't
believe it does."

His logical faculty grew furious with him for
talking so idiotically. "Oh," she said. "Thank you."
He said, "You can ask the driver." She said, "Yes,
I suppose I can. Thank you." He said, "You're
welcome." She obviously wanted to break off the
misbegotten conversation and didn't quite see
how. For his part, he couldn't take any more. The
noises and skins were hollow, no doubt, but they
kept striking at him. He jumped up and crossed
the street. Her eyes pursued him. He hadn't seen
her blink.

The *Idle Hour* was dim. A couple sat in a booth
along one wall; a discouraged man hunched at the
bar opposite; a juke box made garish embers but
remained mercifully unfed. The bartender was a

thin man in the usual white shirt and black bow tie. He was washing some glasses and said without enthusiasm, "Be closing time pretty soon, mister."

"That's all right. Scotch and soda." Speech was automatic, like breath. When he had the glass, he retired to a booth of his own. He leaned back on faded plastic cushioning, set the glass before him and stared at the ice cubes. He didn't want to drink.

Who would want to drink in the ocean? he thought with a touch of wryness.

But this is wrong!

He didn't want to make jokes, he wanted the tides and the plankton swirling into his mouth, the thin warm saltiness, the good sound of rainstorms lashing the surface when he was snugly down among seaweeds. *They* were cool and silken, they caressed. He changed the awkward bony plates that protected him from the others for scales, which were not quite as strong but left him slippery and flexible and alive to the stroking, streaming green weed. Now he could slip through their most secret grottos, nose about on the oozy bottom and look with incurious lidless eyes at the fossils he uncovered.

"Let's examine the superman thesis," he said to his wife. "I don't mean the Nietzschean Uebermensch. I mean Superior, the nonhuman animal with nonhuman powers making him as much stronger than us as we are stronger than the apes. Traditionally, he's supposed to be born of man and woman. In hard biological fact, we know this isn't possible. Even if the simultaneous alternation of millions of genes could take place, the resulting embryo would be so alien in blood type, enzyme system, the very proteins, that it would hardly be created before the outraged uterus destroyed it."

"Perhaps in a million years, man could evolve into superman," she answered.

"Perhaps," he said skeptically. "I'm inclined to doubt it, though. The great apes, even the monkeys, aren't likely to evolve into men. They branched off from our common ancestor too long ago; they've followed their special path too far. Likewise, men may improve their reasoning, visualizing, imagining ability—what we're pleased to call their conscious intelligence—their own characteristic as a species—they may improve that through a megayear or so of slow evolution. But they'd still be men, wouldn't they? A later model, but still men.

"Now the truly superior being . . ." He held his wine glass up to the light. "Let's speculate aloud. What is superiority anyhow, in a biological sense? Isn't it an ability—a mode of behavior, I'll say— that enables the species to cope more effectively with environment?

"Okay. So let's inquire what modes of behavior there are. The simplest, practiced by unicellular organisms as well as higher ones like sunflowers, is tropism. A mere chemical response to a fixed set of stimuli. More complicated and adaptable are sets of reflexes. That's the characteristic insectal mode. Then you get true instincts: inherited behavior patterns, but generalized, flexible and modifiable. Finally, in the higher mammals, you get a degree of conscious intelligence. Man, of course, has made this his particular strength. He also has quite a bit of instinct, some reflexes, and maybe a few tropisms. His ability to reason, though, is what's gotten him as far as he's come on this planet.

"To surpass us, should Superior try to out-human humanity? Shouldn't he rather possess only a modicum of reasoning ability by our standards, very weak instincts, a few reflexes, and no tropisms? But his specialty, his characteristic mode, would be something we can't imagine. We may have a bare touch of it, as the apes and dogs have a touch of logical reasoning power. But we can no more imagine its full development than a dog could follow Einstein's equations."

"What might this ability be?" his wife wondered.

He shrugged. "Who knows? Conceivably in the ESP field—Now I'm letting my hobby horse run away with me again. (Damn it, though, I *am* starting to get reproducible results!) Whatever it is, it's something much more powerful than logic or imagination. And as futile for us to speculate about as for the dog to ponder Einstein."

"Do you really believe there are such super-beings?" She had come to expect almost any hypothesis of him.

"Oh, no," he laughed. "I'm just playing a game with ideas. Like your kitten with a ball of string. But assuming Superior does exist . . . hm. Do mice know that men exist? All a mouse knows is that the world contains good things like houses and cheese, bad things like weatherstripping and traps, without any orderly pattern that his instincts could adapt him to. He sees men, sure, but how can he know they're a different order of life, responsible for all the strangeness in his world? In the same way, we may have coexisted with Superior for a million years, and never known it. The part of him we can detect may be an accepted feature of our universe, like the earth's magnetic field; or an unexplained feature like occasional lights in the sky; or he may be quite undetectable. His activities would never impinge on ours, except once in a while by sheerest accident — and then another 'miracle' is recorded that science never does find an explanation for."

She smiled, enjoying his own pleasure. "Where do these beings come from? Another planet?"

"I doubt that. They probably evolved here right along with us. All life on earth has an equally ancient lineage. I've no idea what the common ancestor of man and Superior could have been. Perhaps as recent as some half ape in the Pliocene, perhaps as far back as some amphibian in the Carboniferous. We took one path, they took another, and never the twain shall meet."

"I hope not. We'd have no more chance than the mice, would we?"

"I don't know. But we'd certainly best cultivate our own garden."

Which, however, he had not done. He wasn't sure how he had blundered onto the Superior plane of existence: or, rather, how his mind or his rudimentary ESP or whatever-it-was had suddenly begun reacting to the behavior-mode of that race. He only knew, with the flat sureness of immediate experience, that it had happened.

His logical mind, unaffected as yet, searched in a distant and dreamy fashion for a rationale. The amplifier alone could hardly be responsible. But maybe the remembrance of his speculative fable had provided the additional impetus necessary? If that were so, then his fate was a most improbable accident. Other men could still go ahead and study ESP phenomena as much as they cared to, learn a lot, use their knowledge, all in perfect safety, with never a hint that on a higher level of those phenomena Superior carried out huge purposes.

Himself, though, was sunk in a gray ocean on a gray world. Let him so remain. Never had he imagined such peace, or the tides or the kissing seaweeds; and as for the lightning storms, he could hide when they flashed. Down he went then, into a green well of silence whose roof coruscated with light shards; further down, the well darkened, the light shrank to spot overhead (if that meant anything here where there was no weight, no heaviness, no force or current or pursuit) and then the dark enfolded him. On the bottom it was always night.

He lay in ooze, which was cool though the water stayed warm, he wrapped the dear darkness around him like another skin, closed the lids he had grown to keep daylight off, he could taste salt and feel the tides go through his molecules. High above rolled the clouds, thunder banged from horizon to horizon, the sky was all one blaze of great lightnings; wind yammered, driving spindrift flat off the crests of the waves, which foamed and snarled and shivered the bones of the world. Even down in the depths—

No! What a storm that must be! Fear tinged him. He didn't want to remember lightnings, which worked their length across heaven and sizzled like hastening scales. He burrowed into the mud until he touched bedrock and, and, and felt it quiver.

Even the storm could not be as dreadful as that deep earthquake vibration. He wailed voicelessly and fled back upward. The others swarmed around him, driven from their grottos by the growing violence. Teeth snapped at him, lidless eyes glowed like twinned globes. Some had been torn apart; he tasted blood in the waters.

Another crash and another went through him, as deeply as ever the tides had done, but bruising and ripping. He burst the surface. Rain and scud whipped him. Wallowing on the wrinkled back of a wave, he looked straight up at the lightning. Thunder filled his skull.

A deeper noise responded. Across many wild miles he saw the mountain rise from the waters. Black and enormous it was lifted; water cascaded off its flanks, fire and sulfur boiled from its throat. Shock followed shock, flinging him to and fro, over and under. He felt, rather than saw, the whole sea bottom lifting beneath him.

He gibbered in the foam and fled, seeking depths, seeking a place where he could not see the mountain. Its pinnacle had already gone through the clouds. In that wounded sky the stars blazed gruesomely.

Somewhere through the explosions, he thought he must be able to get free. Surely all the ocean was not convulsed. But a basalt peak smote him from beneath. The water squirted from his gills; he went sick and dizzy. Raised into naked air, he felt the delicate gill membranes shrivel and drew a breath that burned him down throat and lungs to his inmost cell. The black reef continued rising. Soon it would be part of the mountainside. He made one sprawling flop, all his strength expended: slid off the rock, back down into the sea. But a wave grabbed him in its white teeth and shook him.

He pushed the hand from his shoulder. "All

right, all right, all right," he mumbled. "Let me alone."

"Closing time, I told you," said the bartender. "You deaf or something? I gotta close this place."

"Let me alone." He covered his ears against the screaming.

"Don't make me call a cop. Go on home, mister. You look like you could stand a night's rest." The bartender was thin but expert. He applied leverage in the right places, got his customer to his feet and shambling across the floor. "You just go on home now. Good night. Closing time, you know."

The door swung shut, as if to deny the bartender's existence. Other hollow people were on the street, some going for coffee, some entering the bus that waited on the opposite curb.

My bus, he thought. *The one that may or may not go as far as Seventh Street*. The thought was unreal. All thought was. Reality consisted in a black mountain, rising and rising, himself trapped in a pool on the slope where the surf had cast him, gasping raw air, scourged by rain, deafened by wind and thunder, and lifted toward the terrible stars.

He crouched in his wretchedness, implored the ocean to come back, but at the same time he hissed to the fire and the wind and the sulfurous reek, *If you won't let me go, I'll destroy you. See if I don't!*

Habit had taken him over the street to the bus. He stopped in front of the doors. What was he doing here? The thing was an iron box. No, he must not enter the box. The hollow people sat there in rows, waiting for him. He must tear down the mountain instead.

What mountain?

He knew in the thinking part of himself that somewhere in space and time was an existence not all harm and hatred. The night was too loud now, beneath winter stars, for him to return thither. He must pull down the mountain, so he could regain the ocean. . . . But his logical faculties spun free, down and down a hyperbolic path. They considered the abstract unreal proposition that he would not be hollow if he could become human again. And then he would be happy, though at present he didn't want to be human, he wanted to rip the mountain and re-enter the sea. But as a logical exercise, to pass the time for the unused part of his brain, *why* had he suffered and fought and been hunted, since that moment when he was first sensitized to . . . to Superior's mode of behavior?

He could no more understand the situation with reason than a dog could use instinct to puzzle out the machinery of this bus and the why of its existence. (No, he would not enter that box. He didn't know why, except that the box was hollow and waited for him. But he was sure it went to Seventh Street.) Nonetheless, reason was not absolutely useless. The activities of Superior were always and forever incomprehensible to him, but he could describe their general tendency. Violence, cruelty, destruction. Which didn't make sense! No species could survive that used its powers only for such ends.

Therefore, Superior did not. Most of the time, he/she/it/? was just being Superior, and as such was completely beyond human perception. Occasionally, though, there was conflict. By analogy, mankind—all animals—behaved constuctively on the whole, but sometimes engaged in strife. Superior? Well, of course Superior didn't have wars in the human sense of the word. No use speculating what they did have. Conflicts of some kind, anyhow, where an issue was decided not by reason or compromise but by force. And the force employed was (to give it a name) of an ESP nature.

A mouse could not understand human art or science. In a way, he couldn't even see them. But a mouse could be affected by the crudest, most animal-like manifestation of human behavior: physical combat. A mathematical theorem did not exist for the mouse; a bullet did.

By analogy again, he, the human, was a mouse that had wandered onto a battlefield. By some accident, he had been sensitized to the lowest mode of Superior behavior and was thereby being affected; he was caught in the opposing tides of a death struggle.

Not that he was directly experiencing what Superior actually performed. Everything that had happened was merely the way the forces, the currents, felt to him. Frantically seeking a balance, his mind interpreted those unnatural stimuli in the nearest available human terms.

He thought his sensations must dimly reflect the course of the battle. One side or entity or . . . Aleph . . . had gotten the upper hand and in some sense pursued the other till it found a momentary shelter. Zayin had then had a breathing space until Aleph found it again, pursued it again. Cornered, Zayin fought back so fiercely that Aleph must in turn retreat. Now, having recovered during the lull that followed, Zayin was renewing the battle. . . . But none of this made any difference. The doings of Superior were, in themselves, irrelevant to Sapiens. He was the mouse on the battle-field, nothing else.

With luck, a mouse could escape from bursting shells and burning tracers before they smashed him. A man could escape from this other conflict before it burned out his mind: by desensitizing himself, by ceasing to perceive the transcendent energies around him, much as one could get relief from too brilliant a light by closing one's eyes. But what was the method of desensitization?

Clouds broke further, and he saw the moon flying pocked among the stars. Its light was as cold as the wind. His flesh quivered in the pain of cold and earthquake shocks. But the ocean tumbled not far off, white under the moon. He felt that impact reverberate in the mountain. He began to crawl from his dwindling pool.

How can I get away?

"Hey, mister, you gonna board this bus or not?"

The currents carried me first in one direction, then in another. Down to the depths, up to the stars. Whether I go forward or backward, seaward of skyward, I am still within the currents.

"I said, you comin' aboard? Don't just stand there blocking the door."

Lightning burned his eyes. He felt the thunder in his bones. But louder, now, was the hate in him: for the mountain which had ruined his sea and for the sea which had cast him onto the mountain. *I will destroy them all.*

And then fear smote him, for through the noise and the gigantic white flashes he heard himself asking: "Do you go to Seventh Street?"

The driver said across lightyears, "Yeah, that's the end of my run. Come on, hop in. I got a schedule to keep."

"No—" he whimpered, stumbling backward toward the ocean. His teeth clattered with cold. The waves retreated from him. *I am not going in a box to Seventh Street!*

"Where do you wanna go, then?" asked the driver, elaborately sarcastic.

"Go?" he repeated in a numb voice. "Why . . . home."

Please, he called to the surf. But still the tide withdrew, a monstrous hollow rumble. He turned about, hissing at the mountain where it flamed overhead. *All right, then*, said his hatred. He started to crawl up the wet black rocks. *All right, if you won't tell me the way home, I'll climb up over your peak.*

But you do know the way home, said his human logical faculty.

What? He stopped. The wind hooted and whipped him. If he didn't keep moving he would freeze.

Of course. Consider the pattern. Forward or backward, you are still moving within the currents. But if you remain still—

No! he screamed, and in his fear he reared up and clawed at the stars for support.

It won't take long.

Oh, God no, I'm too afraid. No man should have to do this twice.

The cold and lightning and earthquake struck at him. He cowered on the beach, under the mountain, too frightened to hate. No, I must climb. I can't stay here.

The bus driver snorted and closed the door in his face.

Where the courage came from, he never knew. For an instant he was able to remember his wife's eyes, and that she was waiting for him. He raised his hand and rapped on the door. The driver groaned.

If he goes off and leaves me—if he delays half a minute letting me in—I'll never go aboard. I won't be able to.

The door folded back.

He gathered the last rage of himself around himself, climbed up the step and over the threshold.

Something snatched at him. The wind drove in between his ribs, lightning hit him, he had never conceived such pain. He opened his mouth to yell.

No! That's part of the pattern. Don't do it.

Somehow he maintained silence, clung to the stanchion as the bus got under way and felt the galaxies sundered. The earth-shaken rocks on the mountainside rolled beneath him, thrusting him upward. He planted his feet on the ground and said: "To Seventh Street."

The world drained out of him.

As blackness faded again, he found himself sprawled on one of the longitudinal seats up front. "Now look, buster," said the driver, "drunk or not, you pay the fare, see? I don't want no trouble. Just gimmie the fare."

He drew a breath deep into starved lungs. The bus was noisy, with a stench from the motor; tired people sagged down its length, under improbably bright-colored advertisements. On either side he could see the lighted windows of houses.

How still the night was!

"What is the fare?" he asked. *Ridiculous*, his logical mind scolded him, wearily but not very angrily. After all, the rest of him had shown up well too, when the crisis came. *I've ridden this line a hundred times. But I can't quite remember the cost. It feels so new to be human.*

"Two bits."

"Oh, is that all? I'd have paid more." His knees were weak, but he managed to stand up and fish out a quarter. It clinked in the coin box with a noise whose metal clarity he savored.

Perhaps a little sympathetic, or perhaps from a sense of duty, the driver asked him, "D'you say you was going to Seventh Street?"

"No." He sat down again. "Not tonight, after all. My home isn't quite that far."

WHEN HALF-GODS GO

Morton, of the Harvard Astronomy department, knocked the dottle from his notoriously evil-smelling pipe and looked around the room. There were a dozen or so men gathered here in his home, all professors at his university and neighboring schools, all old friends who could be trusted to keep their mouths shut.

"I hope I wasn't too melodramatic," he said, "but then this whole business is so fantastic that I've long ago given up my usual standards of normality. All you know is that I called each of you up and asked you to come here tonight as discreetly as possible. Now that we're all gathered, there really isn't much more I can tell you."

His eyes traveled around the group which sat quietly smoking and sipping his brandy, and he wondered how to continue. "You remember," he went on as dryly as possible, "that a couple of weeks ago our little discussion club wrote to these *soi-disant* Sagittarians, this couple which claims to be envoys from an intersteller civilization, inviting them to come and speak. We were interested in them and their claims, we hoped to find out how they did their tricks. . . . Well, they wrote back politely saying we were too small a bunch for their purposes, and I thought that was the end of it. When they got in trouble with the law the other day and were officially denounced, I was merely disappointed. Another pair of Cagliostros, eh?

"Then yesterday afternoon they appeared in my office." Morton smiled, a shy smile pleading for belief. "I was sitting alone, the door was closed, and suddenly there they were. They requested me to assemble the club—such members, at least, as I knew wouldn't blab—and said they'd talk to us after all. When I agreed, they vanished again."

The astronomer shrugged. "That's it, gentlemen. Are you game?"

"Certainly," rumbled Johns, the M.I.T. cybernetics man. "For the kind of show they put on, I don't mind harboring a fugitive."

"Y'think they're the genuine article?" asked Foxxe, the British anthropologist currently on loan to Harvard.

"I don't know," said Morton. "I honestly don't know. Maybe we'll find out tonight. We're supposed to think at them simultaneously when we're ready. They're hiding somewhere nearby and will, uh, hear us. Telepathy."

"Rum go," said Foxxe. "One day they're just another show, the next they're wanted for every crime from high treason to selling peanuts without a license. I shall never understand you Americans."

"Sometimes," said Morton, "we don't understand ourselves." He looked around the shabby, comfortable room again. The shades were pulled; night lay beyond the windows. "All set? Okay, let's get on with the seance."

They thought the invitation, feeling a little silly about the whole affair. With a hint whooshing of displaced atmosphere, the Sagittarians stood among them.

There were two, and they looked quite human on the outside, an ordinariness increased by the conventional Earthly garments they wore. They had admitted to having only four toes on each foot —shoes hid that fact—and their ears lacked the intricate Terrestrial convolutions. An X-ray would have shown other differences, and a physiologist would have been surprised by a number of internal details. But all in all, the foreignness was not great. Evolution on Earth-like planets tends to follow very similar patterns.

The man, En-Shan Khorokum, was of medium height, slender and graceful, with high cheekbones and sleek black hair, olive skin and dark eyes. Chi Balkhai, his wife or equivalent thereof, had the same racial characteristics, and was lovely to look on, slim and supple as a finely bred cat. Both seemed young—ageless might be a better term, for there was a vibrant strength and aliveness in them, a depth of mature wisdom under the weary desperation of the hunted.

"Ah . . . how do you do," said Morton..

Khorokum smiled, a flash of white teeth in his mobile face, but the eyes were mostly on Chi. Voices murmured at the newcomers, greetings, good wishes. If they could really scan minds, thought Morton, they'd find here the friendliness

they needed—a high degree of tentative accept-
ance of their story, with no dogmatic rejection
such as had cursed them elsewhere.

He looked awkwardly around. "Please don't try
to do anything special," said Chi. "We're simply
old friends who have dropped in for a visit."

"Well, sit down then, sit down and have some of
this brandy," bellowed Johns. "Our host keeps the
best cellar this side of—what did you say your
home star was called?—this side of Urukand."

"Thank you, thank you." The guests found
chairs, and the professors crowded their own
seats close.

"There is nothing overly melodramatic about
this," said Khorokum. "My wife and I are in no
danger of our lives, not when with an effort of will
we can teleport ourselves off the planet altogether. But we are in a certain amount of profes-
sional jeopardy. This is our first big job as an independent team, and we'd hate to mess it up."

"You mean," said Gray, who taught history,
"that there are many planets in our situation?
That it's a function of your society to—convert
them?"

"Well, quite a few such worlds," replied
Khorokum. "You see, the Galactic Union originated in the Sagittarian star clusters about a
half million years ago and has since been spread-
ing outward, its aim being ultimately to bring all
inhabited planets into itself. Urukand was
civilized 10,000 years or so in the past. But it's a
big job, you can readily see that, so we concentrate
on worlds which have reached approximately
your stage of technology. Their science is sufficiently highly developed to understand the con-

cepts involved, while at the same time they are far behind us and so grasp eagerly at the gifts we offer —the parapsychic powers replacing machines for all but the most routine work, the conquest of age and disease and social ills like war and poverty, membership in the glorious federation of stars— oh, it was a straightforward sort of thing till Earth came along. But there's something unique in your human psychology. You don't believe the evidence of your own senses—I wonder if you *want* a higher civilization. When our scouts reported heavy neutrino emission from your planet, Chi and I were sent on what seemed an easy mission. And we failed. We failed completely." His face twisted a little.

"Our jobs are a very small matter compared to the danger all Earth is in," said Chi softly. "Your unstable society is moving inevitably toward annihilating war and cruel tyranny. Any nation of Earth which joined the Union could no longer wage war, but it would be safe from all attack— but nobody believes that! They've seen what we can do, and still they won't believe. What we want, gentlemen, is advice."

"The savages advise the missionaries?" Van Tyne, of Boston University's English department, raised his shaggy brows.

"You are humans and we are not," said Chi. "One of you may have the vital fact we need."

Foxxe nodded. "I always claimed that the only white men who ever really understood a primitive folk were those who went native," he said. "Trouble always was, y'know, that kind of person just doesn't write for the journals."

Khorokum leaned forward, clasping his hands

between his knees. "Suppose," he said, "that I give you the whole situation—from the very beginning."

At first it had seemed easy. Teleporting across a thousand light years was no more mysterious than willing your arm to move, once you understood the psychophysiological applications of wave mechanics. They took along no equipment except some small powerpacks, the size of cigaret cases, with which to equalize gravitational potentials and trigger the vast cosmic-force flows which their nervous systems could direct to control matter and energy. There had been a month or two of inconspicuous flitting about Earth and reading minds, learning the history, language, mores, filling their trained memories with the key facts. Then, quite simply, they had gone to the leaders of the important nations.

The Union was not a conqueror. That was ruled out by the relative smallness of its population in an enormous Galaxy, by a total lack of any economic necessity for tribute, and by the very structure of a society based on individual development. New planets had to join of their own free will, if they were not to become a dangerous and disruptive element in a carefully balanced civilization. Even the field agents could not exert compulsion of any sort, including hypnosis, except in self-defense; and even after a state had become a member the necessary internal changes were best carried out, gradually, by its own government. The immediate alterations ran in the direction of libertarianism, universal equality, total disarmament—the obvious reforms. After that, field agents would gently guide further de-

velopment, and give training in the fantastic parapsychic powers to qualified natives. The standards
therefore weren't impossibly high—apart from
physical and mental potentiality, there was simply
the ethic of civilized behavior. Usually it took only
four or five generations for all normal dwellers on
a planet to become full citizens; and meanwhile
the benefits of reform, peace, order, higher production for less work, medicine, intersteller trade
and exploration were freely available to everyone.
A nation, a world, would leap at the chance.

Only Earth didn't.

Skepticism, laughter, alarm, malignant slyness
. . . Chi shuddered, there in the quiet Cambridge
room, as she remembered what had been in the
mind of a dictator who had believed. After they
refused him and made it plain what the Union
meant, they had never been quite safe from his
assassins.

America had seemed the best bet. If it joined,
the dam was broken. And while the President had
not accepted them as anything but a pair of bunco
artists, there were the people. Convince enough
of them, and the government of a democratic
country would have to yield. Barnstorming!

Money was no problem. With a slight mental effort, they could duplicate the currency of any
nation, atom by atom. Auditoriums could be hired,
advertisements bought—and a free show had
never lacked for an audience.

It should have worked. Khorokum teleported
himself across the stage. He floated automobiles
and tractors onto the scene, and duplicated them
there from piles of sand. He extracted seventh
roots in his head. He turned the lights on and off
by a thought. He identified individuals and told

them what they were thinking. He asked them to invent tricks for him, and could almost always perform as directed, from controlling the throw of dice to whisking an elephant onstage. At the conclusion of the show, he materialized the full instrument ensemble of an orchestra to play him a grand finale.

It was good. They applauded wildly and shouted for encores. But they didn't believe him. His accompanying lecture about his true nature and purposes, his earnest request that they write their Congressmen and their President, struck them as a smart new line of patter. That was all.

The psychology of it was unique in the known Galaxy. Khorokum could understand some of the reasons. After all, humanity had been exposed to lunatics of one sort or another for centuries, self-styled prophets of this and that, fakers, as well as magicians who never claimed to be more than experts at deception—to say nothing of the visionary fiction which had worn the Galactic Union story a little thin ahead of the reality. Yes, they'd had to develop skepticism, a sort of racial immunity to fantastic claims.

But even so, to reject the evidence of the senses and plain logic . . . !

Then finally, on the blank edge of discouragement, the G-men arriving, an escort to the White House, an interview with the President and his important military and political associates . . .

Khorokum's smile was bitter as he related that part of the story. Almost no one at the conference had believed that the visitors were from outer space, and those who did considered the fact irrelevant. The pair had extraordinary powers. As spies, as projectors of atomic bombs, as shields for advancing troops, the Urukandians could perhaps be useful. But as emissaries ... the United States government could hardly accept formal ambassadors from a country no one had ever seen!

"Someone wanted to be taken back with us," said Chi. "It wasn't a bad idea, except that on a long hop an untrained mind could distort things, would probably kill us all. Besides, they didn't really want to join, even if they were sure. It would have upset the status quo, in which they had attained success."

"The present situation has made them pathologically suspicious and xenophobic," added Khorokum. "It presages ill for your world if you don't get outside help."

"You have become a political issue, you know," said Van Tyne. "Russia at once denies that you exist and accuses us of making a secret weapon of you. Norway is up in arms because you didn't go direct to the U.N. but said it was neither a government nor even a good debating society. France thinks it's some kind of plot. Questions have been asked in the British House of Commons. It's that way all over the world: nobody is sure what you are, but many are aware that you represent some new factor. You may end up precipitating the very crisis you're trying to avoid."

"When we refused to help them with their plans," said Khorokum, "they pointed out that we're guilty of counterfeiting, illegal entry, subversion, inciting to riot, and I don't know what else. They demanded our passports, birth certificates, draft cards, income tax returns ... The land of the free and the home of the brave!"

"And then—?"

"We said we'd go right on taking our case to the people. They replied that we were outlaws; and while they can't successfully hold us in jail, they can break up all our meetings and deluge us under such a barrage of official denunciation that no one will ever listen to us. That's what they've been doing for the past few days, as you know.

"All right, gentlemen." En-Shan Khorokum leaned back in his chair and smiled bleakly. "If you accept our story, you are our last hope. You have to tell us. *How can we convince Earth?"*

The vision went around the circle of men, rapt eyes, indrawn breaths, the realization that they would partake in the rewards the whole planet would have and that most likely all of them could qualify for immediate mind training. Morton said at last, slowly: "If you aren't telling the truth, you're at least the most extraordinary phenomenon science has yet encountered. I, for one, am going to take your truthfulness as a working hypothesis."

"Occam's razor," said Johns, fingering his beard.

"Its application is sometimes a matter of dispute," said the mathematician Lucasczewski. "Is it simpler to believe that these people are from an advanced civilization or that they are merely terrestrial mutants with unusual powers?"

"I'll take the interstellar hypothesis any day," said the geneticist Phillips. "All that ability in one mutation? Hah!"

"I suppose so," said Morton, "though we'll certainly have to revise our physics." His eyes glowed. "God, but we can learn!"

"This is getting us nowhere," said Van Tyne

impatiently. "These young people have a problem. Who has a solution?"

"Another country?" suggested Johns. "Some nation at once more stable and more progressive than ours—oh, say Sweden or Switzerland?"

"Maybe we should have tried that at first," admitted Khorokum gloomily. But certainly not after the United States government has formally branded us as charlatans and criminals."

"I fail to understand," said Phillips. "How people can be so stupid, I mean. I never was too unbearable an intellectual snob, I hope, but when the much-touted Common Man can't see what's as plain as Mendel's law—when he can't reason from the facts that it's at least probable that you two are from outer space—gracious, Foxxe, I often wonder why you Britishers didn't keep your aristocracy in power."

"Oh, Joe Average isn't so very stupid," said Morton. "What the devil, I'll bet half our fathers were from the lower economic brackets. But he's been fooled too often. He knows, or thinks he knows, that all these amazing effects can be produced by perfectly ordinary means. In any case, how many people have actually *seen* you two perform, not over a TV screen but with their own eyes? What you need is something spectacular that everyone can see directly."

"Even then they'd call it a fake," said Johns darkly. "You could light up the sky with letters ten miles tall asking them to join your Galactic Union, and they'd look for a cigaret ad underneath the message. Psychologists would probably call it mass delusion!"

"It's a common enough phenomenon, really," said Foxxe. "I've seen it happen time and again.

Primitive peoples, isolated, hardly seen a white
man in living memory, y'know. Somebody flies an
airplane in. They may be a little scared at first,
though more often than not they'll shoot at it. But
then it's accepted. Just isn't a marvel, y'know, or
rather it's simply another part of a mysterious and
surprising world. It's accepted. Nobody wonders
very much. What really gets a tribe like that excited, a genuine never-ending wonder, something
to be almost worshiped, that's not one of our
clever technical gadgets, oh, no. It's something
just a little beyond what they have but not so far
advanced that the bally old mind refuses to try
t'understand it. An airplane . . . bah, just a large
metal bird, what of it? A truck . . . int'resting. A
horse and cart . . . oh, there's where they bring out
the brass band and the keys to the village!"

"And we're the primitive tribe, eh?" chuckled
Lucasczewski.

"I've read a lot of these science fiction stories,"
said Van Tyne. "Far advanced psychology, subtle
trickery making a population do anything the hero
wanted. How about it?"

"The stories never went into detail, did they?"
asked Khorokum dryly.

"Big impressive fleet, robots, all that sort of
thing?" suggested Foxxe.

"We don't have them," said Chi. "The Union left
such devices behind hundreds of millennia ago."

"The most fantastic part of this business is its
irony," said Johns. "Here you are, like gods
almost, and you can't do a thing. You're *too*
powerful!" He chuckled heavily. "Like a man who
has a sixteen-inch naval rifle but no fly swatter.
Looks as if you'll just have to let us stew in our bed
or whatever the saying is."

Phillips sighed. "Damn it, anyway! I'd give my right arm to the left shoulder for a chance to see—learn—Oh, well . . ."

Khorokum got out of his chair and paced the floor. "I'm tired," he admitted. "It's been a fearful strain. I'm worn down too far to think. Maybe Chi and I had better go into hiding for a few months—that would be easy—and try to think of something in that time."

"Judging by the world situation," said Morton grimly, "you may not have that long."

"What to do, what to do?" Chi buried her face in her hands.

"A tribe," said Khorokum between his teeth. "An isolated tribe of savages, needing the spectacular but not very advanced proof, too blind to understand—"

Of a sudden he stopped. Chi sat bolt upright, and the same thought flamed between them.

"A primitive tribe—"

The circle of humans edged away, uncertain, dimly aware of the sudden mighty surge of will.

Then Foxxe was having his hand shaken almost off the wrist by Khorokum, who was babbling about the natives of Orkhuzan and mass production via atom-by-atom duplication of a covertly prepared prototype—and somewhat to the Englishman's surprise, and very much to his gratification, Chi Balkhai ran up and kissed him.

Four months later the spaceships came.

They blazed mightily out of the sky, filling heaven with flame and thunder. There were three of them, each a good thousand feet long, and they rounded the world six times before settling into a Wisconsin cornfield.

The crews were fairly humanoid, though they had green skins and antennae and seven fingers to a hand. They received visitors graciously and set themselves to learning English, which they did with astonishing ease. As soon as possible, they explained that they were from Orkhuzan, a member planet of the Galactic Union.

When asked about the now almost forgotten pair who had disappeared four months ago, they seemed a little excited and consulted their files. Then they informed the inquirer that, yes, this En-Shan Khorokum and Chi Balkhai were notorious "traders." What was a "trader"? Oh, a petty criminal who traveled ahead of the Galactic Exploratory Service, reaching new planets first and trying to bilk the innocent natives. Fortunately, Earth's wise leaders had seen through this cheap scheme and the evil pair had fled. Alas, the Union was far from perfect.

Still, there were advantages to be gained by joining. The explorers showed copious files of pictures, statistics, specimens. They appeared on radio and television programs and answered all queries with charming frankness. They showed visitors through their ships and let them handle the mighty engines.

Yes, the Galactic Union was anxious to admit all the nations of Earth. There would be gains—well, nothing spectacular, obvious things which a science a couple of hundred years older than that of humanity would be expected to have. Cures for most diseases, regeneration of lost limbs and some organs, improved mental health, tripled lifespan—things like that.

Of course, the offer was not really disinterested. The Union wanted the technical genius of Earth.

Why, even now humanity had three varieties of fission pile which nobody in the Union had ever thought of!

Would the honorable leaders and citizens of Earth care to consider it?

The United States, Great Britain, India, and several European and Latin American countries had joined, and a number of other lands were undergoing revolutions which would soon lead to their admission, when an eager young cub reporter contrived a chance to give one of the great spaceships a really detailed investigation. What he saw made him attempt some detective work, but those he was checking up on had covered their tracks too thoroughly. And since no more orthodox investigator was able (or eager) to pierce the security regulations surrounding the mighty ships, his unsupported word could never convince his editor that several items of control equipment had borne neat brass plates with the legend.

GENERAL ELECTRIC
Schenectady, New York, U.S.A.

PEEK! I SEE YOU!

The father of Sean F. X. Lindquist was an amiable, easygoing Seattle Swede. His mother was, as might be guessed, an O'Kelly with a will of her own. Their genes combined to produce a son who was good-natured, a bit raffish, intelligent, disciplined to toil—but, on occasion, stubborn as Lucifer. And thereby hangs a tale.

Being expelled from college, for reasons having less to do with his grades than the president's daughter, he impulsively joined the Army. True to its promise of showing him the glamorous parts of the world, it shipped him to Thailand, where he served his hitch clerking on what had to be the world's hottest, dustiest, most isolated and dismal station as part of a miniscule military advisory mission which the general truce throughout Asia had made altogether superfluous. Nonetheless, he was enchanted with Bangkok, where he spent his leaves, and pulled wires to be demobbed in that city. In due course, with a certain feeling of mutual relief, the Army gave him his honorable discharge.

The enchantment wore off—she married someone else—and he made a leisurely way home around the world. Whenever his funds ran out, he did odd jobs. Some were very odd indeed. He was twenty-six before he reached the States again, and long out of touch. So he might have caught up on newspapers and technical journals; but he went instead to Las Vegas and updated himself in other fields. A true cliché calls luck a lady, apt to smile most upon men who do not pursue her. Lindquist departed with several thousand dollars in his pocket.

Tourism was booming in the Southwest. Lindquist remembered boyhood camping trips in the area. It occurred to him that he could make a pleasant living, and have his winters free, by starting an air ferry service. Though industry had spoiled much of the Four Corners country, a great deal of solitude and splendor remained in those uplands. But the effort and expense of packing into roadless mountains discouraged most potential visitors. Now if they and their gear could be flown in, and out again at an agreed-on time— if the pilot was available by radio meanwhile, to handle emergencies like lost can openers—

He took lessons and got his license. Then he bought himself a used VTOL aircraft and went to scout the territory.

Thus it was that he saw the spaceship.

He was droning leisurely along at about 3500 meters. The peaks were not extremely far below him. Their landscape was awesome: vast, steep, cragged, a ruddiness slashed by mineral ochers and blues, a starkness little relieved by scattered mesquite, greasewood, and sagebrush. Here and there, a streamlet turned the bottom of a canyon green. But mostly this was desert land, people-empty land, hawk, buzzard, jackrabbit, and coyote land. The sun was westering in a deep, almost purple sky. Updrafts boomed briefly and trickily, shaking the plane in its course.

Lindquist's lean, sandy-haired, shabby-clad form sat relaxed. He puffed a corncob pipe and hummed a bawdy song. But alertness was in him. Before he tried carrying passengers, he must get familiar with this kind of flying. And he needed a place to roost for the night, preferably containing water and firewood. His eyes roved.

The vision slanted down before him. It moved at incredible speed, banked at impossible angles. Yet its passage was so silent that his own motor, his very pulse hammered at him. The shape, as nearly as he could tell, was roughly like a disk thickened in the middle. But the lambent, shifting colors that played across it, enveloped it in aurora, made such things hard to gauge.

It swung around, slid near, and his magnetic compass went crazy. For a moment he stared at what seemed to be a row of ports, glowing as if furnaces burned behind them. Far in the back of his mind, a reckoner clicked: *Diameter something like thirty meters*. Otherwise he felt sandbagged.

The thing spun off. He grew aware that the pipe had dropped from his jaws. No matter. His hands were a-dance across the radar controls. He locked on. Reflection, yes! His compass steadied again. The vision dwindled . . . a mile away, two miles, three, shrinking to a rainbow dot, like the diffrac-

tion dots you see when you look sunward through
your lashes ... vanishing to nothing against
mountain flanks and canyon shadows.

But it was real. Not just his rocking mind said
so. His instruments did.

Other memories from boyhood and youth boiled
up. "Judas priest," he whispered. "That's a sho-
nuff flying saucer."

He opened the throttle. His plane leaped forward, roaring and shivering with power. He
hadn't a chance of overhauling in a flat-out chase.
But the thing did seem to be on a long downward
track. Could he but stay within range, would it but
land—

"Well, what then, laddy?" he challenged himself.

He didn't know. But he relived vividly the arguments that had once fascinated him. The radicals
had insisted that flying saucers were ships from
outer space, operated by benevolent though green
little men. The conservatives denied that anyone
had ever seen anything. In this hour he, S. F. X.
Lindquist, had been handed a chance to investigate personally. He had nothing to lose, and perhaps—if he could solve the mystery—a great deal
to gain. Like fame and money.

Though no intellectual, he followed the news
around him. Had he not spent the past several
years in out-of-the-way places, he would have
known that pursuit was a waste of time, that the
riddle had in fact already been answered. But no
one had mentioned this to him. Quite simply and
naïvely, he lined out after the vision.

In the different cultures of the galaxy, Dorek's
Law is known by many different names. Some call

it Shepalour's Rule, some the Basic Law of Thermodynamics, some the Principle of Most Effort, and so on for millions of languages. But the formulation is invariant, because we all inhabit the same universe.

"Everything that can go wrong, will."

On their present voyage, the partners in the hypership had seen it in full glorious operation. There is no need to detail their woes with rickety hull, asthmatic engines, and senile computer. Nor need one describe what cargoes they carried, with what infinite trouble, from planet to planet. A tramp has to take anything she can get, and this is apt to be stuff too weird for the sleek cargo liners.

But they did think their fortunes had turned when they reached Zandar. A message from the brokers lay waiting for them. After discharging their load of sandorads—and, hopefully, getting most of the mercaptan odor out of the vessel—they were to pick up some machine tools for New Ystankikkinikkitantuvo. Plain machine tools, harmless crated metal! Of course, the destination was far out on the Rim. So much the better, though. It would be a peaceful haul, with lovely pay accumulating; and then, having been gone as long as they'd signed for, they would head home, loaded or not; and the fleshpots of the Core had better be filled in advance for them.

But a summons came from the port coordinator.

Pazilliwheep Finnison went alone to the office. The coordinator was not of any species he recognized, possessing three eyes and a good many tentacles. They studied each other for a few seconds.

The spacefarer was from Ensikt. He was a diopt

himself, though the eyes were quite large and dark, contrasting with blue stripes upon glabrous orange skin. (The air being thicker, wetter, and hotter than he was used to, he went nude except for a musette bag.) His body was slender, centauroid, with a gracefully waving tail. He breathed through rows of gill-like organs on either side of his long neck, which alternated with aural tympani. Albeit he thus had no nose, he did sport a muscular trunk above his mouth. It split into two arms that ended in boneless four-fingered hands. This was entirely practical on Ensikt, where gravity is comparatively weak and animals comparatively small. Pazilliwheep stood one meter high at the rump.

"Ah . . . Navigator-Pilot Finnison, H/S *Grumdel Castle* . . . yes, yes. Welcome," said the co-ordinator in Interlingo-5 with a flatulent accent. He punched a button on his data screen and regarded what appeared. "Yes. Correct what I was informed. You are clearing for . . . yes, that part of the Rim . . . with a stopover at—what is the name of the planet?"

Pazilliwheep automatically jerked his tail, then said in haste: "My gesture indicated indifference."

"Were you afraid it might be objectionable in my culture? No, we have no tails. Now about this . . . yes . . . confounded planet. Never heard of it till the other day. Cataloged as— But what's the name?"

"Tierra, Earth, Mir, Jorden, die Erde, et cetera, et cetera." Pazilliwheep's vocal apparatus formed the sounds rather well, except for a lack of nasal quality. "Hundreds of autochthonous words. Most of them translate as 'Dirt.'"

"So. Yes. I see." The co-ordinator had kept one

eye on the unrolling data. "Primitive world. What do you call it?"

"Restocking Station 143."

The co-ordinator waved a tentacle in the air. "I indicate assent and understanding. Well, Navigator-Pilot, this is quite fortunate. Yes, fortunate. You came at, shall we say, the strategic moment. You are therefore able to be of material assistance to the Galactic Federation. Intergovernmental Department of Planetary Development, Bureau of Supervisions, to be exact."

Oh, oh! thought Pazilliwheep, and braced himself for bad news. But it was worse than he feared:

"Yes, you can, and therefore you . . . are herewith instructed to . . . furnish transportation and every necessary assistance . . . to the Sector Inspector."

"No!" Pazilliwheep cried. His four hoofs clattered on the floor when he sprang backward. "Not the Sector Inspector!"

"Yes. The Sector Inspector. New one, you know. Anxious to make a good showing in . . . this latest assignment. Came here to check local records. Found no official investigation of that particular planet had been made for a long time. Yes, much overdue. Entire intelligent species being neglected. Perhaps, even, slyly exploited by the less scrupulous. Eh?"

"Exploited, my lowest left operculum!" Pazilliwheep protested. "What the entropy would there *be* to exploit? Besides, their principal culture belongs to the Federation. They have any complaints, they can go through regular channels, can't they? And say, why doesn't the Inspector go in his own ship?"

Remorselessly, the co-ordinator answered: "Economy drive at GHQ. Inspectors for outlying regions do not, shall we say, rate their own vessels any longer. They use available transportation. Yes, I know, that delays them in their work, but they're always behindhand anyway. Too many planets. And a sector like this—not even important enough for records on it to clutter central data banks on any Core world—do you see?"

"But . . . listen, the *Grumdel*'s an old wreck. We've got the stingiest owners in the galaxy. My engineer's trying to repair a fusion tube right now. The interior maintenance units keep breaking down too. Our top hyperspeed is a hypercrawl. Anything would be better!"

"No doubt. No doubt. But nothing else available. Not soon. Every other vessel due here within the next several weeks is a liner or else on time charter. Or, of course, not crewed by oxygen breathers. You may be old, Navigator-Pilot Finnison; you may be rusty; you may be underpowered, vermin-infested, and all but certifiably unspaceworthy; but you are the best I can do for the Sector Inspector. And, yes, my own career—promotion off this dreary mudball—his reports to GHQ—you understand. Yes. You are hereby commandeered." And the co-ordinator handed over the official orders with a flourish.

Thus Hypership *Grumdel Castle* departed Zandar with a third being aboard.

The Inspector was a good fellow at heart: young, inclined to take himself and his work overly seriously, but well intentioned. He apologized for the trouble he was causing, and reminded his hosts that their owners would be compensated according to law. His hosts showed no great enthusiasm at this. He explained that a major reason for his having picked their ship was that she was already scheduled to lay over on 143—"And might I inquire, out of a wish to become more intimately acquainted with my companions as well as for the technical information itself, not to mention simple curiosity, what activities you have planned on this planet?"

He used Interlingo-12 rather than any language of his own world, Ittatik. Unfortunately, Pazilliwheep did not speak Interlingo-12. Engineer-Supercargo Urgo the Red did, more or less, and translated into his version of Interlingo-7:

"He says what're we gonna do there?"

"Well, no reason not to tell him the truth," Pazilliwheep replied. "Unless you've got some or other little racket you haven't told me about."

"When we touch maybe once in three years? Don't make me laugh. It hurts."

In point of fact, Pazilliwheep had a racket of his own. It was a mild one, and might even be legal, for all he knew. He swapped small quantities of ondon oil, which had turned out to have powerful aphrodisiac effects on the natives of 143, for kitchenware. The latter was unusual and artistic enough to command good prices on several more advanced worlds. This was one reason he did his restocking on 143 whenever possible.

"Let's answer his question by reciting common, elementary knowledge," he suggested to Urgo. "Might put him to sleep, at least."

"Is any knowledge common?" wondered the engineer-supercargo. "Like, it's a big galaxy. *I* never heard o' whatzisname's muckin' civilization till now. And still he says it fills a whole muckin' star cluster! Maybe he don't know how we operate in this spiral arm."

"Oh, I suppose the basic procedures are similar everywhere. If nothing else, in the course of ten thousand years or however long it's been around, wouldn't the Federation have had some leveling influence on the member species?" Pazilliwheep tail-shrugged. "We haven't anything better to do. Suppose you translate as I talk." He filled his lungs and began:

"It's a long way between stars in this thin outer part of the galaxy. And it's even longer between up-to-date systems that are normal ports of call. So ships are apt to need fresh supplies en route. Maybe the deuterium runs low, or the protein, or —lots of things. Or else, because no ship has perfect biochemical balance, it's necessary to stop on a homelike world and flush out accumulated by-products with fresh air. Planets suitable for the various types of space-going life forms are listed in the *Pilot's Data Bank and Ephemerides* for each region."

"He says we gotta tank up," Urgo told the Inspector.

Klat't'klak of Ittatik nodded, signifying assent in the same way as most 143an cultures. The head he used for this purpose also resembled the 143an, and those of both his shipmates, in that it had two eyes and a mouth. However, mouth and nostrils were set in a beak that brought the narrow skull to a point. A fleshy aileron grew from the top, counterpart to the rudderlike fluke at the end of a thin tail. The body in between had, like Pazilliwheep's, evolved from a hexapod. But on Ittatik the rear limbs had become legs terminating in claws to grasp branches; the middle limbs had become skinny arms with six-digited hands; the

forelimbs were now leathery wings. A keelbone
jutted from the deep-chested torso. When he stood
erect, Klak't'klak's nude gray-skinned frame was
of slightly less stature than Pazilliwheep's; but his
wingspan was easily four meters. Nonetheless, he
could not fly here. The ship's gee-field was set
lower than his home gravity, but the air was so
much thinner that he couldn't stay healthy
without artificial help. This took the form of a
pomander which he kept lifting to his face. The
oxygen-generating biochemicals within smelled
like rich swamp ooze.

"The requirement is understood," he said, "And
obviously biological maintenance problems alone
suffice to compel your descent into the planetary
atmosphere. The point, however, which it was
desired to make, is that a primary reason for the
selection of this vessel as my transport was that
you were, indeed, planning to restock on the world
in question. Furthermore, your cargo is not
perishable nor urgently required by the consignee.
Thus the sum total of inconvenience and delay is
minimized. Admittedly, I may be the cause of your
remaining for more than the few 37.538-hour
periods you presumably reckoned with. But if all
appears to be in order, if there is no clear need at
this point in time for further investigation of the
possibility that ameliorative action may be
required somewhere upon the globe, then we
should be able to proceed within two or three
months. I will not insist upon being returned to
Zandar, but will rather continue with you to the
Rim, where I shall debark in order to instigate a
study of conditions prevailing upon that frontier."

"Oh," said Urgo. To Pazilliwheep: "He says we'll
be stuck there for at least two or three months."

"Oh!" said the navigator-pilot, rather more pungently. "Will you ask his unblessed bureaucratship why the inferno he wants to excrete away so loving much time on one unseemly little ball of fertilizer?"—likewise rather more pungently.

"No fair," grumbled Urgo. "I can't talk to him like that."

Klat't'klak explained. He wasn't really much interested in 143. His primary mission was to make sure that things were going well on the civilized planets of the Rim, and recommend remedies to the Federation authorities for whatever he found amiss. Still, 143 was overdue for inspection—seeing that it housed one nation that belonged to the great confraternity.

Such membership confers certain privileges. They are not many, because a galactic-scale league is necessarily a loose one, little more than a set of agencies serving the common interests of wildly diverse cultures. But a member is entitled to some things: for example, technical assistance if it wishes to modernize in any way.

"No," said Pazilliwheep, "our friends on 143 aren't what you would call the go-getter type. They're content to sell us their services, use of landing space, a few kinds of goods. Mainly they take biologicals in exchange—you know, longevity pills and, uh, other medicines. Ask them yourself if you doubt my word."

"I do not, of course," Klak't'klak answered through Urgo. "But I gather the planet holds numerous cultures. Perhaps they are being treated unfairly. Might they not, for example, be worthy of Federation membership too?"

"Chaos, no!" Pazilliwheep paused. "Well, I suppose they're no worse than some I could name.

But no better, either. We do make spot checks, we traders, in the hope of finding new potential markets. But the majority of 143ans haven't shown any improvement in the more than two centuries that the blob's been visited. They've got a drab, fragmented, quarrelsome, early-mechanical kind of civilization. Last time I was there, we noticed traces of manned landings on the single moon. That indicates the stage they're at. If they learned the Federation exists—"

"They would have to be admitted to membership if they asked."

"Exactly! And can you imagine the results? Those dismal characters would yell for so much technical assistance that their whole planet would be one gigantic college for the next fifty years. Sector taxes would go up ten percent, I'll bet, to finance it. We'd have to stop using our base, probably, because of their confounded nationalistic regulations about passports and I don't know what other nonsense. And there isn't as handy a planet for us within a hundred light-years." Pazilliwheep gestured violently. "And all this sacrifice on our part for what? To add one more lousy space-traveling species—competing right in our trade lanes to the Rim!"

"You are satisfied with the status quo, then?"

"Right. The 143ans who do know about us and do have membership are friendly, dignified, unaggressive, mind-their-own-business people who'll work for us when we need help at an honest wage for honest labor, and who produce salable handicrafts. Do you wonder that we hide our existence from everyone else?"

"No. Frankly, I cannot help suspecting you underpay your native help; that is what "honest wage for honest labor" usually means. But I am more concerned with ascertaining whether the planet has other civilizations that would, on balance, prove an asset to the Federation. Rather than read the sporadic reports of untrained and biased observers, I want to investigate and decide for myself."

Even through Urgo's translation, Pazilliwheep noted how Klak't'klak had dropped his elegant periods for shorter sentences in a sharper tone. The navigator-pilot sighed and resigned his soul. All right, he'd be hung up for a while on 143, chauffering the Sector Inspector around, assisting with instruments, catching natives for interviews. (This was done in such wise that, after they were released, no one believed their story. Experience had shown that the best ploy on 143 was the Benign Observers of Elder Race.) He and Urgo would be at once busy and bored.

Yet . . . eventually they'd start drawing overtime pay. And the mission on 143 wouldn't likely be prolonged. If nothing else, *Grumdel Castle* was uncomfortable. Her cramped cabins, vibrating decks, rusty metal, chipped plastic, wheezy ventilators, and uninspired galley saw to that. In addition, she carried so few books and tapes suitable for Klak't'klak that he would have them memorized in weeks. Pazilliwheep and Urgo always laid in recreational materials before a voyage. But what use to an Ittatikan were Ensiktan murder mysteries and Bontuan pornography?

And so *Grumdel Castle* creaked and groaned the long dark way to the Solar System. She took up orbit around the third planet while Pazilliwheep checked for indications of excessive radioactivity, smog, and other hazards of an early-mechanical culture. Meanwhile, Urgo the Red went outside to install camouflage tubes on the hull.

His shipmates saw his fur as bright blue; but then, they didn't use a visual spectrum identical with the Bontuan. The engineer-supercargo was a tailless biped, three meters tall and broad to match. His head was round, short-muzzled, big-eyed, fuzzy, and rather endearing. His hands were five-fingered, his feet four-toed. In spite of his hirsute skin, he affected white coveralls, sandals, and an ornate tool belt.

He clumped in again and shed his spacesuit. "Guess they'll hang together awhile," he reported, "but if the owners don't spring for a new set when we get home, I'm gonna look for another berth. How's the planet doin'?"

"About as before. I note more air traffic each time, though, damn it," Pazilliwheep said. "Also, today, what appears to be a manned orbital satellite. We'll have to wait here till the stupid thing's on the opposite side of the globe."

Klak't'klak inquired why they lingered. Urgo explained. *Grumdel Castle* used a camouflage standard on worlds of this atmospheric type, where it was desired to fly unbeknownst. The natives could not detect an operating hyperdrive; if they had that capability, they'd soon be making their own star ships! And antiradiation screens served to control air molecules as well as atomic particles, making even the fastest travel soundless. But you were still stuck with the fact that your ship was a solid, visible, radar-reflecting object.

So you wrapped her in the gaudiest ionized gas-discharge effect you could generate. You added

powerful magnetic and electrostatic fields, and
varied them randomly. You sailed in, alerting
every eye and every instrument for a hundred
miles around—

Just like a natural traveling plasmoid.

But since those erratic masses of molecules and
electrons occur in atmosphere, and the ship was in
space, she must first sneak down.

Presently she did. Near her destination, she
spied a native aircraft. At Klak't'klak's request,
she veered closed so he could get a good look.
Then she headed off for the home of that 143an
people who, during the past two hundred years,
had been members in good standing of the
Galactic Federation.

On the assumption that the flying saucer would
continue in a straight line, Sean Lindquist zig-
zagged along the same general path. After half an
hour he was rewarded. He crossed above an
immense red ridge. Its farther slope tumbled into
a canyon whose bottom was the most vivid green
he'd spied in a long while. Squarish adobe buildings were stacked against one rock wall, overlooking a stream lined with trees. But what made his
pulses jump afresh was the object that lay before
the houses. The dazzling, confusing play of colors
was gone; the shape had definite outlines and a
dark gray hue; but it was surely the thing that had
buzzed him. And by all the saints and any heathen
gods who cared to join in—it *was* a vessel!

He tilted his airplane's wings, crammed on
power, and whipped back the way he had come. A
thermal nearly tossed him from control. But he
must get out of sight before he was observed
and—

And what? Some kind of ray gun shot him down? He ran his tongue across lips gone sand-papery. The ship had to be from outer space: real outer space, the unimaginable abysses that held the stars. He'd followed the progress of flybys and landings within the Solar System. Hence he knew that, while the saucerians might be little and emerald-colored, they were not from any neighborhood planet. He also knew enough aero-dynamics to be sure no Terrestrial organization was experimenting with stuff that advanced. Even if he had been ignorant of the engineering require-ments, he was learned in the ways of public re-lations offices. . . . "Stop maundering, will you?" he croaked.

What to do?

He kept the plane wobbling back and forth on the far side of the mountain while, feverishly, he studied his charts and tried to discover where he was. Uh, yes . . . "Wuwucimti," plus the symbol for Pop. 0-1000 . . . evidently a pueblo, and lonely as hell, to judge from the fact that nothing led away from it except a dim mule trail. . . . Numbly, like parts of a machine rather than a body, his fingers activated the radio. If he could raise, oh, Gallup or Durango or wherever . . . make his location known, so it wouldn't do the aliens any good to destroy him. . . . A distant seething filled his earphones. Whether atmospherics or They were responsible, he couldn't get through.

He got his pipe off the floor, reloaded and relit it, and fumed himself into a measure of calm. A long gulp from a bottle that lived in his sleeping bag was equally helpful. *Consider, Lindquist*, he thought. *You've stumbled on a secret to shake the world. But this is hardly our first visit from yonder.*

Leaving aside the mistakes, the hoaxes, and the claims of the nut cults, there always was a certain amount of saucer observation that couldn't be explained away. At least, it was easier to believe in spaceships than in some of those concatenations of coincidences that the orthodox scientists postulated! And now you've got proof that the ship hypothesis is right. Only, who's going to take your unsupported word? Supposing you could go fetch witnesses, the thing's bound to be gone when you return. You'd get classed with Adamski and his breed.

For which sane reason, you'll keep your mouth shut.

Hey! he reflected in rising eagerness. *How many people have actually met saucerians, and been disbelieved afterward? And, on that account, how many more have met them and—not wanting to be laughed at—simply kept mum?*

After all . . . what little consistent evidence there is—indicates the saucerians aren't evil. They're shy, or snobbish, or something, but I can't remember anyone ever claiming that they do any deliberate harm. So maybe, this time, I can—

Allowing himself no second thoughts, Lindquist brought the plane about. He roared back over the mountain, chose his position, tilted wings, and commenced vertical descent.

Updrafts were tricky; and this was a somewhat battered, cranky craft he had. For a while he was too occupied with controls, instruments, hiss and shudder around him, to heed much else. He did see how the saucer squatted imperturbable in the bright late sunlight. Tawny mud-brick walls, red canyon sides, deep blue sky, green meadows and cornfields, green cottonwoods and willows along the quicksilver stream, dusty sage and juniper farther back—and in the middle, a spaceship from the stars!

His landing gear touched. He cut the power. Silence hit him like a thunderclap. He unharnessed, opened the door, and sprang shakily forth. The air was thin, dry, pungent with resinous odors. Except for a breeze, tinkle of water, bleating from a pasture shared by sheep and goats, the silence continued.

It was not broken by the approaching locals. They were ordinary Pueblo types, a few hundred medium-sized dark-complexioned folk of every apparent age. Men and women both wore their hair in braids. Clothing varied, from more or less traditional breechcloths, gowns, and blanketes, to levis and sport shirts. Lindquist's sharpened perceptions noted that the people were better clad, seemed more healthy and prosperous, than the average Southwest Indian. And they were strangely uncordial. Not that they threatened him. But they drew up in a kind of phalanx, and stared, and said never a word. Even the littlest children sucked their thumbs in a marked manner.

Lindquist gulped. "Uh . . . hello," he said. His voice sounded very small to him. "I'm afraid I, uh, don't speak your language." They might know Spanish. *"Buenas días, mis amigos."* Trouble was, that damn near exhausted his Spanish.

A grizzled, weather-beaten man called softly, "sikyabotoma." Lindquist said, "I beg your pardon?" but decided it was the name of a young man who stepped to the elder. They put heads together and conferred in mutters.

Lindquist gulped again, nodded, pasted on a smile, and started toward the flying saucer. At once he grew so conscious of it—so astonished, for instance, at the pitted, corroded metal of what had once been a smooth unitized shape—that the Indians faded from his mind. Colliding with them was a shock. Several had moved to intercept him.

They were embarrassed. The pueblo dwellers are among the politest beings on Earth. They smiled, in a forced way, bobbed their heads, and waved their hands. They pushed gently on Lindquist's arms, as if to urge him toward their houses.

Anger flared. "No, thanks!" he snapped, and planted his heels.

The young man rescued the situation. He was among those who wore modern clothes, including the gaudiest sombrero Lindquist had ever met. He sauntered forth, tapped the newcomer on the back, and said, "Excuse me, buddy. That's not the way."

"What?" Lindquist whirled to confront him.

"Welcome to Wuwucimti Pueblo," the Indian said. "I'm Sikyabotoma. But in the Army I used the name Joe Andrews. Picked that because it's handy being near the head of the alphabet. So if you want, call me Joe. Come on inside and have a drink."

"I—I thought—you—"

"You needn't be surprised. Sure, the Hopi don't approve of liquor as a rule. But they need somebody like me, who's equipped to handle white men. Like, I interpret when we take the mules to town and stock up on things. And I did do a military hitch. So I've gotten a few outsider habits. It's good bourbon."

"But—I mean—" Lindquist twisted his neck to

goggle what now lay behind his back. "I never imagined—"

"Yes, it is unusual," Sikyabotoma agreed cordially. He linked arms with Lindquist, who must needs come along as he ambled in the direction of the village. "We're the most isolated pueblo in the country. Not awful old. A bunch of Shoshonean-speaking Hopi moved here to get away from the Spaniards after the revolt of 1680 was put down. So we have a tradition of minding our own affairs, and we discourage visitors. Nothing rude, you understand. We just don't do anything interesting when the anthropologists come. And we got rid of the missionaries by telling the last padre who showed that we'd already been converted to hard-shell Baptists."

The other Indians trailed after at some distance. They kept their silence. "Please don't think we're hostile," Sikyabotoma urged. "We're only satisfied. We combine the old and the new as suits us best; and we do quite well for ourselves, on the whole; and everybody among us knows a Regular contact with the outside world would upset our applecart. So we act pretty unanimously to defend our privacy. Unanimity comes natural in the Hopi culture anyhow. If you're in trouble, we'll help you, Mr., uh—"

"Lindquist," said Lindquist feebly.

"We'll do what we can for you. But if you dropped in out of curiosity, well, I hate to sound inhospitable, but the fact is you'd find Wuwucimti a mighty dull place. Lively young fellow like you, huh? I'd suggest you proceed right away. And, uh, I'd take it as a favor if you don't mention this stop you made. We're not after tourist business and that's that. You savvy?"

"Dull?" Lindquist tore loose. He spun, flung out both arms toward the great spaceship, and shouted, "You call that dull?" so echoes rang.

"Well, not to me, of course," Sikyabotoma said. "I get my kicks. And the average pueblo dweller is staid by nature."

"Flying saucers and—and—"

Sikyabotoma regarded Lindquist narrowly. "Do you feel okay?" he asked.

"Sure I feel okay! What about that flying saucer over there?"

Sikyabotoma squinted. "What flying saucer?"

"What do you mean? I, I, I chased it . . . to here . . . and there it sits!"

"Awa-Tsireh," called Sikyabotoma, "do you see a flying saucer?"

A middle-aged Indian looked solemnly back and shook his head. "No," he grunted. "No see fly sawsuh."

"I'll ask the others in Hopi if you want," Sikyabotoma offered. "But you know, Mr. Lindquist, when people aren't used to this thin air and sunglare, they can mistake mirage effects for some of the damnedest things. I'd be careful about that if I were you. Flitting around in an airplane, a guy has to be mighty sure what's real and what's an optical illusion. Doesn't he?"

Lindquist stared for an entire minute into the broad bland face. The others moved closer, and had also begun to smile and murmur soothing words. Briefly, in his tottering mind, he wondered if he was not indeed the crazy one.

No! He sprang back and launched himself. His legs flew. Dust spurted, the footfalls slammed through his shins, and he made an end run around the tribe. Meanwhile he bawled:

"Do radars have illusions? Do compasses? By heaven . . . let me . . . at my instruments . . . and I'll show you!"

He reached the ship. Its curve swelled immense above him, casting a knife-edged shadow. He snatched a rock and pounded the metal. It boomed. A lizard ran away. The sandstone crumbled under repeated impacts. "Is that optical?" he screamed.

The Hopi had been running toward him. But once more they halted at a distance. Sikyabotoma came nearer. The young Indian stopped, regarded Lindquist, and sighed.

"Okay," he said. "I didn't really expect it'd work. Have your way, Charlie."

He semaphored with his arms.

Lindquist stepped back from the ship, panting, sweating, trembling. The canyon brooded in a quiet immense and eternal; only the wind had voice. Then came a rusty creak.

Someone had been watching from inside, through some kind of television. And in some fashion, a part of the hull detached itself on three sides and unrolled, to make a gangway to the ground. Three creatures came forth. Lindquist saw them and strangled on an oath that was half a prayer.

Sikyabotoma took a philosophical attitude. "You ought to see what membership in the Galactic Federation has done to our kachina dolls," he remarked. "The real ones, that we don't show the anthropologists."

"This is most annoying," Klak't'klak said. He flapped his wings. They made a parchment rustle where he squatted in the sunshine, under the spaceship, confronting the bug-eyed 143an.

"Sure is," Urgo the Red agreed. "We gotta get rid of this bum. And then we gotta stay away from here for several days—prob'ly go into orbit—in case he does somehow talk somebody into comin' back with him. Right when I was hopin' to get that Number Three regulator tuned!"

"I was thinking more personally," the Inspector admitted. "I am not prepared to conduct interviews. That is, my translating computer has not yet assimilated the records of this planet's dominant languages which the autochthons brought me from their—ah—what did they call it?—their kiva. And I hate working through interpreters."

"So don't."

"No, as long as we have captured this being, I feel my duty is to examine him for whatever information he can give. And, no, I should endeavor to allay his fears. To this poor unsophisticated semi-savage, we must resemble veritable demons. Consider how he staggered to his aircraft for that bottle of tranquilizing medication he now clutches so tightly."

Urgo waved a massive blue hand. Pazilliwheep trotted over, using his nose-tendrils in turn to summon one of the Indians. "I don't speak this barbarian's jabber," the navigator-pilot explained, "but Sikyabotoma does." Urgo passed on the datum.

The galactics, including the Pueblo man, formed a semicircle confronting Lindquist. The rest of the village watched aloofly. Klak't'klak lifted a gaunt arm. "Greeting to you, O native," he said in Interlingo-12. "Rest assured that you are in the grasping organs of civilized and benevolent entities who intend you no harm; who may, indeed, prove to be the promoters of a benign revolution upon your planet. Whether this eventuality materializes or not is dependent upon my official judgment as to whether a general announcement of the existence of a galaxy-wide Federation of technologically and sociologically advanced races will serve the larger good, including your own good. Hence the outcome is to a small extent dependent upon what you yourself, individually, today, choose to give me in the way of information. May I therefore initially request—request, mind you; we shall not compel you—request and advise that you relate to me in circumstantial detail what I wish to be apprised of, beginning with the events which led to your untoward arrival."

"He wants to know how the bum got there," Urgo said in Interlingo-7.

"The honorable envoy of the Federation's guiding council asks what gods led hither the stranger's path," Pazilliwheep said in Hopi.

"The pterodactyl character is a kind of inspector," Sikyabotoma said in English. "He won't hurt you, but he would like to know a few things, like how come you stopped by."

Lindquist took another pull on his bottle. "I . . . I saw the flying saucer . . . and followed it," he whispered.

"Yeah, sure. Look, pal, I don't believe you can tell him a thing that I can't. But let's go through with the game and make him happy, okay? The other two are plain merchant sailors. Old buddies of mine; I even made a voyage with 'em once, to help establish an outplanet market for our local handicrafts. But Beak-and-Wings, he's come to find out whether the galactics ought to let the rest of the Earth know about them; whether they should invite every country to join their Federation. In other words, he's one of those do-gooder types."

"You—don't think—we should join?" Lindquist gave forth.

"Frankly, no." Sikyabotoma shrugged. "Not that the pueblo is selfish, or holds a deep grudge against the white man, or anything. However, you can't expect we'll fall over ourselves to do the white man a favor, can you? Especially when that'd end our own comfortable monopoly on trade and services with the galaxy. We're not ostentatious about it, and of course we're pretty small potatoes in the Federation . . . but you'd be surprised at some of the stuff we keep in our adobes."

Lindquist braced himself. "*I* look at the matter differently," he said. "Can I trust you to give him my side of the story?"

"Sure. I may be prejudiced, but I'm honest. Besides, he figures to study the whole planet. Don't loft your hopes though. One dollar gets you ten that he turns thumbs down."

"How can he?" Lindquist cried.

Sikyabotoma looked closed. "I'll be damned, you're right. He has thumbs on both sides of his palms. . . . Oh. You mean how can he refuse the USA, and the USSR, and France, Britain, and China, and—Well, it's easy. They haven't anything unique to offer. Not in a galaxy loaded with civilizations. All that Wuwucimti has, really, is a convenient location, and people who don't swarm over every ship that lands, stealing things and asking stupid questions. You start letting in the riffraff, and first you've got to disestablish institutions like war, and then you've got to give them technical assistance, and then—anyhow, it's a mess. That's why secrecy is preserved, you know. If you guys ever found out the truth, collectively, you'd have to be invited to join. Otherwise, the do-gooders say, your precious little egos would be so bruised that what culture you have would fall to pieces." The Hopi checked himself. "Sorry. I didn't mean to sound smug. Or malicious. It's just the way the ball bounces."

"How about my ego?" Lindquist demanded, close to tears.

Sikyabotoma patted his shoulder. "Nothing personal, Charlie," he said. "Individual humans who got interviewed in the past don't seem to've suffered harm. Look at it this way: You won't be any worse off than you were. Huh?"

"I'll tell the world!" Lindquist said furiously. "I'll call in the FBI, the news reporters, the—"

"For both our sakes," the Indian answered, "I wish you wouldn't. You'd only make a fool of yourself. At most, you'd bring in somebody else, and the village 'ud have to go through the same old cover-up schtick as before. You wouldn't do that to us, would you, now? A nice guy like you?"

"No, I'll keep watch—" Lindquist snapped his mouth shut.

"Till another ship arrives, eh?" Sikyabotoma chuckled. "You'd wait a mighty long time, podner."

"Not many come?"

"M-m-m, well, it varies. With thousands of shipping outfits plying these lanes, we can expect several craft per year to stop by, though we never know in advance. However, what we do know is if anybody's within thirty-forty kilometers. A little gadget that detects thoughts. So you can't monitor us unbeknownst. We can warn off ships; they do radio us from orbit before landing. Chances are they'd come down anyway, but maintain camouflage. All you'd observe or photograph would be a colored blur like ordinary ball lightning. If worst comes to worst, a bunch of us can deal with a spy. Nothing violent, understand. We'll kind of escort him away, no more. If we have to break his camera, we'll pay him full value. You see, we're Federation members; we live by Federation rules."

The Inspector spoke words which went along the chain of interpreters. Sikyabotoma nodded and sat down on his haunches. "You might as well relax," he said. "Over here, in the shade. You're about to be interviewed."

Time passed. Shadows lengthened. The Pueblo women cooked dinner. They brought some to Lindquist. It was Hopi food, based on cornmeal tortillas, but the filling was like nothing on Earth. Quite literally so. Sikyabotoma explained that a lot of interstellar trade was in spices.

When the sun went below the mountains, stars leaped arrogantly forth. Coyotes yipped across a gigantic silence. Lindquist stared heavenward and shivered in the sudden cold.

Sikyabotoma rose, yawning. "That's that," he said. "They'll fly you out now, to make sure you don't hang around. Any special place you'd like to go?"

"Colorado Springs?" Lindquist faltered.

"I wouldn't. NORAD headquarters, remember. They spot your plane on their radars without any flight plan filed, they might get a little unpleasant."

"That's my problem." Lindquist could scarcely keep his tone level. He had not dared hope his precarious scheme would work to this extent.

"Okay, then. Hm, I think I'll ride along. You might enjoy being shown around a genuine hypership. Something to tell your grandchildren, if you don't mind 'em thinking you're an awful liar."

The three aliens embarked. Lindquist and Sikyabotoma followed, after the village elders had bidden the former good-bye with every ritual courtesy. A larger opening gaped elsewhere in the hull; the aircraft rose on some silent, invisible beam of force; it was stowed aboard. The great ship closed herself. Soundlessly, but swathed again in rainbow haze, she lifted and swung north.

Inside, she was less impressive. In fact, she was grimy, battered, noisy and ill-smelling. Sikyabotoma shrugged when Lindquist dared remark on it. "What do you expect in an old tramp with cheapskate owners? Red plush toilet seats? C'mon, we better stash you in your plane. Be over Pike's Peak soon."

When Lindquist was harnessed, the Hopi stuck a hand through the open cabin door of the aircraft. His brown face was bent in a wry smile. "Shake," he offered. "I hope there aren't any hard feelings. You're a right guy. I could damn near wish Birdbrain does certify this whole planet for membership. But I know he won't. So long, Charlie, and good luck to you."

He closed the door. For a minute Lindquist sat alone, in the thrumming, coldly lit cavern of the hold. The hull opened. Stars glittered in the aperture, brilliant against crystalline black. Air puffed outward, popping his eardrums, and chill flowed inward. He started his engine. But it was the impalpable force beam that carried him forth and released him.

Town lights glittered far beneath. The spaceship hovered close, like a swirling, shifting, many-hued light-fog. She departed, gathering speed until no human-built rocket could have paced her. Night swallowed the vision.

Lindquist shuddered. His radio receiver squawked with challenge. An interceptor jet winged toward him. "Sure," he said. "I'll come down. Any place you want." Excitement torrented through him. "And then . . . take me to your leader!"

In the morning they turned him over to Lieutenant Harold Quimby. Maybe that press officer could get rid of him.

Sunlight slanted through a window, beyond which stretched the neat buildings and walked the neat personnel of a United States Air Force base. Light glowed on immaculate office furniture, on Quimby's polished insignia and practiced toothpaste smile. Lindquist grew doubly aware of how unshaven, sweaty, and haggard he was. His eyes burned; the lids felt like sandpaper.

"Cigarette?" Quimby invited. "Coffee?"

"No," Lindquist grated. "Some common sense. That's all I ask. The common sense and common decency of listening to me."

"Why, surely our people—"

"Yeah, they grilled me. For most of the night. Oh, polite enough. But they kept after me and after me."

"Well, you must realize, Mr. Lindquist, when

you suddenly appear over a sensitive area like this, you must expect that men charged with the national defense will ask for details."

"Damn it, I *gave* them details! Every last stinking detail I could dredge up. Look, the fact that I did appear, without your fool radars registering me till I was there . . . doesn't that mean anything?"

"It means that the plasmoid blanketed your approach. Not unknown. An unusually fine plasmoid, wasn't it?" Quimby leaned forward with a sympathetic air. "I can easily understand why you would follow such a beautiful and fascinating object. And, ah, how the interplay of colors . . . hypnotic, even epileptogenic effects . . . mistaking a vivid dream for reality—no, wait!" He lifted his hand. "The Air Force is not calling you a lunatic, Mr. Lindquist. What happened to you could happen to anyone. I talked with Major Willians of our psychiatric division before my appointment with you today. He assured me that illusion and confusion are the normal result of lengthy exposure to certain optical phenomena. We lodged you overnight precisely in order that our intelligence officers could make a few phone calls, checking on your background and recent activities. I assure you, Mr. Lindquist, we are careful here. We have established that you are sane and well intentioned. We appreciate the patriotism that led you to seek us out, even in your, ah, slightly delirious condition. You are free to go home, Mr. Lindquist, with the warmest thanks of the United States Air Force."

Quimby paused for breath. "But you saw the spaceship yourselves!" Lindquist groaned. "You radared the thing. You recorded electric and mag-

netic effects. Your technical man admitted as
much to me. How can you call it an illusion?"

"We don't, sir, we don't," Quimby beamed. "It
was absolutely real. The Air Force is not dogmatic.
The Air Force has been interested in this subject
for many years. When the first so-called flying
saucer reports were made in the later 1940s, the
Air Force mounted its own investigation. Here."
He handed Lindquist a glossy-paper pamphlet off
a stack on his desk. "A brief summary of Project
Blue Book. Certain people continued unsatisfied.
They charged—quite wrongly, I assure you—they
charged distortion and suppression of evidence.
Accordingly, to clear its good name, in the late
1960s the Air Force supported a new, independent
investigation under the leadership of the late distinguished Dr. Condon. An unclassified project,
mind you." He gave Lindquist another pamphlet.
"Here is a history of that effort." And another.
"Here is information on the final effort, which
produced a theory to account for the facts. This is
a summary of the technical findings. Here is a
somewhat more popular account, and here is a
reprint of what proved to be the key physical data,
and here is a—"

Lindquist slumped. "I know," he said. "They
told me last night what they believe. Ball lightning."

"Well, no, not exactly that," Lindquist said.
"The subject is pretty complicated. Yes, sir, pretty
complicated, if I do say so myself. Flying saucer
reports had many different sources. Early during
the furore, it was shown that most were caused by
sightings of weather balloons, or mirages, or re-
flections, or Venus, or any of several other things.
There did remain a certain small percentage

which could not be accounted for in that way. But at last it was shown that nature can generate plasmoids in the atmosphere. You know, traveling masses of ionized gas, held together for a few minutes or hours by a kind of self-generated magnetic bottle. Ball lightning is one kind of plasmoid. There are others. Including the kind that shines, produces erratic magnetic and electric fields, reflects radar, shuttles about at incredible speed but with never a sound, and is roughly disk-shaped. In short, the classical flying saucer apparition. This was *proven*, Mr. Lindquist. It was observed, analyzed, and reproduced in the laboratory. By now, any good electrophysicist who wanted to take the trouble could fake his own flying saucer. Here is an account by the Nobel Prize winner Dr.—"

"Never mind," Lindquist mumbled. "I don't doubt there are natural neon signs zipping around. So the saucerians don't need anything for camouflage except a false one."

"Well, Mr. Lindquist," Quimby replied, the least bit severely, "don't you believe it's high time you looked at the matter like the reasonable man you are? You had a, ah, an involuntary psychedelic experience. You would not have had it if you had known the truth. Then you would have realized there was no point in chasing that plasmoid. Nobody does anymore, you know. Because of your, ah, long foreign residence, you weren't kept up to date. But the truth is that the flying saucer hysteria vanished years ago. Once the clear light of science was thrown on this murky subject, the American people realized that everything had been due to an easily explainable natural phenomenon. They turned their attention to better topics. You won't find anyone any longer who claims that flying saucers are, ah, spaceships crewed by little green men."

"Would you believe a surly blue giant?"

"No, Mr. Lindquist, I would not. Nor, ah, pterodactyls and centaurs with arms on their noses. Least of all that a bunch of poverty-stricken, mostly illiterate Pueblo Indians are— Well, you have a very imaginative subconscious mind, sir, but I'm afraid no one cares to listen. So you had better settle for everyday reality."

Lindquist raised eyes in which hope still struggled with exhaustion. "No one?" he asked. "Absolutely no one in the world?"

"Oh, I suppose a few cranks are left, like in California," Quimby laughed. "People to whom the outer-space—visitors idea became a sort of religion that they still can't bear to give up." His tone sharpened. "It would not be advisable to prey on their gullibility. Not that you would, Mr. Lindquist. But some confidence man who, ah, tried to squeeze a dollar from those poor deluded souls— yes, I think the authorities might deal rather harshly with him."

Lindquist rose. "I know when I'm licked," he said bitterly. "I won't take any more of your time."

"Well, thank you, that's appreciated." Quimby stood too, with almost indecent haste. "We are rather busy at the moment, preparing press kits about General Robinson's promotion to four-star rank."

Lindquist ignored the proffered hand and shambled toward the door. "Too busy to bring Earth into the Galactic Federation!" he spat.

"That's not the job of the Air Force," Quimby reminded him. "Foreign relations belong to the State Department."

The bar which Lindquist found was noisy with college students. He didn't mind that. For the most part he sat hunched over his beer. When his awareness did, occasionally, return from interstellar immensities—to order more beer—he got a little encouragement from the sight of coeds passing by. A universe which had produced girls couldn't be all bad.

Contrariwise, it must be a hell of a good universe. Rich, wonderful, various, exciting, mind-expanding, soul-uplifting: if only you could get out into the damned thing.

"Rats!" Lindquist muttered around his pipestem. "Got to be *some* way to make a buck with what I know."

He wasn't entirely cynical. The galactics were, he thought. They denied to the human race every marvel, opportunity, insight, help, comfort that a millennia-old science must have to give. Not that they were monsters. With—how many suns in the galaxy? a hundred billion?—they rated intelligent species at a dime a dozen, and probably this was inevitable. Indeed, it was astonishing how altruistic they were. They could have conquered Earth in an afternoon. But instead, they slunk about in disguise for fear of what the knowledge of their presence might do to men ... if, following the revelation, they did not promptly act to lift man to their own level.

Sure, you can't blame them. Why should they solve our problems for us? Especially when it'd be a lot of trouble or expense to them. What did we ever do for the galactics?

Lindquist fumed smoke into the racketing, beer-laden air. *That's not the point*, he thought grimly. *The point as far as I'm concerned is that I and my whole ever-lovin' species will keep on being poor, ignorant, war-plagued, tyrannical, restricted, short-lived, and I don't know what else —unless the Federation can be forced to take us in.*

Which it can be, if we the people of the United States learn for sure that the Federation exists.

How? The galactics, including those damn Injuns, understand how to keep us blindfolded. They didn't even bother to silence me. Who'd listen?

Maybe, momentarily, the chance had existed. In 1950, whenever the flying saucer craze started, human civilization had advanced to the point where it could imagine extraterrestrial visitors; and it had not yet gotten the idea of plasmoids or rather, it was denying that any such thing could be. So a standard spaceship disguise had been ineffective for a decade or two. Unfortunately, though, no one had happened to see a sitting spaceship during those years. At least, not any people had happened to do so, and their unsupported word was insufficient. Now research had established that flying saucers could be plasmoids. Therefore, humankind concluded, they were plasmoids. As the galactics had foreseen. The bastards.

Today no one would believe the crazy truth. Except maybe some pathetic remnants of the discredited saucer cults. They might. But what could they do, except invite the narrator into their mutual admiration society?

What . . . could . . . they . . . do?

Sean Lindquist leaped to his feet. His table went

over, scattering beer and broken glass. His pipe fell to the floor. "Eureka!" he bellowed.

The bartender approached. "You had enough, buster," he said ominously. "Start taking off your clothes and I call a cop."

The Reverend Jacob Muir, pastor of the First United Church of the Cosmic Brotherhood, was a surprise. Though Lindquist had done considerable research beforehand, he had expected someone more, well, far out. Reverend Muir was soft-spoken, self-contained, and conventionally dress-ed: for Los Angeles, at least. He lived with his wife in an apartment near the shop that earned him his daily bread. The place could have belonged to any middle-class, middle-aged couple. Only the books were unusual. They formed prob-ably as complete a library of sauceriana as existed anywhere on Earth.

"Please sit down, Mr. Lindquist," he invited. "Would you care for some coffee?—Joan, brew us a pot, will you dear?—Smoke if you wish. It's bad for the health, but until the Elder Brethren see fit to raise us to the next rung of revolution's ladder, we can't much help our frailties. Pardon me. I didn't intend to preach at you. You came to tell me something, not vice versa."

Lindquist wondered what his best gambit was. From what he could learn of the C. B. Church, its few score active members, and its influence on several hundred saucerists of other kinds, he didn't believe that he could be entirely truthful. Muir's credo held that the extraterrestrials were the benevolent, well-nigh omnipotent agents of a civilization which was the chosen instrument of God. That wouldn't fit well with a rusty old tramp ship, pinchpenny owners, and so forth. Would it?

"I've had an Experience," he said.

"Really?" Muir's tone did not alter. "Do you know, I never have been vouchsafed one. Few who were are left alive; and the last confirmed report of a talk with Them was fifteen years ago." His gaze was quite steady. Traffic noises came through the window, to underscore his voice with muted thunder. "Hoaxes are not unheard-of."

Lindquist achieved a smile. "You're skeptical, Reverend?"

"Well, let us say I'm open-minded. I've often stated, in sermons and articles, that I think the Elders have abandoned us for a while because we grew too skeptical. They will come back when faith has come back. But—forgive me—there have been deliberate frauds, and there have been far more honest mistakes. For your sake as well as ours, we must sift your story carefully—whatever you tell."

"You're very tactful, sir." Lindquist's lanky frame relaxed in the armchair. As he felt his way into the situation, he gained confidence. "And I might as well confess at the outset, I want money. Furthermore, I haven't a scrap of physical evidence. Only the recent sighting over Colorado Springs, which thousands of people saw." He drew a breath. "However, if I can get financing, your auditors will keep track of every nickel. What we need is to build and transport a certain device which the Elders have described to me. For this, we'll have to buy materials and hire expensive technicians. We'll have to do a little R & D, perhaps, because the Elders didn't give me any blueprint, only a general verbal account. We'll have to do this on the QT until we're ready to roll, or you can imagine what a field day the news media will have."

Muir opened his mouth. Lindquist hurried on:

"In earnest of my sincerity, as well as to help, I can mortgage what little I own and toss several thousand dollars into the kitty. If you can double that, I believe we'll have the necessary. I checked on your people before I phoned you. They're not rich by a long shot. But between your congregation and, uh, its sympathizers—if you launch an appeal yourself—a few dollars contributed per person—the thing can be swung financially without hurting any individual except me if it fails."

He paused. "I do not guarantee success," he finished.

Muir sat quiet for a long time. His eyes never left his visitor. Finally he whispered, "You're not a con artist. You may be a crank, but you're honest. Go on, in God's name."

Lindquist saw tears. However noble his purpose, he felt a touch guilty as he gave his doctored account. The benevolent Elders had returned. They found Earth in dire straits. Disaster was imminent. Yet they could not destroy the human spirit by acting as dictators. They could only work through such persons as had faith in them.

Nor could they linger here. Other planets also needed their attention. But if enough humans had faith—if the veritable mustard seed existed upon Earth—then they could manifest themselves at last, and lead mankind to salvation. To this end, let the faithful build a communication device such as they demonstrated and explained to Sean F. X. Lindquist. In time, they would receive its message and they would come.

Did no such call reach them, they would sadly know that man was beyond redemption.

Passing through the ship's observation veranda —an elegant phrase for a crummy little cabin outfitted with an exterior visiscreen and a few seats adjustable to most species—Urgo the Red saw Klak't'klak. The Sector Inspector stood hunched before the view that slid beneath. The scene was of high desert, raw mineral hues under a blazing sun. His winged shape was etched in black by contrast. And yet he looked so frail, bowed, utterly tired and discouraged, that Urgo's equivalent of a heart went out to him. The engineer-supercargo had grumbled at length during the past tedious weeks. Nevertheless, against his will, he had come to like the official passenger. It hurt him, now, to see the little Ittatikan stand thus alone. He went and joined him.

"You're really quittin', huh?" he asked inanely.

Klak't'klak uttered a mournful whistle. "Yes. Not that the natives have no potential. They seem about average, insofar as any such concept is meaningful. But I could not justify a recommendation that missions be sent to elevate them."

"Troublemakers. Yeh, I could'a told you that right off," Urgo rumbled.

"No. Not really." Klak't'klak spread his wings and folded them again. "They would not be a detriment to the Federation. But neither would they be an outstanding asset as far as I can judge on the basis of my examinations. They would, in short, be . . . merely one more member species. Therefore, as long as they remain in happy ignorance of us, I cannot honestly say that the Federation taxpayer should be burdened with the cost of incorporating them. Let them invent the hyperdrive for themselves, in a thousand or two years."

Urgo belched, which out of him corresponded to a sigh of relief. "That's the spirit, Inspector! I knew you'd decide right. But how come are you lookin' down in the chops you haven't got?"

"I don't rightly know," Klak't'klak said. "Depression, I suppose. So much time, effort, expense, inconveniencing you and Navigator-Pilot Finnison —you've been extraordinarily kind, you two, and I won't forget it when I write my official report— but for nothing."

Urgo waved his mighty arms. "Ah, don't worry. The job was a drag, sure, but it's over with now. We'll stop off at the pueblo to snatch a rest and some trade goods. Then ho for the Rim!"

At that moment, the buzzer sounded. Pazilliwheep's voice followed. *"Attenta!"* He had amused himself by acquiring a few 143an phrases as *Grumdel Castle* prowled around the globe. *"Pericolo!* All hands to stations!"

"What the blazes?" Urgo was already loping for the engine room. Klak't'klak flapped and hopped toward his quarters, where he would at least be out of the way. You don't argue when someone calls emergency on a hypership. The deck gonged to the engineer-supercargo's footfalls. "What's'a matter?" he roared.

"I don't know," Pazilliwheep said tautly over the intercom. "Electromagnetic field . . . variable . . . registered a few seconds ago. Might be a natural plasmoid, but we'd better have a look."

Urgo felt relieved. The news could have been something nasty, like the bottom dropping out of this hull. "Where are we, anyhow?" he asked.

"About a hundred kilometers west of Wuwu-cimti. Which is to say, the emanations could be from a galactic ship in distress—a little ways beyond mind detector range from the pueblo." Pazilliwheep swung his craft through a ninety-degree turn. The acceleration compensators were so badly out of phase that Urgo slipped on the deck and hit his nose.

Nevertheless, the engineer-supercargo confirmed his remarks to a muttered *"Snagabaga-bartbats!"* That was cruel country below, especially for beings who had not evolved on this planet. A vessel grounded helpless in those arid mountains and canyons might soon be crewless. And that—aside from every moral consideration—invited the disaster of discovery by non-Hopi autochthons. It was well that *Grumdel Castle* had happened by in time.

Once in the engine room, Urgo activated his own visiscreen. He saw a wild landscape, heat shimmers and dust devils . . . and, yes, a saucer shape on a small mesa. Its outlines were blurred by a weak camouflage field, and neither he nor Pazilliwheep could identify the make of ship. But with millions of different makes—

"Why aren't they transmitting?" Pazilliwheep wondered.

"Transmitter busted, I guess," Urgo said. "They could'a lain here for, cometfire, days or weeks, you know. Aimin' to land at Wuwucimti but not makin' it. Expectin' somebody else'd come by eventually, and keeping' their field goin' so's they be detectable at a distance."

"But not daring to strike out on foot for the pueblo," Pazilliwheep added. "Right you are. Let's get down."

Grumdel Castle descended to the mesa and cut her own camouflage and her engines. The galactics emerged in a brilliant, silent, sagebrush-pungent air. Hulking Urgo, graceful Pazilliwheep, broad-winged Klak't'klak moved across the sand toward the beached hypership.

Only, now that they were close, it looked less and less like a hypership. It looked more and more like—

"Surprise, surprise!" caroled a native voice. Sean F. X. Lindquist's lean form sprang from the false hull. He ran to meet them, arms spread in welcome, face wide open in a silly grin. "Am I glad to see you! Two weeks waiting! And you turn out to be the very same guys who— Come on and have a cold beer!"

Klak't'klak had brought his translator machine, which was keyed to several federation as well as 143an languages. But it was his pomander behind which he retreated. His eyes rolled. He gasped. Urgo bawled, "Oh, no!" and Pazilliwheep looked ill.

Other humans emerged. So did a television camera on a dolly. "We alerted the news services," Lindquist said happily. "Of course they thought this was a lunatic-fringe project, but they did agree to stand by, in case we came up with anything good for laughs. Smile, you're on candid camera. Now we better break the news gently to my assistants, though you aren't quite the godlike beings most of them think you are." He stopped, blushed through his stubble, and beckoned to a companion. "Pardon me. I was so excited I forgot. Here's Professor Rostovtsev from Colorado U. He speaks Hopi."

Klak't'klak had already adjusted his machine to

English. He turned it off for a minute, while he expressed himself in his own tongue. Then he closed the circuit again.

"Never mind," he said resignedly. "Welcome to the Galactic Federation."

DETAILS

The most austerely egalitarian societies—and the League is a mature culture which has put such games behind it—soon learn they must cater to the whims of their leaders. This is true for the simple reason that a mind on whose decisions all fate may turn has to function efficiently, which it can only do when the total personality is satisfied and unjarred. For Rasnagarth Kri the League had rebuilt a mile-high skyscraper. His office took up the whole roof, beneath a dome of clear plastic, so that from his post he could brood by day over the city towers and by night under the cold radiance of the Sagittarian star-clouds. It was a very long walk from the gravshaft door to the big bare desk.

Harban Randos made the walk quickly, almost jauntily. They had warned him that the High Commissioner was driven by a sense of undying haste and that it was worth a man's future to spill time

on a single formality. Randos fairly radiated brisk-
ness. He was young, only a thousand years old,
plumpish and sandy-haired, dressed in the latest
mode of his people, the Shandakites of Garris. His
tunic glittered with starry points of light and his
cloak blew like a flame behind him.

He reached the desk and remained standing. Kri
had not looked up. The harsh blue face was intent
over a bit of paper. Around him the sky was sunny,
aircraft flittered in dragonfly grace, the lesser
spires glowed and burned, the city pulsed. For the
blue man in the plain gray robe, none of it existed,
not while he was looking at that one sheet.

After all, its few lines of text and paramathe-
matical symbology concerned eight billion human
lives. In another lifetime or so—say 10,000 years—
the consequences might well concern the entire
League, with a population estimated at ten to the
fifteenth power souls.

After an interminable minute, Kri scribbled his
decision and dropped the report down the outgoing chute. Another popped automatically from
the incoming slot. He half reached for it, saw
Randos waiting, and withdrew his hand. That was
a gaunt hand, knobby and ropy and speckled with
age.

"Harban Randos, sir, by appointment," rattled
off his visitor. "Proposed agent-in-chief for new
planet in Section two-three-nine-seven-six-two."

"I remember now. Sit down." Kri nodded curtly.
"Coordinator Zantell and Representative Chuing
urged your qualifications. What are they?"

"Graduated in seventy-five from Nime Psychotechnic Institute in the second rank. Apprenticeship under Vor Valdran on Galeen V, rated as
satisfactory." Damn the old spider! What did he

think the Service was . . . the Patrol?

"Galeen was a simple operation," said Kri. "It was only a matter of guiding them along the last step to full status. The planet for which you have been recommended is a barbarous one, therefore a more difficult and complex problem."

Randos opened his mouth to protest that backward planets were, mathematically, an elementary proposition . . . Great Designer, only a single world to worry about, while the Galeenians had reached a dozen stars at the time he went there! Wisely, he closed it again.

Kri sighed. "How much do you know of the situation on this one?—No, never mind answering, it would take you all day. Frankly, you're only getting the job for two reasons. One, you are a Shandakite of Garris, which means you are physiologically identical with the race currently dominant on the planet in question. We have no other fully trained Shandakite available, and indeed no qualilfied man who could be surgically disguised. Everyone I would like to appoint is tied up elsewhere with more important tasks. Two, you have the strong recommendation of Zantell and Chuing.

"Very well, the post is yours. The courier boat will take you there, and supply you en route with hypnotic instruction as to the details. You already know the Service rules and the penalties for violating them.

"I wanted to see you for just one reason . . . to tell you personally what your job means. You're a young man, and think of it as a stepping stone to higher things. That's an attitude which you'll have to rub off. It's an insignificant planet of an undistinguished star, out on the far end of the galaxy, with a minimum thousand years of guidance ahead of it before it can even be considered for full status. I know that. But I also know it holds more than a billion human creatures, each one fully as valuable as you and I, each one the center of his own particular universe. If you forget that, may the Great Designer have mercy on them and on you.

"Dismissed."

Randos walked out, carefully energetic. He had been prepared for this, but it had still been pretty raw. Nobody had a right to treat a free citizen of a full-status planet like . . . like a not very trustworthy child. Damn it, he was a man, on the mightiest enterprise men had ever undertaken, and—

And someday *he* might sit behind that desk.

Kri allowed himself a minute's reflection as Randos departed. It was so tinged with sadness that he wondered if he weren't getting too old, if he hadn't better resign for the good of the Service.

So many planets, spinning through night and cold, so many souls huddled on them . . . a half-million full-status worlds, near galactic center, members of interstellar civilization by virtue of knowing that such a civilization existed . . . and how many millions more who did not know? It seemed that every day a scoutship brought back word of yet another inhabited planet.

Each of them had its human races—red, black, white, yellow, blue, green, brown, tall or short, thin or fat, hairy or bald, tailed or tailless, but fully human, biologically human, and the scientists had never discovered why evolution should work thus on every terrestroid world. The churches said it was the will of the Designer, and perhaps they were right. Certainly they were right in a pragmatic sense, for the knowledge had brought the concept of brotherhood and duty. The duty of true civilization was to guide its brothers in darkness—secretly, gently, keeping from them the devastating knowledge that a million-year-old society already existed, until they had matured enough to take that bitter pill and join smoothly the League of the older planets. Without such guidance . . . In his younger days, Kri had seen the dead worlds, where men had once lived. War, exhaustion of resources, accumulation of lethal genes, mutant disease . . . it was so hideously simple for Genus Homo to wipe a planet bare of himself.

The old blue man sighed, and a smile tugged at his mouth. You didn't work many centuries in the Service without becoming an idealist and a cynic. An idealist who lived for the mission, and a cynic who knew when to compromise for the sake of that mission. Theoretically, Kri was above political pressures. In fact, when there was no obvious disqualification, he often had to give somebody's favorite nephew a plum. After all, his funds and his lower echelons were politically controlled. . . .

He started, realizing how much time had passed and how many decisions had yet to be made before he could quit for the day. His wife would give him Chaos if he stayed overtime tonight. Some damned card party. He bent over the report and dismissed from his mind the planet called Earth.

The doorman was shocked.

He was used to many people going in and out of the gray stone building, not only toffs and tradesmen but foreigners and Orientals and even plain tenant farmers, come down from Yorkshire with hayseeds in their hair. Benson & McMurtrie, Import Brokers, were a big firm and had to talk to every sort. He'd served in India as a young fellow and considered himself broad-minded. But there are limits.

"'Ere, now! An' just where d'yer think you're going?"

The stocky, sunburned man with the tattered clothes and the small brass earrings paused. He had curly black hair and snapping blue eyes, and was fuming away on an old clay pipe. A common tinker, walking into Benson & McMurtrie cool as damnit! "In there, ould one, in there," he said with an Irish lilt. "Ye wouldn' be denyin' me a sight of the most beautiful colleen in London, would ye?"

"That I would," said the doorman. A passing car stirred up enough breeze to flutter the tinker's rags, flamboyant against the grimed respectability of Regent Street. "On yer wye before I calls a constable."

"Sure an' it's no way to be addressin' a craftsman, me bhoy," said the tinker. "But since ye seem to be sharin' of the Sassenach mania for the written word, then feast your eyes on this." Out of his patched garments he produced a letter of admittance, dated two years ago and signed by McMurtrie himself.

The doorman scanned it carefully, the more so as McMurtrie was eight months dead, the nice white-haired old gentleman, struck down by one of these new-fangled autos as he crossed this very street. But it gave a clear description of Sean O'Meara, occupation tinker, and set no time limit.

He handed it back. "In yer goes, then," he conceded, "though why they—Nev' mind! Behyve yerself is all I got ter sye."

Sean O'Meara nodded gaily and disappeared into the building. The doorman scratched his head. You never knew, you didn't and those Irish were an uppity lot, a bad lot. Here Mr. Asquith was trying to give them Home Rule and the Ulstermen were up in arms about it!

Sabor Tombak had no trouble getting past the private secretary, who was a Galactic himself, but he sadly puzzled the lesser employees. Most of them concluded, after several days of speculation, that the tinker was a secret agent. It was well known that Benson & McMurtrie had sufficient financial power to be hand in glove with the Cabinet itself. They weren't so far off the mark at that.

The inner office was a ponderosity of furniture and sepia. Tombak shuddered and knocked out his pipe. Usrek Arken, alias Sir John Benson—grandson of the founder, who had actually been himself—started. "Do you have to bring that thing in here?" he complained. "The London air is foul already without you polluting it."

"Anything would be welcome as a counterirritant to this stuff," answered Tombak. His gesture included the entire office. "Why the Evil don't you guidance boys get on orbit and guide the English into decent taste? An Irish peasant without a farthing in his pocket has better-looking quarters than this kennel."

"Details, details." The sarcastic note in Arken's voice did not escape Tombak. The word had somehow become a proverb in his absence.

"Better get hold of the boss and let me report," he said. "I've an earful to give him."

"An eyeful, you mean," replied Arken. "Written up in proper form with quantitative data tabulated, if you please."

"Oh, sure, sure. Gimme time. But this won't wait for—"

"Maybe you don't know we have a new boss," said Arken slowly.

"Huh? What happened to Kalmagens?"

"Killed. Run over by a bloody Designer-damned petroleum burner eight months ago."

Tombak sat down, heavily. He had had a great regard for Kalmagens, both professionally—the Franco-Prussian business had been handled with sheer artistry—and as a friend. He dropped into fluent Gaelic for a while, cursing the luck.

At last he shook himself and asked: "What's the new man like?"

"Harban Randos of Garris. Arrived six weeks back. Young fellow, fresh out of his apprenticeship. A good psychotechnician, but seems to think the psychotechnic laws will cover every situation." Arken scowled. "And the situation right now is nasty."

"It is that," agreed Tombak. "I haven't seen many newspapers where I've been, but it's past time Kaiser Wilhelm was put across somebody's knee." He jumped back to his feet with the restless energy of two years tramping the Irish roads. "Where's Randos now? Damn it, I want to see him."

Arken lifted his brows. "All right, old chap. If you really insist, I'll call him for you, and then I'll crawl under the desk and wait for the lightning to subside."

He buzzed for the secretary and told him in English: "Send Mr. Harrison to me, please." That was for the benefit of the non-Galactic employees. When the door had closed, he remarked to Tombak:

"You know how complicated the secrecy requirement can make things. Bad enough to always have to look your Earth-age, and officially die every fifty years or so, and provide a synthetic corpse, and assume a new face and a new personality. But when you're at the top, and the leading autochthons know you as an important man— Chaos! We have to fob Randos off as a senior clerk, freshly hired for nepotistic reasons."

Tombak grinned and tamped his pipe. He himself was in the lowest echelon of the five thousand Galactics serving on Earth, and refused to study for promotion. He liked the planet and its folk, he liked being soldier and sailor and cowboy and mechanic and tramp, to gather knowledge of how the Plan was progressing on the level of common humanity. He did not hanker for the symbological sweatshop work and the identity problem of the upper brackets.

A plump, undistinguished form, in somber clothes that looked highly uncomfortable, entered. "You sent for me, sir?" The door closed behind Harban Randos. "What's the meaning of this? I was engaged in an evaluation of the political dynamics, and you interrupted me precisely as I was getting the matrix set up. How many times do I have to tell you the situation is crucial? What the Chaos do you want now?"

"Sir Randos . . . Sabor Tombak, one of our field agents, returned from a survey of Ireland," murmured Arken. "He has important new information for you."

Randos did not bow, as urbanity demanded. He

looked tired and harried. "Then file it and mark it urgent, for Designer's sake!"

"Trouble is," said Tombak imperturbably, "this is not stuff that can be fitted into a mass-action equation. This concerns individual people ... angry people."

"Look here—" Randos drew a ragged breath. "I'll take time to explain to you." His tone grew elaborately satirical. "Forgive me if I repeat what you already know.

"This planet wasn't discovered till seventeen ninety-eight, and three years went by before a mission could be sent. The situation was plainly critical, so much so that our men couldn't take a century to establish themselves. They had to cut corners and work fast. By introducing techno-logical innovations themselves and serving with uncanny distinction in several countries' armed forces and governments, they barely managed to be influential at the Congress of Vienna. Not very influential, but just sufficiently to get a stopgap balance-of-power system adopted. They couldn't prevent the anti-democratic reaction and the subsequent revolutions ... but they did stave off a major catastrophe, and settled down to building a decent set of governments. Now their whole work is in danger.

"We're too damned few, Tombak, and have to contend with too many centuries of nationalism and vested interest. My predecessor here did manage to get high-ranking agents into the German leadership. They failed to prevent war with Denmark, Austria, and France, but a fairly humane peace treaty was managed after eighteen seventy. Not as humane as it should have been, it left the French smarting, but a good job under the circumstances."

Tombak nodded. He had seen that for himself. He had been a simple krauthead officer then moderating the savagery of his troops . . . less for immediate mercy than for the future, a smaller legacy of hatred. But rumors had filtered down, which he later gleefully confirmed: British pressure secretly put on Bismarck to control his appetite, and the pressure had originated with the Prime Minister's good friend "Sir Colin McMurtrie." And the Boer War had been unavoidable, but the quick gestures of friendship toward the conquered had not— The Plan called for a peaceful, democratic British Commonwealth to dominate and stabilize the world.

"Kalmagens' death threw everything into confusion," went on Randos. "I suppose you know that. You fellows carried on as best you could, but the mass is not identical with the sum of the individuals concerned. There are factors of tradition, inertia, the cumbersome social machinery . . . it takes a trained man to see the forest for the trees. Things have rapidly gone toward maximum entropy. An unstable system of checks and balances between rival imperialisms is breaking down. We have less than a year to avert a general war which will exacerbate nationalism to the point of insanity. I have to develop a program of action and get it into effect. I have *no* time to waste on details!"

"The Turkish-Italian war was a detail, of course," said Tombak blandly.

"Yes," snapped Randos. "Unfortunate, but unimportant. The Ottomans have had their day.

Likewise this Balkan business."

"Saw a paper on the way here. Sun Yat-sen's government is having its troubles. Are all those Chinese another detail?"

"No, of course not. But they can wait. The main line of development toward full status is here in Western Europe. It happened by chance, but the fact is there. It's European civilization which has got to be saved from itself. Do you realize that Earth is only an angry turn around the office. "All right. I'm trying to work out a new balance, an international power alignment that will hold German ambition in check until such time as their Social Democrats can win an unmistakable majority and oust the Prussian clique. After that we can start nudging Europe toward limited federalism. That's the objective, sir, the absolute necessity, and your report had better have some relevance to it!"

Tombak nodded. "It does, Chief, I assure you. I've talked with thousands of Irish, both in Ulster and the south. Those two sections hate each other's intestinal flora. The southerners want the present Home Rule bill and the Ulstermen don't. They're being whipped up by the Carson gang, ready to fight . . . and if they do, the Irish-Irish are going to revolt on their own account."

Randos' lunar face reddened. "And you called me in to tell me this?"

"I did. Is civil war a detail?"

"In this case, Sir Tombak, yes." Randos was holding back his temper with an effort that made him sweat. "A single English division could put it down in a month, if it broke out. But it would take all Britain's and France's manhood to stop Germany, and we'd have to drag in a dozen other countries to boot. The United States might get involved. And the USA is the main line after Europe, Sir Tombak. They have to be kept out of this mad-dog nationalism, to lead the world toward reason when their day comes." He actually managed to show his teeth. "I'll forgive you this time on grounds of ignorance. But hereafter submit your reports in properly written form. The next time you disturb me with a piddling detail like Ireland, you'll go back to Sagittarius. Good day!"

He remembered to assume a meek look as he was opening the door.

There was a silence.

"Whoof!" said Tombak.

"Second the motion," said Arken. "But I warned you."

"Where's the nearest pub? I need one." Tombak prowled over to the window and looked gloomily down at the traffic. "Kalmagens was an artist," he said, "and artists don't worry about what is detail and what isn't. They just naturally see the whole picture. This chap is a cookbook psychotechnician."

"He's probably right, as far as he goes," said Arken.

"Maybe. I dunno." Tombak shrugged. "Got a suit of clothes here I can borrow? I told the doorman I was coming in to make a date with a beautiful girl, and I noticed a most nice little wench with a sort of roundheeled look at a typewriter out there. Don't want to disappoint the old fellow."

Peter Mortensen was born north of the Danevirke, but after 1864 his people were reckoned German, and he was called up in 1914 like anyone else. Men died so fast on the eastern front that promotion was rapid, and by 1917 he was a captain. This did not happen without some investigation of his background—many Schleswig Danes were not overly glad of their new nationality—but Graf von Schlangengrab had checked personally on him and assured his superiors of his unquestionable loyalty. Indeed, the count took quite a fancy to this young man, got him transferred to Intelligence, and often used him on missions of the utmost importance.

Thus the official record, and in the twentieth century Anno Domini the record was more than the man—it *was* the man. A few rebellious souls considered this an invention of that supreme parodist, the Devil, for now the Flesh had become Word. To Galactics such as Vyndhom Vargess and Sabor Tombak, it was convenient; records are more easily altered than memories, if you have the right gadgets. So Vargess became von Schlangengrab and Tombak called himself Peter Mortensen.

A thin, bitter rain blew across muddy fields, and the Prussian pines mumbled of spring. Out in the trenches to the west, it meant little more than fresh lice and fresh assaults, human meat going upright into the gape of machine guns. To the east, where Russia lay sundered, the spring of 1917 meant some kind of new birth. Tombak wondered what sort it would be.

He sat with a dozen men in a boxcar near the head of the sealed train. The thing was damp and chilly; they huddled around a stove. Their gray uniforms steamed. Beneath them, the wheels clicked on rain-slippery rails. Now and again the train whistled, shrill and lonesome noise across the graves of a thousand years of war.

Captain Mortensen was well liked by his men: none of this Junker stiffness for him. They held numbed hands toward the stove, rolled cigarettes, and talked among themselves. "Cold, it's been a long time cold, and fuel so short. Sometimes I wonder what it ever felt like to be warm and dry."

"Be colder than this in Russia, lad. I've been there. I know."

"But no fighting this time, thank God. Only taking that funny little man toward St. Petersburg. . . . Why the devil's he so important, anyway? Hauled him clear from Switzerland in his own special train, on orders of General Ludendorff, no less, one runty Russian crank."

"What say, Captain?" asked someone. "Are you allowed, now, to tell us why?"

Tombak shrugged, and the faces of peasants and laborers and students turned to him, lost between military caps and shoddy uniforms but briefly human again with simple curiosity. "Why, sir? Is he a secret agent of ours?"

"No, I'd not say that." Tombak rolled himself a cigarette, and a corporal struck a match for him. "But the matter's quite simple. Kerensky has overthrown the Czar, you see, but wants to keep on fighting. This Ulyanov fellow has a good deal of influence, in spite of having been an exile for so long. Maybe he can come to power. If he does, he'll make peace on any terms . . . which is to say, on German terms. Then we'll no longer have an eastern front to worry about." Tombak's leathery face crinkled. "It seems worth trying, anyhow."

"I see, I see . . . thank you, Captain . . . very clever. . . ."

"My own chief, Graf von Schlangegrab, urged this policy on the General Staff," confided

Tombak. "The idea was his, and he talked them into it." He always had to remember that he was Peter Mortensen, doubly anxious to prove his Germanness because it had once been in doubt, and would therefore brag about the nobleman with whom he was so intimate.

What he did not add was that von Schlangengrab had been given the idea and told to execute it by a senior clerk in an English brokerage house, over an undetectable sub-radio hookup. This clerk, Mr. Harrison, had checked Galactic records on Ulyanov—whom Kalmagens had once met and investigated in London—and run a psychotechnic evaluation which gave the little revolutionary a surprising probability of success.

"Maybe then we can finish the war," muttered a sergeant. "Dear God, it's like it's gone on forever, not so?"

"I can't even remember too well what began it," confessed a private.

"Well, boys—" Tombak inhaled the harsh wartime tobacco and leaned back in a confidential mood. "I'll tell you my theory. The Irish began it."

"Ach, you joke, Captain," said the sergeant.

"Not at all. I have studied these things. In nineteen fourteen there was a great deal of international tension, if you remember. That same year the House Rule bill was so badly handled that it alienated the Ulstermen, who were egged on by a group anxious to seize power. This caused the Catholic Irish to prepare for revolt. Fighting broke out in Dublin in July, and it seemed as if the British Isles were on the verge of civil war. Accordingly, our General Staff decided they need not be reckoned with for a while, and—"

—And the Sarajevo affair touched off the

powder. Germany moved in accordance with long-laid plans because she did not expect Britain to be able to fulfill her treaty obligations to Belgium. But Britain wangled a temporary Irish settlement and declared war. If the English had looked more formidable that year, the Germans would have been more conciliatory, and war could have been postponed and the Galactic plans for establishing a firm peace could have gone on toward their fruition.

"Captain!" The sergeant was shocked.

Tombak laughed. "I didn't mean it subversively. Of course we had to fight against the Iron Ring. And we will conquer."

Like Chaos we will. The war was dragging into a stalemate. Neither side could break the other, not when Russia had gone under.

If Russia did make peace, Randos had calculated, then the stalemate would be complete. Peace could be negotiated on a basis of exhaustion in another year, and America kept out of the mess.

Privately, Tombak doubted it. On paper the scheme looked fine: the quantities representing political tensions balanced out nicely. But he had lived in America some twenty years ago, and knew her for a country which would always follow an evangelist. Like Wilson—whose original nomination and election had hinged on an unusual chance. Randos assured him that the personality of the leader meant little . . . was a detail . . . but . . .

At any rate, the main immediate objective was to get Russia out of the war, so that she might evolve a reasonably civilized government for herself. Exactly how the surrender was to be achieved, was another detail, not important. This queer, bearded Ulyanov with the bookish diction and the Tartar face was the handiest tool for the job, a tool which could later be discarded in favor of the democrats.

The train hooted, clicking eastward with Ulyanov aboard.

His Party name was Lenin.

Tombak had not been in New York for three decades. The town had changed a lot; everywhere he saw the signs of a feverish prosperity.

On other planets, in other centuries, he had watched the flowering and decay of a mercantile system, big business replacing free enterprise. For certain civilizations it was a necessary step in development, but he always thought of it as a retrogression, enthroned vulgarity grinding out the remnants of genuine culture, the Folk became the People.

This was a brisk fall day, and he stepped merrily along through the crowds, a short, sunburned, broad-shouldered young man, outwardly distinguished only by a cheerful serenity. Nor was he essentially different inside. He was a fully human creature with human genes, who simply happened to have been born on another planet. His environment had affected him, balancing anabolism and catabolism so well that he had already lived two thousand years, training mind and body. But that didn't show.

He turned off onto Wall Street and found the skyscraper he was looking for and went up to the sacrosanct top floor. The receptionist was female this time, and pretty. Woman suffrage had eased the team's problems by allowing them to use their wives and girl friends more openly. For a moment he didn't recognize her; the face had been changed. Then he nodded. "Hello, Yarra. Haven't seen you since . . . good Designer, since the Paris Exposition!"

"We had fun," she smiled dreamily. "Care to try it again?"

"Hmmmm . . . yes, if you'll get rid of that godawful bobbed hair and cylindrical silhouette."

"Aren't they terrible? Usrek ran a computation for me, and the Americans won't return to a girl who looks like a girl for years."

"I'll get myself assigned back to Asia. Bali, for choice." Tombak sighed reminiscently. "Just worked my way back from there—deckhand on a tramp steamer to San Francisco, followed a harvesting crew across the plains, did a hitch in a garage. Lots and lots of data, but I hope the boss doesn't want it tabulated."

"He will, Sabor, he will. Want to talk to him? He's in the office now."

"Might as well get it over with."

"He's not a bad sort, really. A basically decent fellow, and a whiz at psychomath. He tries hard."

"Someday, though, he'll have to learn that— Oh, all right."

Tombak went through the door into the office of the president. It was Usrek Arken again, alias the financier Wolfe . . . a name chosen with malice aforethought, for wolf he was on Wall Street. But what chance did brokers and corporations, operating mostly by God and by guess, have against a million-year-old science of economics? Once Randos had decided England was declining as a world power, and become an American, Wolfe's dazzling rise was a matter of a few years' routine. Arken was in conference with Randos, but both rose and bowed. The chief showed strain, his plumpness was being whittled away and the best total-organismic training could not suppress an occasional nervous jerk. But today he seemed genial. "Ah, Sir Tombak! I'm glad to see you back. I was afraid you'd run afoul of some Chinese war lord."

"Damn near did. I was a foreign devil. If it hadn't been for our Mongoloid agent in Sinkiang—well, that's past." Tombak got out his pipe. "Had a most enjoyable trip around the world, and got friendly with thousands of people, but of course out of touch with the big events. What's been happening?"

"Business boom here in the States. That's the main thing, so I'm concentrating on it. Tricky."

Tombak frowned. "Pardon me, but why should the exact condition of business in one country be crucial?"

"Too many factors to explain in words," said Randos. "I'd need psychodynamic tensors to convince you. But look at it this way . . .

"Let's admit we bungled badly in 'fourteen and again in 'seventeen. We let the war break out, we let America get into it, and we underestimated Lenin. Instead of a republic, Russia has a dictatorship as ruthless as any in history, and paranoid to boot; nor can we change that fact, even if the rules allowed us to assassinate Stalin. We hoped to salvage a kind of world order out of the mess: once American intervention was plainly unavoidable, we started the 'War to end war' slogan and the League of Nations idea. Somehow, though, the USA was kept out of the League, which means it's a farce unless we can get her into it."

Thanks for the "we," thought Tombak grimly.

With the benefit of hindsight, he knew as well as Randos why the Russian revolution and the Versailles peace had gone awry. Lenin and Senator Lodge had been more capable than they had any right to be, and Wilson less so. That poor man had been no match for practical politicians, and had compounded the folly with his anachronistic dream of "self-determination." (Clemenceau had passed the rational judgment on that idea: *"Mon Dieu!* Must every little language have a country of its own?") But individual personalities had been brushed aside by Randos as "fluctuations, details, meaningless eddies on the current of great historical trends."

The man wasn't too stupid to see his own mistakes; but subconsciously, at least, he didn't seem able to profit by them.

"We still have an excellent chance, though," went on Randos. "I don't quite like the methods we must use, but they're the only available ones. Wall Street is rapidly becoming the financial capital of Earth, a trend which I have been strengthening. If finance can be maintained as the decisive power, within twenty years America will be the leader of the world. No one else will be able to move without her okay. Then the time will be psychologically ripe for Americans to get the idea of a new League, one with armed force to maintain the peace. The Soviets won't stand a chance."

Tombak scowled more deeply. "I can't argue with your match, Sir Randos," he answered slowly, "but I got a hunch . . ."

"Yes? Go on. You were sent around the world precisely so you could gather facts. If those facts contradict my theories, why, of course I'm wrong and we'll have to look for a new approach."

Randos spoke magnanimously.

"Okay, buster, you asked for it," said Tombak in English. He returned to Galactic: "The trouble is, these aren't facts you can fit into mass-action equations. They're a matter of, well, *feel*.

"Nationalism is rising in Asia. I talked with a Japanese officer in Shanghai . . . we'd gotten drunk together, and he was a fine fellow, and we loved each other like brothers, but he actually cried at the thought that someday he'd have to take potshots at me."

"The Japanese have talked about war with the United States for fifty years," snorted Randos. "They can't win one."

"But do they know that? To continue, though— people, Western people, don't like the present form of society either. They can't always say why, but you can tell they feel uprooted, uneasy . . . there's nothing about an interlocking directorate to inspire loyalty, you know. The trade unions are growing. If capitalism goes bust, they're going to grow almighty fast."

"To be sure," nodded Randos, unperturbed. "A healthy development, in the right time and place. But I'm here to see that capitalism does not, ah, go bust. Mass unemployment—You know yourself how unstable the Weimar Republic is. If depression is added to its other troubles, dictatorship will come to Germany within five years."

"If you ask me," snapped Tombak, "we've got too bloody damn much confidence around. Too many people are playing the stock market. It has a hectic feel, somehow. They'd do better to save their money for an emergency."

Randos smiled. "To be sure. I'll admit the market is at a dangerous peak. In this month, it's already shown some bad fluctuations. That's why Wolfe is selling right now, heavily, to bring it down."

Usrek Arken stirred. "And I continue to think, Sir Randos," he muttered, "that it'll cause a panic."

"No, it won't. I have proved, with the help of games theory, that—"

"Games theory presupposes that the players are rational," murmured Tombak. "I have a nasty suspicion that nobody is."

"Come, now," chided Randos. "Of course non-rational elements enter in. But this civilization is in a highly cerebral stage."

"What you ought to do," snapped Tombak, "is get away from that computer of yours and go out and meet some Earthfolk."

Frost congealed on Randos' words: "That is your task, Sir Tombak. Please report your findings and stand by for further assignment. Now, if you'll pardon me, I'm busy."

Tombak swapped a glance with Arken and went out. He chatted for a while with Yarra and, silhouette or no, made a date for the next evening: Thursday, October 24, 1929.

> Now play the fife lowly and beat the drums
>   slowly,
> And play the dead march as you carry my pall.
> Bring me white roses to lay on my coffin,
> Roses to deaden the clods as they fall.

The flames jumped up, lighting their faces: grimy, unshaven, gaunted by wind and hunger, but American faces. Tombak thought he had fallen in love with America. A Galactic had no business playing favorites, and it was perfectly obvious that in another hundred years Earth's power center would have shifted to Asia, but something in this country suited him. It still had elbow room, for both body and soul.

He finished the song and laid his guitar down as Robinson gave the can of mulligan another stir. Far off, but coming along the rails near the hobo jungle, a train whistled. Tombak wondered how many times, how many places, he had heard that noise, and always it meant more lonesomeness.

"I looked at the schedule in the station." A thin man with glasses jerked his thumb at the town, a mile away. "Be a freight stopping at midnight, we can hop that one."

"If the dick don't see us," mumbled Robinson. "They got a mean dick in this place."

"I'll handle him, if it comes to that." Tombak flexed stumpy strong fingers. Maybe a Galactic shouldn't take sides, but there were some people whose faces he enjoyed altering. That storm trooper in Berlin two years ago, for instance, the lout who was kicking an inoffensive Jew around. Getting out of Germany had been like getting out of jail, and even riding the rods in the States was a welcome change.

"Be careful, Jim," murmured Rose McGraw. She leaned against Tombak with a pathetic posessiveness.

In a better age, he thought, she would have been somebody's contented housewife, minding the kids in suburbia, not tramping over a continent in a ragged print dress, rain in her hair, looking for work ... any kind of work. Too late now, of course, at least till the war with Japan made jobs. But Randos had predicted Japan would not attack till early 1942, give or take six months, and he was usually right about such things. Almost six years to go. True, initially he had thought the Japanese would never fight, but contrary evidence piled up . . .

"Don't worry about me," said Tombak gruffly. He felt again the tugging sadness of the quasi-immortal. How many years on Earth, how many women, and with none of them could he stay more than a few months. They must not be taken off the road and fed, they must not be told the truth and comforted, Rose McGraw had to become a fading memory fast bound in misery and iron for the sake of her descendants a thousand years hence.

At least he had warned her. *"I'm not a marryin' man, I won't ever settle down."*—Not till his tour of duty on Earth ended, another seventy-five years of it and then a hundred-year vacation and then another planet circling one of those stars blinking dimly overhead. . . . Why had he ever gone into the Service?

"Think Roosevelt's gonna win?" asked Robinson. He mispronounced the name.

"Sure, Landon hasn't got a prayer." The man with glasses spoke dogmatically; he had had some education once.

"I dunno, now. Old man Roosevelt, he's for us, but how many of us stay in one place long enough to vote?"

"Enough," said Tombak. He had no doubt of the election's outcome. The New Deal under one name or another was foregone, once the Depression struck. Hoover himself had proposed essentially the same reforms. Randos had not even had to juggle the country—through propaganda, through carefully planted trains of events—to get FDR elected the first time. Tombak would be able to return from this trip and report that the changes were popular and that there was no immediate danger of American fascism or communism.

The main line of history, always the main line. Since the Rhineland debacle this year, war in Europe was not to be avoided, nor was war in the Pacific. Japanese pride and hunger had not been so small a factor after all. Tombak's mind slipped to the Washington office where Randos was manipulating senators and brain trusters.

"The important thing will be to keep the two wars separate. Russia will be neutral, because she has Japan to worry about, and Germany alone cannot conquer Britain. The United States, with British help, can defeat Japan in about five years while the European stalemate is established. Then and only then must Germany and Russia be goaded into war with each other . . . two totalitarianisms in a death struggle, weakening as they fight with America armed from the Japanese war and ready to step in and break both of them. After that we can finally start building an Earth fit to live on."

An Earth which had so far gone from bad to worse, reflected Tombak. He didn't deny the bitter logic of Randos' equations; but he wondered if it was going to develop that way in practice. Roosevelt, who would surely run for a third term, had strong emotional ties—he *could* not see England fight alone, and he could make the country agree with him. And Hitler, now . . . Tombak had seen Hitler speak, and met a lot of Nazis. A streak of nihilistic lunacy ran through that bunch. Against every sound military principle, they were entirely capable of attacking Russia; which would mean the emergence of the Soviet Union, necessarily

aided by America, as a victorious world power.
Well . . .

"Wonder if we're someday gonna find a steady job," said someone in the night.

"Ought to have a guy like Hitler," said another man. "No nonsense about him. He'd arrange things."

"Arrange 'em with a firing squad," said Tombak sharply. "Drive men like Einstein out of the country. At that," he added thoughtfully, "Hitler and his brown-shirted, brown-nosed bastards are doing us a favor. If this goes on, we'll have more talent in this country, refugees, than anybody ever had before."

And if somebody had the idea of gathering it into one place, what would all that embittered genius do to Randos' plans?

Bob Robinson shrugged, indifference clothed in faded denim. "To hell with it. I think the stew's about done."

Harban Randos' eyes looked ready to leap out of their sockets. "No!" he whispered.

"Yes." Usrek Arken slapped the papers down on the desk with a cannon-crack noise. "Winnis knows his physics, and Tombak and the others have gathered the essential facts for him to work on. They're making an atomic bomb!"

Randos turned blindly away. Outside, Washington shimmered in the heat of midsummer, 1943. It was hard to believe that a war was being fought . . . the wrong war, with the issues irretrievably messed up, the Soviets fighting as allies of the democracies, Japan half shunted aside to make way for a Nazi defeat that would plant Russian troops in the middle of Europe . . . and meanwhile gnawing away at Nationalist China, weakening the nation for Communists who had made a truce which they weren't respecting.

"They're able to," said Randos huskily.

Tombak nodded. "They're going to," he said.

"But they don't *need*—"

"What has that got to do with anything? And after the uranium bomb comes the thermonuclear bomb and— Write your own ticket." Tombak spoke flatly, for he had come to like the people of Earth.

Randos passed a shaking hand over his face. "All right, all right. Any chance of sabotaging the project?"

"Not without tipping our hand. They've got this one watched, I tell you; we've not been able to get a single Galactic into the Manhattan District. We could blow up the works, of course ... fake a German operation ... but after the war, when they go through German records ..."

"Vargess can handle the records."

"He can't handle the memories. Not the memories of thousands of people, instrinsically just as smart as you and I." Tombak bit his pipestem and heard it crack. "Okay, Randos, you're the boss. What do we do next?"

The chief sat down. For a moment he shuddered with the effort of self-control, then his body was again disciplined.

"It will be necessary to deal firmly with the Russians, force them to agree to a stronger United Nations Organization," he said. "Churchill already understands that, and Roosevelt can be persuaded. Between them, they can prepare their countries so that it'll be politically feasible. The West is going to have a monopoly of nuclear

weapons at the war's end, which will be helpful
... yes ..."

"Roosevelt is not a well man," declared
Tombak, "and I was in England only a month ago
and can tell you the people aren't satisfied. They
admire Churchill, love him, but they're going to
want to experiment with another party...."

"Calculated risk," said Randos. His confidence
was returning. "Not too great."

"Nevertheless," said Tombak, "you'd better
start right away to handpick those men's successors and see they get exposed to the facts of life."

"For Designer's sake, leave me alone!" yelled
Randos. "I can't handle every miserable little
detail!"

Rasnagarth Kri did not want to spend time
interviewing a failure. It seemed as if each day
brought a higher pile of work to him, more decisions to be made, a million new planets struggling toward an unperceived goal, and he had had
to promise his wife he would stop working nights.

Nevertheless, a favorite nephew is a favorite
nephew.

He hooded his eyes until a glittering blankness
looked across the desk at Harban Randos.

"We are fortunate," he said, "that an experienced man of your race was available to take
charge. For a while I actually considered breaking
the rules and letting Earth know the facts immediately. But at this stage of their society, that would
only be a slower damnation for them; extinction is
more merciful. Whether or not the new man can
rescue the planet remains to be seen. If he fails,
the whole world is lost. At best, progress has been
retarded two centuries, and millions of people are

needlessly dead."

Randos stiffened his lips, which had been vibrating, and answered tonelessly:

"Sir, you were getting my annual reports. If I was unsatisfactory, you should have recalled me years ago."

"Every agent is allowed some mistakes," Kri told him. "Psychodynamics is not an exact science. Furthermore, your reports, while quantitatively accurate, were qualitatively ... lifeless. They conveyed nothing of the feel. Until the fact leaped out that nationalism and atomic energy had become contemporaneous, how could I judge?"

Feel! Randos thought of Sabor Tombak. The smug, pipesucking pig! He hoped Tombak would be killed; plenty of chance for that, in the next fifty or a hundred years of Earth's troubles.

No—he was doing the man an injustice. Tombak had simply been right. But Randos still couldn't like him.

"I used the standard methods, sir," he protested. "You have seen my computations. What else could I do?"

"Well—" Kri looked down at his desk. "That's hard to answer. Let me just say that human nature is so complicated that we'll never have a complete science of it. All we'll ever be able to do mathematically is predict and guide the broad trends. But those trends are made up of millions of individual people and incidents. To pervert an old saying, in government we must be able to see the trees for the forest. It takes an artist to know how and when to use the equations, and how to supplement them with his own intuitive common sense. It takes not only a technician, but a poet to write a report that will really let me know what is really going on."

He raised his eyes again and said mildly: "You can't be blamed for being neither an artist nor a poet. I gather you wish to remain in the Service?"

"Yes, sir." Randos was not a quitter.

"Very well. I'm assigning you to a chief technicianship in my own evaluation center. Consider it a promotion, a reward for honest effort. At least, you'll have higher rank and salary. You may go."

Kri thought he heard a gasp of relief, but returned to his papers.

One might as well face truth. You can't kick a favorite nephew anywhere but upstairs. The fellow might even make a good technical boss.

As for this planet called Earth, maybe the new man could salvage it. If not, well, it was only one planet.

CAPTIVE OF THE CENTAURIANESS

The hero is the child of his times, in that his milieu gives him his motives and means. Yet he seizes the world as he finds it and reshapes it as he will; and he remains eternally an enigma to his contemporaries and to the future.

Nowhere is this better illustrated than in the famous but ever strange story of the three whose discoveries and achievements, late in the twenty-third century, set entire races of beings upon wholly new courses. The driving idealism and military genius of Dyann Korlas; the wisdom, mighty, profound, and benign, of Urushkidan; above all, perhaps, the inspired leadership of Tallantyre—these molded history, but we will never truly understand them. The persons who embodied them are still further beyond us. The essential selves of the glorious three will always be mysterious.

—Vallabhai Rasmussen,
Origins of the Galactic Era

Floodlit, the tender loomed against night, above the swarm of humanity, like a great golden bullet. Ray Tallantyre quickened his steps. By George and dragon both, he'd made it! The flight from San Francisco to Quito, the nail-gnawing wait for an airbus, the ride to the spaceport, the walk through a terminal building that seemed to stretch on forever—all were outlived and there she was, there the darling stood, and ready to carry him up to the *Jovan Queen* and safety.

He kissed his fingers at the craft and shoved rudely through the crowd. He'd already missed the first trip up to the liner, and the thought of standing around till the third was beyond endurance.

"Hey, you."

As the voice fell on his ears, a hand did on his arm. Ray could have sworn he felt his heart slam against his teeth and his spine fall out of his trousers. Somehow he turned around. A large man was comparing his thin features with a photograph held in the unoccupied paw. "Yes, it's you, all right," this person said. "Come along, Tallantyre."

"¡ *Me llama Garcia!*" the fugitive gibbered. *"No hablo inglés."*

"I said come along," the detective answered. "We figured you'd try to leave Earth. This way."

Sometimes desperation breeds inspiration. Ray's own free hand crammed the fellow's hat down over his eyes. Wrenching loose, he bolted for the gangramp. En route, he upset a corpulent lady. A volley of Latin imprecations pursued him. Shoving aside another passenger, he sped up the incline —and bounced off the wall which was a Jovian officer.

"Your ticket and passport, please," said that man. He was a tall, muscular blond, crisply white-uniformed, who regarded the new arrival with the thinly veiled contempt of a true Confed for the lesser breeds of life.

Ray shoved the documents at him, meanwhile staring backward. The detective had gotten entangled with the lady, who was beating him around the head with her purse and volubly cursing him. Agonizingly deliberate, the Jovian scanned the engineer's papers, checked them against a list, and waved him on.

The detective won free, followed, and struck the same immovable barrier. "Your ticket and passport, please," said the ship's representative.

"That man's under arrest," panted the detective. "Let me by."

"Your ticket and passport, please."

"I tell you I'm an officer of the law and I have a warrant for that man. Let me by!"

"Proper authorization may be obtained at the security center," said the immovable barrier. The detective tried to rush, encountered a bit of expert judo, and tumbled back into a line of passengers who also grew indignant with him. Every able-bodied Jovian was a military reservist.

"Proper authority may be obtained at the security center," the gatekeeper repeated. To the next person: "Your ticket and passport, please."

In the airlock chamber, Ray Tallantyre dashed the sweat off his brow and permitted himself a laugh. By the time his pursuer had gone through all the red tape, he himself would be on the space liner. Before one of his own country's secret police, the ship's officer would have quailed. However, this was Earth; and the Confeds loved to bait

agents of the Terrestrial government; and there
was no better way than by putting the victims
through channels. Where it came to devising
these, the bureaucracy of the Confederated Satellites of Jupiter was beyond compare.

Being in orbit, the vessel counted as Jovian
territory; and Ray's alleged offense did not rate
extradition.

He went on inside, was shown to a seat, and
secured the harness. He was clear! No matter how
long, the arm of the Vanbrugh family did not
reach as far as he was bound. He could stay till the
whole business had blown over. To be sure, he
might have difficulty getting a job meanwhile, but
he'd worry about that when the time came. *Always
did want to see the Jovian System anyway*, he
rationalized.

Sighing, he tried to relax: a medium-sized, wiry
young man with close-cropped yellow hair and a
countenance a little too sharp to be handsome.
Likewise, his scarf was overly colorful, his jacket
a trifle extravagantly flared.

The last passenger boarded. The lock valves
closed. A stewardess went down the aisle handing
out cookies which, Ray knew, contained medication to prevent space sickness. She had the full-
bodied Caucasoid good looks of the ideal Jovian
together with the faintly repellent air of total effi-
ciency. "No, thanks," he said. "I've been out
before. Acceleration and free fall don't bother
me."

"The cookies are compulsory," she told him,
and watched while he ate his. A throbbing went
through the vessel as the engine came to life; outside the hull, a warning siren hooted.

He turned to the passenger beside him, obsessed

with the idiotic desire for conversation found in most recent escapers from the law or the dentist. "Going home, I see," he remarked.

That person sat tall in the gray Jovian army uniform, colonel's planets on his shoulders and a haberdashery of ribbons across his chest. He looked about forty-five years old, Terrestrial, though his shaven pate made it hard to estimate; Ray gauged by the deep facial creases running down to the craggy jaw. Fixing the Earthling with a glacier-pale eye, he responded: "And you, I see, are leaving home. Two scintillating deductions." Though English was his mother tongue also—the one on which his polyglot ancestors had agreed even before the Symmetrist Revolution laid a single ideology on them—he made it sound as if it had been issued him.

"Um-m-m, uh, well," said Ray and looked elsewhere, his ears ablaze. The Jovian clutched tighter to his side the large briefcase he bore.

Announcements and orders resounded. The spacecraft shivered, howled, and sprang into the sky. Ray let acceleration pressure push him back into the cushions; the seat flattened itself into a couch; he gazed upward through a viewport and saw splendor unfold, stars and stars and stars, blackness well-nigh crowded out of sight by brilliance. His companion declined to recline.

The boost did not take long, then they were on trajectory and the *Jovian Queen* appeared. At first the liner was a mere needle to see, shimmery-blue by the light of the Earth she was orbiting. Soon she was close by, and the sun struck her as she swung clear of the planet's shadow cone, and she became huge and radiant. Despite her weight-giving spin, the tender made smooth contact.

Whatever you could say against the Jovians—and some people said quite a bit—they did maintain the best transport in the Solar System. Every national fleet on Earth and most private companies were finding it nearly impossible to compete.

The stewardess directed the passengers through joined airlocks and toward their quarters. She promised that luggage would be delivered "in due course." That reminded Ray that he'd checked in a single tiny suitcase containing little but a few changes of clothing. And his third class ticket meant that he'd have to share a cabin, which it would be ludicrous to call a stateroom, with two others. The decline and fall of the Tallantyre credit account was so depressing a subject that the pseudo-gravity, low though it was, bowed his shoulders; and, forgetting to allow for Coriolis force, he bruised a toe as he rounded a corner in the passage. Well and good to have gotten away from Earth free, he thought; but he'd hit Ganymede damn near broke, and he hadn't really considered as yet how he was going to survive there. This had simply been the sole destination in space for which he could get a ticket at exceedingly short notice. . . .

A number identified the door assigned him. He opened it.

"Put—me—down!"

Ray gaped at the spectacle of a Martian struggling in the clutch of a woman two meters tall.

"Put—me—down!" the Martian spluttered again. He had coiled his limbs snakelike around her arms and torso, and the four thick walking tentacles were formidably strong. She didn't seem to notice, but laughed and shook him a bit.

"I beg your pardon," Ray gasped and backed away.

"You are forgiven," the woman replied in a husky contralto with a lilting accent. She shot out one Martian-encumbered hand, grabbed him by the jacket, and hauled him inside. "You be the yudge, my friend. Is it not yustice that I have the lo'er berth?"

"It is noting of te sort!" screamed the Martian. He fixed the newcomer with round, bulging, indignant yellow eyes. "My position, my eminence, clearly entitle me to ebery consideration, and ten tis hulking monster—"

The Earthling's gaze traveled up and down the woman's form before he said softly, "I think you'd better accept the lady's generous offer. But, uh, I seem to have the wrong cabin."

"Is your name Ray Tallantyre?" she asked.

He pleaded guilty.

"Then you belon vith us. I have asked about the passenyer list. You may have the sofa for sleepin."

"Th-thanks." Ray sat down on it. His knees felt loose.

The Martian gave up the struggle and allowed the woman to place him on the upper bunk. "To tink of it," he squeaked. "Tat I, Urushkidan of Ummunashektaru, should be manhandled by a sabage who does not know a logaritm from an elliptic integral!"

Astounded, Ray stared as if this were the first of the race that he had met in his life. Urushkidan's gray-skinned cupola of a body balanced 120 centimeters tall on the walking tentacles; above them, two slim, three-fingered arms writhed bonelessly on either side of a wide, lipless mouth. Elephantine ears and flat nose supported a pair of horn-rimmed spectacles, his only garb except for a poisonously green vest full of pockets with all kinds of things in them.

"Not *the* Urushkidan?" Ray breathed—the mathematician acclaimed throughout the Solar System as a latter-day Gauss or Einstein.

"Tere is only *one* Urushkidan," the Martian informed him.

For a moment of total irrelevance, Ray's rocking mind wondered how different history might have been if the first probes to Mars hadn't happened to land in two of the Great Barrens—if civilizations upon that world had gone in for agriculture or architecture identifiable by instruments in orbit— if, even, the weird biochemistry of the natives had been unable to endure Terrestrial conditions—

A Homeric shout of laughter brought him back to what he must suppose was reality. The woman uttered it where she loomed over him. "Velcome, male Tallantyre," she cried. "You are cute. I think I vill like you. I am Dyann Korlas of Kathantuma." She took his hand in a friendly grip.

He yelped and got it back not quite crushed. "You're one of the Centaurians, then," he said feebly.

"Yes, so you call us."

He found himself regarding her with some pleasure, overwhelming though her presence was. Hitherto he had only seen her kind on television.

Except for the pointed ears, which her braids concealed, she looked human enough externally, albeit not of any stock which had ever evolved on Earth. The similarities extended to all the most interesting areas, he knew. Memories came back to him of scientific arguments he had read as to whether this was mere coincidence or whether form had to follow function that closely on every globe of a given type. There were plenty of internal differences, of course, among them being bone and flesh which were considerably harder and denser than his. Alpha Centauri A III—or Varann, as its most advanced nation had decided to name it after learning from the first Solar expedition that it was a planet—had, among other striking non-resemblances to his world, half again the surface gravity.

Her size reminded him of alienness which went deeper than appearance. Men of her race were smaller and weaker than women. In every known culture, they stayed home and did the housework while their wives conducted public business. In warlike Kathantuma and its neighbor lands, public business usually meant raids on somebody else with the objective of stealing everything that wasn't bolted down.

Nevertheless, this . . . Dyann Korlas . . . was well worth staring at. She was built like a statuesque tigress. Her skin was smooth and golden-hued. Bronze hair coiled heavy around a face which would have inspired an ancient Hellenic sculptor; but exotic touches, such as a slight tilt to the big, storm-gray eyes, made it look not only Classical but sexy. Her outfit consisted of a knee-length tunic, sandals, a form-fitting steel cuirass with twin demonic visages sculptured on the bust, a round helmet decorated with bat-like bronze wings, a belt upholding purse and sheath knife, and a sword which Lancelot might have reckoned just a trifle too heavy.

Ray found his voice: "Are you sure I belong in this cabin? Hasn't somebody made a mistake?"

She grinned. "Oh, you are safe."

He recalled that the titles of aristocrats in her home country translated into expressions like "chief," "district ruler," "warrior," and the like. A few males had accompanied the Centurian ladies to the Solar System. Arrogantly indifferent to details of ethnology, the Jovians must have assumed from her honorific, whatever it was—doubtless written down on her behalf by some Extraterrestrial Secretariat underling told off to assist these visitors—that she was among those males.

Well, why should Ray Tallantyre disabuse the ship's officers? The overworked third-class steward wasn't likely to care, or perhaps even notice. Not that the Earthling expected any action with his cabin mate, especially in Urushkidan's presence. Indeed, the idea was somewhat terrifying. However, from time to time the view in here ought to get quite nice. They had no nudity taboo in Kathantuma.

Reminded of the Martian and his manners, Ray glanced toward the upper berth. Urushkidan was morosely stuffing a big-bowled pipe. Tobacco-smoking was a vice on which his race had eagerly seized; they didn't exactly breathe, but by the bellows-and-membrane organ which they also used to form human speech, they could keep the fire going. They usually described the sensation as "tinglesome."

"Uh, sir, I'd like to say I know of your work," the human ventured. "In fact, since I am—was—a nucleonic engineer, I can appreciate what it means."

The Martian inflated his body, his way of smiling or preening. "Doubtless you habe grasped it quite well," he replied graciously. "As well as

any Eartling could, which is, of course, saying
bery little."

"But if I may ask, uh, what are you doing here?"

"Oh, I habe a lecture series arranged at te
Jobian Academy of Sciences. Tey are quite com-
mendably aware of my importance. I will be glad
to get off Eart. Te air pressure, te grabity, pfui!"

"But a . . . a person . . . of your distinction,
traveling third class—"

"Naturally, tey gabe me a first-class ticket. I
turned it in, bought a tird-class, and banked te
difference." He glowered at Dyann Korlas. "To' if
I am treated like tis—" He shrugged. A Martian
shrugging is quite a sight. "No real matter. We of
Uttu—Mars, as you insist on calling it—are so in-
comparably far adbanced in te philosophic birtues
of serenity, generosity, and modesty tat I can
accept barbaric mistreatment wit te scorn tat it
deserbes."

"Oh," said Ray. To the Centaurianess: "And may
I ask why you are bound for Jupiter, Ms.—Ms?—
Korlas?"

"You may," she allowed. "And let us use first
names, no? That is sveet. . . . Vell, I vish to see
Yupiter, though I do not think it vill be as
glamorous as Earth." She sighed. "You live in a
fable! Your beastless carriages, your flyin
machines, your auto—auto-*matic* kitchens, your
clocks, your colorful clothes, your qvaint customs
—*haa*, it vas vorth the long travel yust to see such
things."

Long, for certain; fantastically powerful though
they were, the exploratory ships needed ten years
to cross the interstellar gulf, and there had only
been three expeditions to date. Dyann had arrived

with the latest, part of a delegation and inquiry group dispatched by her queen. Ray had heard that the crew had quite a time with that turbulent score until everybody settled down in suspended animation. The visitors had now spent about a year on Earth and Luna, endlessly curious, especially as to what their hosts did to pass the time since the World Union had arisen to terminate the practice of war. By and large, they'd caused remarkably little trouble. A couple of times tempers had flared and Terrestrial bones gotten broken, but the Varannians were always apologetic afterward. To be sure, once one of them had been scheduled to address a women's club. . . .

"Tell me this I am not clear about," Dyann requested. "The Yovians, they did begin on your planet?"

Ray nodded. "Yes. They colonized the moons partly for economic reasons, partly because they didn't like the way Europe was becoming homogenized. Asian and African immigrants were getting numerous, and so on. About sixty years ago, they declared their independence. After a lot of debate, the leaders of Earth decided the issue wasn't worth fighting about. That may have been a mistake."

"Vy?"

"M-m-m . . . well, it's true they had certain economic grievances, after the heroic work their pioneers had done—and they themselves are still doing, I must admit. Nevertheless, they live under a dictatorship that keeps telling them they're the destined masters of the Solar System. Last year they occupied and claimed the Saturnian moon colonies. Their pretext was almighty thin, but the Union was too chicken-livered to do more than squawk. Not that it has much of a navy compared to theirs."

Dyann beamed. "Ha, you might really have a var vile I am here to see? Lovely, lovely!" She clapped her hands.

A knock on the door interrupted, and the steward bore in the luggage marked "Wanted on Voyage." When he was gone, the cabin occupants got busy unpacking and stowing. Dyann changed into a fur-trimmed robe, confirming Ray's guess that the scenery was gorgeous. Urushkidan slithered to the deck, extracted from his trunk several books, papers, penstyls, and a humidor, and appropriated the dresser top for these.

Unease touched Ray. "You know, sir," he said, "apart from the honor of meeting you, I wish you weren't aboard."

"Why not?" demanded the Martian huffily.

"U-u-uh-h . . . it was your formulation of general relativity that showed it's possible to travel faster than light."

"Among many oter tings, yes," said Urushkidan through malodorous clouds.

"I can't believe the Jovians are interested in your work for its own sake. I suspect they hope to get your guidance in developing that kind of ship. Then we'd all better beware."

"Not I. A Martian is not concerned wit te squabbles of te lower animals. Noting personal, you understand."

Dyann took forth a small wooden image and placed it on the shelf above her bunk. It was gaudily painted and fiercely tusked; each of its arms held a weapon, one being a Terrestrial tommy gun. "Qviet, please," she said, raising an arm. "I am about to pray to Ormun the Terrible."

"An appropriate god for the likes of you," sneered Urushkidan.

She stuffed a pillow from the bunk into his mouth. "Qviet, please, I said," she reproached him with a gentle smile, and prostrated herself before the idol.

After a while, during which she had chanted a prayer full of snarling noises, she got up. Urushkidan was still speechless, with rage. Dyann turned to Ray. "Do you know if this ship has any live animals for sale?" she asked. "I vould like to make a sacrifice too."

After the *Jovian Queen* got under weigh, her captain announced that, given the present planetary configuration, she would complete her passage, at a steady one Terrestrial gee of positive and negative acceleration, in six standard days, 43 minutes, and 12 ± 10 seconds. That might be braggadocio, though Ray Tallantyre would not have been surprised to learn it was sober truth. He soon started wishing the time would prove over-estimated. His roommates wore on his nerves. Urushkidan filled the place with smoke, sat up till all hours covering paper with mathematical symbols, and screamed if anybody spoke above a whisper. Dyann meant well, but limited vocabulary soon caused her conversation to pall; besides, she was mostly off in the gymnasium, working out. When she wasn't, her forcefulness often reminded him of Katrina Vanbrugh, occasioning shudders.

On the second day out, he slouched moodily into the bar and ordered a martini he could ill afford. The ship's food was so wholesome that he wasn't sure he could choke any more down otherwise.

The chamber was quiet except for Wagnerian music in the background, discreetly enough lit that the murals of pioneers and soldiers weren't too conspicuous, and not very full. At one table sat the colonel who had accompanied Ray aloft, still clutching his briefcase but talking with quite human animation to a red-headed female tourist from Earth. Her shape, in a skin-tight StarGlo gown, left small doubt as to his objective. The purity of the Jovian race, "Hardened in the fire and ice of the outer deeps, tempered by adversity to form the new and dominant mankind," had been set aside for a while in favor of international relations.

She didn't look as fascinated as she might have. *If I had some money,* sighed within Ray, *I bet I could pry her loose from him.*

For lack of that possibility, he fell into conversation with the bartender. The latter informed him, in awed tones, that yonder he beheld Colonel Ivan Hosea Domenico Roshevsky-Feldkamp, late military attache of the Confederation's Terrestrial embassy, an officer who had served with distinction in suppressing the Ionian revolt and in asserting his nation's rightful claims to Saturn.

Things got livelier when a couple of fellows entered from second class. North Americans like Ray, they were quick to make his acquaintance and ready to stand him drinks. After an hour or two, they suggested a friendly game of poker.

Oh, ho! thought the engineer, who was less naïve than he often appeared. "Sure," he agreed. "How about right after dinner?"

Joined by a third of their kind, they met him in a proper stateroom and play commenced. It went on for most of the following two days and evenings.

Fortune went back and forth in a way that would have impressed the average person as genuine. Ray kept track, and made occasional bets that ought to have proven disastrous, and when he was alone ran off statistical analyses on his calculator. He was winning entirely too much, and the rate of it was increasing on far too steep a curve. These genial chaps were setting him up for disaster.

When he was a couple of thousand Union credits to the good, he let febrile cupidity glitter from him and said, "Look, boys, you know I'm traveling on the cheap, but I do have money at home and this game is too good for kiddie antes. Suppose I lase my bank to transfer some credit to the purser's office here, and tomorrow we can play for real stakes."

"Sure, Ray, if you want," said the lead shark, delighted to have the suggestion made for him. "You're a sport, you are."

At the appointed hour, he and his companions met again around the table, lit anticipatory cigars, and waited.

And waited.

And waited.

Ray had found the redhead remarkably easy to pry loose from the colonel.

She thought it would be great fun to go slumming and join him in the third-class dining room for the captain's dinner. First class was too stuffy, she said. He escorted her down a corridor, thinking wistfully, and a trifle wearily, that soon the trip would end and he'd disembark in Wotanopolis as broke as ever. She'd made him free of the luxury and spaciousness of her section, but since he avoided the bar—and possible embarrassing confrontations therein—she tacitly assumed that he would pay for refreshments ordered from the staff. Besides, she liked to gamble, and the ship's casino was not rigged.

The sight of Urushkidan distracted him from his generally pleasant recollections. Awkward under Earth weight, the Martian was creeping along toward the saloon reserved for his species; the choice between mealtime segregation and decorum by either standard had been made long ago. He condescended to give the human a greeting: "Well, tere you are. I hope you habe not been found obnoxious."

The trouble actually began with Dyann Korlas, who appeared a moment later in finery of leather boots, fur kilt, gold armbands, necklace of raw gemstones, and polychromatic body paint. Striding up behind Ray, she clapped a hand on his shoulder which almost felled him.

"Vere have you been?" she asked reproachfully. "You vent avay, and you vere so long."

The redhead blushed.

"Oh, hello," Ray said, feeling a touch awkward himself. "What have you been up to?"

Dyann's glance scuttled back and forth. "I think better we ask vat have you been up to," she laughed. "Ah, you dashin, glamorous Earthmen!" —looking down on him by about fifteen centimeters. She pushed in between him and his date, amiably linking arms with both. "Come, ve go feed together, no?"

They reached the companionway leading to the dining room, and there stood three much too familiar figures. Ray felt a thunderbolt go through his head. He'd not counted on this.

"Hey, Tallantyre!" exclaimed the largest of his

poker buddies. Somehow the entire trio seemed bigger than before. "What the hell happened to you? We were going to have another game, remember?"

"I forgot," Ray said around a lump in his gullet.

"Aw, you couldn't've," another man replied. "Look, a sport like you wouldn't quit when he's way ahead, would you?"

"We still got time for a session," added the third.

"But I don't have any more money," Ray protested.

"Now, wait a minute, pal," said the largest. "You want to be a good sport, don't you? Sure you do. You don't want to make any trouble. It wouldn't be good for you, believe me."

The trio crowded close. Backed against the bulkhead, Ray stared past them. Passengers on their way to dinner ignored the unpleasantness, as people generally do. An exception was, of all possible individuals, Colonel Roshevsky-Feldkamp. Though his table was in first class, he must have been getting a drink in the bar—or was his presence more significant than that? Certainly he stood and watched with his iron features tinged by smugness.

Did he put these gullyhanses up to accosting me? Ray wondered wildly. *He could very well be bearing a grudge and—and—would this kind of threat be possible without some kind of* sub rosa *hint that the ship's officers won't interfere?*

"Now why don't you come on back to my cabin and we'll talk about this," proposed the largest. Three tight grins moved in on the engineer. The redhead squeaked and shrank aside.

Dyann scowled and touched the hilt of her

sword. "Are these men annoyin you, Ray?" she asked.

"Oh, no, we just want a quiet little private talk with our friend," said the chief card player. He closed a meaty hand on the engineer's arm and tugged. "You come along now, okay, Tallantyre?"

Ray ran a dried-out tongue over unsteady lips. "Dyann," he mumbled, "I think they are starting to annoy me."

"Oh, vell, in that case—" She grinned happily, reached out, and took hold of the nearest man.

Something like a small explosion followed. The man went whirling aloft, struck the overhead, caromed off a bulkhead, hit the deck, and bounced a couple of times more before lying stunned.

Almost by reflex, his companions had attacked the amazon. "Ormun is kind!" she shouted in joy and gave one a mouthful of knuckles. Teeth flew.

The third had gotten behind her. He plucked the dagger from her belt and raised it. Ray seized his wrist. Bigger and stronger, he tore loose with a force that sent the engineer staggering, and followed. Ray lurched against Roshevsky-Feldkamp. Without thought for anything except a weapon to use when the knife confronted him, he yanked the colonel's briefcase free, raised it in both hands, and brought it down on his enemy's head. It made a dull *thwack* and stopped the gambler in his tracks. Ray hit him again. The briefcase burst open and papers snowed through the air. Then Dyann, having put her second opponent out of the game, turned to this third and proceeded with martial arts practice.

Save for the redhead, who had departed screaming, spectators milled about at a respectful distance. Now Roshevsky-Feldkamp advanced from among them, livid. "I'm terribly sorry, sir," gasped Ray, who didn't think he needed such a personage angry at him. "Here, let me help—"

He went to his knees and began to collect scattered papers and stuff them back into the briefcase. In a dazed fashion he noticed that a number of them bore diagrams of apparatus. A polished boot took him in the rear. He skidded through the mass of documents. "You unutterable idiot!" Roshevsky-Feldkamp yelled.

"You vould hurt my friend?" Dyann said indignantly. "I vill teach you better manners."

The colonel drew his revolver. "Stand where you are," he snapped. "You are both under arrest."

Dyann's broad smooth shoulders sagged. "Oh," she said in a meek voice. "Let me yust carry him" —she pointed at the gambler who was totally unconscious—"for a doctor to see." Bending over, she picked him up.

"March," the Jovian ordered her.

"Yes, sir," she said, and tossed her burden at him. He went over on his backside. She kicked him in the belly and he too lost interest in further combat.

"That vas fun," she chuckled. "Vat shall ve do next?"

"You," said Urushkidan acidly, "are a typical human."

Through the open door of a cabin which had been declared the ship's brig for his benefit, Ray gazed in appeal at his visitor, who had come by request. There was no guard; a chain around his ankle secured the Earthling quite well. "What else could I do?" he pleaded. "Try fighting the entire crew? As was, it took every bit of persuasion I had in me to get Dyann to surrender."

"I mean tat you fought in te first place," Urushkidan scolded. "I hear it started ober a female. Why don't you lower species habe a regular rutting season as we do on Uttu? Ten you could perhaps act sensibly te rest of te year."

"Well—Please, sir! You're the only hope I've got. They won't even tell me what's become of Dyann."

"Oh, tey questioned her, found she cannot read, and dismissed te charges of mayhem and mutiny. Roshevsky-Feldkamp himself agreed she had acted 'in te heat of te moment,' alto' I beliebe I detected a sour note in his boice. She will be all right."

"I'm glad of that much," Ray said, a trifle surprised to notice his own sincerity. "Of course, no doubt the Jovians figured punishing one of our first interstellar visitors would raise more stink on Earth than it could be worth to them. But what's her illiteracy got to do with it? And how do you know they inquired about that?"

"She mentioned it to me afterward. I ten recalled how carefully I had been interrogated, like ebery witness, to make sure I could not habe seen what was in te colonel's papers from tat briefcase. Obbiously tey are top secret and I suspect tey are information about Eart's military situation, gatered by spies for him to take back in person. You are being held prisoner because you did see tem."

"What? But damn it, I never stopped to read anything!"

"You must habe unconscious memories which a hypnoquiz could bring out. If noting else, tat would alert te Union to te existence of a Jobian espionage network. Dyann lacks te word-gestalts, she could not retain any meaningful images, but you— Well, tat is your bad luck. I suppose ebentually te Terrestrial embassy can negotiate your release, after te Jobians habe had time to cober teir tracks on Eart.''

"No, not then," Ray groaned. "They'll never bother. There's a warrant out for me at home. Besides, old Vanbrugh will be only too pleased to see me get the rotary shaft."

"Banbrugh—te Nort American member of te World Council?"

"Uh-huh." Ray slumped where he stood. "And to think I was a plain underpaid engineer till Uncle Hosmer left me a million credits in his will. I hope he's frying in hell."

Urushkidan's eyes bugged till they seemed about to push off his spectacles. "A man left you money and you resent it? Ten why habe you talked about being poor?"

"Because I am. I spent the whole sum."

"Shalmuannasar! On what?"

"Oh, wine, women, song, the usual."

Urushkidan winced as if in physical pain. "A million credits, and not a millo inbested."

"Meanwhile I got into high society," Ray explained. "I made out as if I had more than I actually did, not to defraud anybody, only so as not to be scoffed at. Katrina Vanbrugh—that's the Councillor's daughter—got the idea I'd make a good fifth husband, or would it have been the sixth? I forget. Well, she's not bad-looking, and she has a headlong way about her, and the upshot was that we became engaged. Big social event. Except then a reporter grew nosy, and found out my fortune was practically gone, and Katrina decided I'd only been after her money and now she and her parents were a laughingstock. . . . Vanbrugh had me charged with criminal misrepresentation. Quite false—oh, maybe I had shaded the truth a little, but I honestly didn't think it'd make any difference to Katrina when I got around to admitting it, she being as rich as she is—the family just wanted revenge. How could I fight that kind of power? I panicked and skipped. Maybe that was foolish; certainly it's made my case worse. The upshot is that the Jovians can do anything to me they feel like."

He flung out his arms. "Sir, can't you put in a good word for me?" he begged. "You're famous, admired, influential if you choose to be. Couldn't you please help?"

The Martian inflated himself in the equivalent of simper, then deflated and said with mild regret, "No, I cannot entangle myself in te empirical. It is too distracting, and my work too important. My domain is te beauty and purity of matematics. I adbise you to accept your fate wit philosophy. If you wish, I can lend you a copy of Ekbannutil's *Treatise on te Insignificance of Temporal Sorrows.*"

Ray collapsed onto his bunk and buried face in hands. "No, thanks."

Urushkidan waved affably and waddled off.

Presently the spaceship entered orbit around Ganymede. A squad of soldiers arrived to bring Ray down to the moon. Roshevsky-Feldkamp took personal charge of that.

"Where am I going?" the Earthling asked.

"To Camp Muellenhoff, near Wotanopolis," the colonel told him with pleasure. "It is where we keep spies until we have completed their interrogation and are ready to shoot them."

Dyann Korlas needed a couple of Terrestrial days to decide that she didn't like Ganymede.

The Jovians had been entirely courteous to her, offering a stiff apology for the unfortunate incident en route and assigning her a lieutenant in the Security Corps for a guide. Within limits, he indulged her curiosity about armaments, and she found her conducted tours of military facilities more impressive than anything corresponding that she had seen on Earth. However, granted that plasma-jet spacecraft, armored gun carriers, and nuclear missiles had capabilities beyond those of swords, bows, and cavalry, still, they took the fun out of combat and left nothing to plunder. She missed the brawling mirth of Kathantuman encampments among these endlessly and expressionlessly marching ranks, these drab uniforms and impersonal machines.

The civilians were still more depressingly clad, and their orderliness, their instant obedience before any official, their voluminous praises to her of the wonders of Symmetrism, the tiny apartments in which they were housed, soon made her nerves crawl. The officer caste did possess a certain dash and glamour which she would have enjoyed, had it not been exclusively male. She had found the Terrestrial concept of sexual equality interesting, even perversely exciting; but the Jovians had not simply changed the natural order of things, they had turned it upside down, and she found herself regarding them as a race of perverts.

The standard sights were often fascinating. Below ground, Wotanopolis was a many-leveled

hive of industry; she admired especially the count-
less engineering accomplishments which made
human life here so triumphantly safe and ordinary. The views above ground were often magnificent in their stark fashion: Jupiter like a huge
moon, softly lambent, in a twilit heaven; an
auroral shimmer in the phantom-thin air, where
the force-fields created by enormous generators
warded off radiation that would otherwise have
been lethal; crags, craters, mountains, glaciers; a
crystalline forest, a splendidly leaping animal, the
marvel that life had arisen here too, here too.

Yet the impression grew upon her that she was
being hurried along, from sight to sight and conversation to conversation, without ever a chance
really to talk to anyone, to glimpse whatever soul
there dwelt beneath the busy flesh. True, she
heard lectures about the superiority of Jovian
society and its clear right to leadership of the
Solar System, till she lost count. Nonetheless she
wondered if the people she met would have been
that monomaniacal had her guide not been
present. Besides, if they felt they ought to rule,
why didn't they just hop into their spaceships and
have at the Earthlings?

Everywhere she saw portraits of the Leader, a
short and puffy-faced man named Martin Wilder.
Once Lieutenant Hamand, the person conducting
her, said in awe that, if the Leader was not too
occupied with cares of state, she might actually be
introduced to him. Hamand looked hurt when she
yawned.

Meanwhile, she fretted about Ray Tallantyre.
Though she hadn't really seen much of her erst-
while roommate, she had found him uncommonly
appealing. In part, she recognized, that was no

doubt because, what with one thing and another, she hadn't gotten laid for some time when she boarded the liner, nor had she since. But in part, also, she liked his liveliness and wry humor. They contrasted vividly with the humble men of her homeland. She had confirmed for herself that male Earthlings often deserved the reputation they had won among female Varannians; she suspected that Ray exceeded the average. It was unlikely that he'd adjust well to harem life, but she had no such plans for him. It was impossible that he, belonging to a different species, could father a child of hers. Right now, that was no drawback at all.

She'd been looking forward to developing the acquaintance on Ganymede. Then he got into trouble, and she'd not been able to discover a thing about his present situation. Under pressure, Hamand had put her in touch with an officer of the political police, who said that the case was under consideration and advised her not to get involved. If nothing else, he said, her tour of the Jovian System would end before the matter had been disposed of. He concluded with assurances that Tallantyre would "receive justice," which she did not find very satisfactory.

Her concern sprang from more than attraction. That had caused her to think of Ray as a friend—and in Kathantuma, one did not abandon a friend. They hadn't exchanged blood oaths or anything like that. Nevertheless, the fact that she had enjoyed his company led her warrior conscience toward the illogical conclusion that she owed him her help.

This did not come about overnight, nor in any such clear terms. What she experienced was simply an anxiety which grew and grew. It fed upon her distaste for the civilization which currently surrounded her. If Ray had offended these creatures, well, they needed offending. Could she be less brave?

Ganymede swung once about Jupiter, a period of a week, while Dyann Korlas wrestled ever more with her emotional and ethical dilemma. At last she did the proper thing according to her own beliefs: alone in her quarters, save for a bottle of whiskey, she brought the matter out before herself, considered it explicitly, realized that it was indeed important to her, and resolved that she would no longer stay idle. In the morning she would seek divine guidance.

That decision made, she slept well.

At 0600 hours, as always, lights flashed on throughout Wotanopolis to decree a new day. Dyann bounded out of bed, sang a cheerful song of clattering swords and cloven skulls while she washed and dressed—cuirass, helmet, sword, dagger above tunic and sandals—and sought the kitchenette of her apartment, where she prepared a breakfast that would have sufficed two Terrestrial laborers. Ordinary Jovians knew no such luxuries, but she rated diplomatic housing.

When she entered the main room, she found Hamand present; crime was alleged to have been stamped out of Symmetrist society, and locks on civilian doors were thought to suggest that those within might be talking sedition. A powerfully built young man, immaculate in gray cloth and shiny boots, he bowed from the waist. "Good day," he greeted. "You will recollect that we are going topside to visit the Devil's Garden. At 1145 we will proceed to Heroville, where we will appreciate the

Revolutionary Cenotaph and have lunch. At 1300 hours we have an appointment to fill out the necessary documents for your forthcoming visit to Callisto. Thereafter—"

"Hold," Dyann interrupted. "First I have a reliyious rite."

"I beg your pardon?"

"Vy? You have done no wrong." Dyann gestured to the image of Ormun, standing ferocious on a table. "I must ask for the counsel of this god." She paused, struck by a thought. "You better—vat is the vord?—you better prostrate yourself too."

"What?" cried the lieutenant.

"She does not like atheists," Dyann explained.

Hamand flushed and stiffened. "Madame," he said, "I have been educated in the scientific principles of Symmetrism. They do not include groveling before idols."

Dyann took him by the back of his neck, bore him down to his knees, and rubbed his nose in the carpet. "You vill please to grovel," she said amiably. "It is good manners." She spread herself prone, while keeping a grip on him, and recited a magical formula. Thereafter she let him go, rose to a crouch, dredged three Kathantuman dice from the purse at her belt, and tossed them.

"*Haa,*" she murmured after study. "The omen says—vell, I am not a *marya*, a certified vitchvife, but I do think the omen says I should seek Urushkidan. See, here the Visdom sign lies right next to the Mystery sign, with the Crossed Axes over here . . . Yes, I am sure Ormun tells me I need to see Urushkidan." She bowed to the image. "Thank you, sveet lady. *Laesti laeskul itorum.*" Rising: "Shall ve go?"

Hamand, who had finished swallowing his resentment for the sake of public relations, was taken aback all over again. "Do you mean the Martian scientist?" he yelped. "Impossible! He is doing critically important work—"

Dyann strolled out into the corridor. She had been shown the Academy of Sciences earlier. No matter how alien this warren of passages was to her native forests, she retained a huntress' sense of direction and landmarks. Hamand trailed her, gabbling, barely able to keep her in sight. There were no slideways. Except in the tunnels where authorized vehicles moved, everybody walked. It was a result of the government's concern over preserving public physical fitness in Ganymede's low gravity. Dyann felt feather-light. She proceeded in three- and four-meter bounds. When a clump of people got in the way of that, she sprang over their heads.

The Academy occupied 50 hectares on a high level of town, a pleasant break in an environment where the very parks were functional. Here, grass, trees, and flowerbeds made lanes of life between walls which, admittedly roofless, were at least covered with plastic ivy. Overhead, a teledome gave an awesome vision of Jupiter, stars, Milky Way, the shrunken sun. The air bore faint, flowery perfumes and recorded birdsong. Upon this campus, moving from building to building, were a number of persons, several obviously military personnel but most just as obviously scholars, little different from their colleagues on Earth.

Dyann stopped one of the latter, loomed over him, and asked where Dr. Urushkidan might be. "In Archimedes Hall—over there," he gasped, and tottered off, perhaps in search of a reviving cup of tea.

She might have known, Dyann thought. In front
of that door, a soldier on guard clashed with the
general atmosphere. She guessed his presence was
due to the military significance of Urushkidan's
work. Though her appearance startled him, too,
rather badly, he slanted his rifle before him and
cried, "Halt!"

Dyann obeyed. "I must see the Martian," she
told him. "Please to let me by."

"Nobody sees him without a pass," he replied.

Dyann shoved him aside and took hold of the
door switch. He yelled and batted at her with his
rifle butt. That was his great mistake.

"You should show more respect for ladies," she
chided, and removed the weapons from his grasp.
Her free hand flung him across the greensward.
He collided with Hamand, who had panted onto
the scene, hard enough that neither was of much
use for some time to come. Dyann admired the
rifle—Earthlings on Varann were deplorably
stingy about giving such things to her folk—before
she slung it across her back by the strap. By now,
too many passersby had halted to stare and
chatter. Best she keep on the move. She opened
the door and passed on through.

For a minute she poised in the hallway beyond,
cocking her ears this way and that. They were
keen. A faint sound of altercation gave her the clue
she hoped for, and she bounded up a flight of
stairs. Before another door she stopped to listen.
Yes, that was the voice of Urushkidan, bubbling
like an infuriated teakettle.

"I will not, sir, do you hear me? I will not. And I
demand immediate return passage from tis
ridiculous satellite."

"Come now, Dr. Urushkidan, do be reasonable."

Was that Roshevsky-Feldkamp? "What is your complaint, actually? Do you not have generous financial compensation, Mars-conditioned lodgings, servants, every imaginable consideration? If you wish something further, inform us and we will try to provide it."

"I came here to lecture and to complete my mathematical research Now I find you habe arranged no lectures and expect me to superbise an—an *engineering* project—as if I were a mere empiricist!"

"But your contract plainly states—"

"Did you tink I would waste my baluable time reading one of your pieces of printed gibberish? Sir, in human law itself, a proper contract requires tat tere habe been a meeting of minds. Te mind of your goberment neber met te mind of myself. It was not capable of it."

The man attempted ingratiation: "You are a leading scientist. As such, you realize that science advances by checking theory against fact. If, with your help, we create a faster-than-light ship, it will be a total confirmation of your ideas."

"My ideas need no confirmation. Tey are a debelopment of certain implications of general relatibity, true. Howeber, tat is incidental. In principle, what I habe produced is a piece of pure matematics, elegant and beautiful. If it agrees or disagrees wit te facts, tat is of no concern to any proper philosopher. And furtermore—" The squeaky tone approached ultrasonic frequencies. "—not only do you want experimental tests, you want to me lend my genius to bulgar military applications! No, no, and again no! Do you understand? I want a ticket on te next ship bound for Mars!"

"I am afraid," said the man slowly, "that that will not be possible."

Dyann opened the door and trod through. "Are they annoyin you?" she asked.

Urushkidan goggled at her from the chair across which he was draped. The room was so thick with the fumes of his pipe that one of the two Jovians present, a bald man in the black tunic of the political police, was holding a handkerchief to his nose. The other was, indeed, Roshevsky-Feldkamp, who sprang to his feet and snatched for his revolver.

Dyann had already unlimbered the expropriated rifle. She aimed it at his midriff. "Better not," she warned him. He froze.

"What . . . you . . . what are you doing here?" stammered the political officer.

"Lookin for Ray Tallantyre," she answered. "Could you tell me vere he is?"

"Guards!" Roshevsky-Feldkamp bellowed fearlessly. "Help!"

Dyann made a leap across the room, seized him by the neck, and hammered his forehead against the desk. With her right hand she kept the second Jovian covered. "I asked you vere is Ray Tallantyre," she reminded him.

"I am glad you came," Urushkidan told her. "Shall we leabe tis uncibilized place?" Two soldiers appeared in the doorway. "Perhaps not."

Dyann swung her rifle around. She was a trifle slow. Both newcomers already had weapons unlimbered, and opened fire. She dropped behind the desk. Twin streams of slugs pierced its mass, seeking her. She took it by the legs and heaved. It arced high over the floor and landed on the soldiers in a burst of drawers, papers, penstyls, and books. They went down beneath it and stayed there, stunned.

The secret police officer had taken advantage of the distraction to snatch forth his sidearm. He trained it on Dyann as she rose. Urushkidan snaked forth a tentacle and pulled him off his feet. Dyann paused to knock Roshevsky-Feldkamp unconscious before she closed fingers around the other man's Adam's apple. "Vere you not listenin?" she growled. "Vere is Ray Tallantyre?"

"Come, no delay, prudence requires we get out of here," urged the Martian.

Perforce, Dyann agreed. She hadn't really intended to get into a brawl. Things had just sort of happened. "Vat's a safe vay to go?" she inquired.

"Tis way. I'be been shown around. Follow me." Urushkidan paused to relieve both officers of their pistols. He carried one in either hand, gingerly, as if he feared they might explode. Dyann frogmarched the political policeman out into the hall after him. Shouts of alarm rang through it, coming nearer; she heard the thud of military boots.

"Hurry," Urushkidan gasped. "Shalmuannasar, we habe te entire Jobian Confederacy after us!" Since he could not move as fast as a human or Centaurian, Dyann expedited matters by picking him up and draping him over her prisoner's head.

They rounded a corner and clattered down several flights of stairs to a steel door marked HANGAR. AUTHORIZED PERSONNEL ONLY. It wasn't locked. Passing through, they found themselves in a cavernous enclosure where several small spacecraft rested on mobile cradles. Mechanics stared at the trio.

"Tese are bessels for scientific use around te

surface," Urushkidan explained. "We want one."

A superintendent hurried up, obviously puzzled but afraid to comment. "You heard vat ve vant," Dyann whispered, and squeezed her captive at the shoulder, quite gently, only enough to make bones creak.

"Yes," the officer gasped through the tentacles that curtained his face. "Practice maneuvers. We ... we have immediate requirement of a fully-equipped craft. Mission confidential and—ow-w-w!—urgent."

"Yes, sir," responded a lifetime's training in blind obedience. However, the crew was a little less efficient than usual. They kept stealing looks.

As a teardrop-shaped boat trundled forth, Dyann held most of her attention on the door through which she had entered. Pursuit might re-open it at any instant. Surely by now Roshevsky-Feldkamp and the soldiers had been found. It shouldn't take somebody long to think of the possibility that her group had fled hither.

"I'll start the warmup, sir," the head mechanic said.

"No, don't bother, ve'll take her straight out," Dyann replied.

Aghast, he protested, "Madame, you don't understand. That'll cause carbon deposits in the tubes. You'll risk engine failure, a crash—"

"You find that an acceptable risk," Dyann told the secret policeman.

"Yes, of course I do," he choked. "The ... the Leader tells us no hazard is too great for the cause."

Dyann propelled him ahead of her through the airlock. In the control cabin, she pushed him into the pilot's recoil chair, which she recognized from her travels around Earth. "I hope you can fly vun of these," she said.

"I hope so too," added Urushkidan. He slithered off the Jovian, secured the airlock, and knitted himself to a passenger seat.

"Ve are goin to find Ray Tallantyre," Dyann instructed the man. Part of her thought that she was beginning to sound obsessive. Yet, given the wtich's brew of events in which she had somehow submerged herself, it was as reasonable a plan of action as any. Ray's shrewdness and sophistication might lend her the vital extra help, when Ormun was being left behind. In fact, this appeared to have been Ormun's intention.

"What do you mean?" the officer asked. He seemed a trifle disconcerted and confused.

"Ray Tallantyre, the Earthman that was arrested off the *Yovian Qveen*," Dyann said with what she congratulated herself was exemplary patience. "You in your service ought to know vere he is kept. Vould some blows refresh your memory?"

"Camp Muellenhoff, you savage!" he got out. "North of the city. You'll never succeed. You'll kill us all."

Dyann smiled. "Then ve vill feast forever vith the gods, in the Hall of Skulls," she comforted him. "Von't that be nice?"

The cradle got into motion, rumbling toward the hangar airlock. Up a long ramp ... into the chamber ... darkness outside, as valves closed ... hollow noise of pumps, withdrawing air.... Urushkidan relit his pipe with shaky tendrils. Dyann whistled tunelessly between her teeth.

"I am not so sure we are wise," the Martian said. "Tis bessel cannot carry us away from te Jobian System, or eben to anoter satellite of te planet."

"No, you are not wise," the political officer agreed eagerly.

"Hindsight will show," Dyann responded. "Meanvile, *you* vould be most unvise not to pilot like I tell you."

The outer valve opened. The cradle rolled out onto the field. Behind that flat expanse, the dome which covered Wotanopolis glowed against sawtoothed mountains, rearing above a near horizon, and starlit sky. The dwarfed pale sun cast luminance from the west. Only one other spacecraft was in sight, a black shape which Dyann could identify as a patrol ship.

"They vill come out after us in force pretty soon," she said. "Vat can ve do about that boat yonder, ha?" She reached a decision. "Ah, yes." Her involuntary pilot received his orders. When he clamored refusal, she reminded him, briefly but painfully, that he was no volunteer but, indeed, an impressed man. The engine thuttered and the little scientific craft rose.

Having reached altitude, she descended again, sufficiently to play her jets across the patrol ship. That was not good for the patrol ship.

Dyann didn't bother to receive whatever they were trying to tell her from the control tower. "Now," she stated as her boat rose anew, "you, my policeman friend, take us to this prison and make them release Tallantyre to us. If this goes okay, ve vill set you free somevere. If not—" she passed the edge of her knife across the back of his hand, neatly shaving off hairs, "you may still be a police, but you might not be a man."

"You unutterable monster," he said.

"It is nicer droppin nuclear missiles on cities?" she asked, genuinely bemused.

"Yes," Urushkidan snickered, "I habe had a digestibe pouch full of you Jobians talking about te glories of war and destiny and te will of te Race and historical necessity and suchlike tings. Perhaps in future you will wish to employ more logical rigor."

The flight was short to Camp Muellenhoff. It lay out on the surface, a cluster of pressure huts around a watchtower. There was no barbed wire; the Ganymedean environment gave ample security. If a spacesuited prisoner did slip away from a work detail, the sole question was whether a local monster would get him before his oxygen or his heatpack was exhausted.

When the boat landed in the area, such a figure was urged toward her airlock by a couple of others. The political officer had radioed ahead the demand he was supposed to, quite convincingly. A voice did rattle out of her receiver: "Sir, I've been ordered to ask if you really want to bring this prisoner back to town. We've lately been alerted to watch out for a party of escaped desperadoes."

"Yes," the secret policeman said between clenched teeth, "I want him back in town. Oh, how I want him back in town!"

The captive stumbled into the cabin. Ice promptly formed over his armor. Dyann gave a command, the boat stood on her tail and screamed off toward parts unknown, the newly rescued person clattered against the after bulkhead and lay asprawl.

Presently, when they were flying on an even keel, he opened his faceplate. Slightly battered, the countenance of Ray Tallantyre emerged. "*Haa-ai*, dear sveetheart!" Dyann cried. She reached for him, touched his suit, and withdraw her hand with a yelp. "How are you?" she asked, not very distinctly since she was sucking frostbitten fingers.

"Well . . . I . . . well, not too bad," he answered out of his bewilderment. "A rough time but . . . mainly it was truth drugs . . . they told me I'd be shot as a, a precautionary measure—"

"Poòr, dear Ray! Poor little Earthlin! Lie easy. I vill soon take care of you."

"Yeah, I'm afraid you will."

"Te immediate question," Urushkidan said, "is, Tallantyre, can you pilot a behicle of tis type?"

"Well, uh, yes, I suppose I can," Ray answered. "Looks like a modified Astrid-Luscombe. . . . Yes, I can."

"Good. Ten we can drop tis creature here. I do not like and/or trust him. He smells of phenylalanine—Dyann! Do you mean we are not simply going to *drop* him?"

"I made my promise," the woman said.

They descended on a rocky plateau, gave the secret policeman a spacesuit, and dismissed him. He should be able to reach the camp, given reasonable luck. Nevertheless he bemoaned his maltreatment.

"And now, vat next?" Dyann asked blithely.

"Lord knows," Ray sighed. "I suppose we find us a place in the wilderness where we aren't likely to be spotted for a while, and take stock. Maybe, in some crazy fashion, we can contact the Union embassy. You and Urushkidan ought to rate diplomatic intervention, and I can ride on your cloaks. Maybe. First we find that hideyhole, and second we prepare to skedaddle if we spy a Jovian flyer."

He strapped into the master seat and tickled the controls. The boat lifted readily, but after a moment began to shake, while ominous noises came through the engine-room radiation wall.

"Could tat be te effects of carbon deposits in te tubes tat we were warned about?" wondered Urushkidan.

Ray grimaced. "You mean you took off without proper warmup? Yes, I'm afraid it is." His fingers danced across the board. The response he got was erratic. "We'll have to land soon. Eloc we crash. It'll take a week before the radioactivity is low enough that we can go out and clean the jets."

"And meanvile is a satellite-vide hunt after us." Dyann's clear brow wrinkled. "Is Ormun offended because I did not invite her alon? It does seem our luck is runnin low."

"And," said Ray, "how!"

He used the last sputter of ions to set down in a valley which appeared to be as wild and remote as one could hope for. However, when he got a look through a viewport, he wondered if he hadn't overdone it.

Around the boat was a stretch of seamed and pitted stone, sloping up on every side toward fang-cragged hills. The glow of Jupiter shimmered, weirdly colored, off a distant glacier and a closer pool of liquid methane. The latter had begun boiling; its vapors obscured the tiny sun and streamed ragged across a stand of gaunt, glassy plants. Quite a wind must be blowing out there, though too tenuous for him to hear through the hull. At this time of day, when the hemisphere had warmed, the air—which still didn't amount to much more than a contaminated vacuum—consisted mostly of carbon dioxide, with some methane, amonia, and nitrogen: not especially breathable. Even Urushkidan couldn't survive those conditions without proper gear. This craft's heating and atmosphere regeneration plants had better be in good working order.

An animal passed across the view in kangaroo-like bounds. While small, it gave him another reason not to want to go outdoors. Ganymedean biochemistry depended on heat-absorbent materials; the thermal radiation of a spacesuited human attracted animals, and carnivores were apt to try eating their way directly to the source.

Ray turned to his companions. "Well," he sighed, "what shall we do now?"

Dyann's eyes lit up. "Hunt monsters?" she suggested.

"Bah!" Urushkidan writhed his way toward the laboratory compartment, where there was a desk. "You do what you like except not to disturb me. I have an interesting aspect of unified field teory to debelop."

"Look," said Ray, "we've got to take action. If we sit here passive, waiting for the time when we can clean those tubes, we're too bloody likely to be found."

"What do you imagine we can effect?"

"Oh, I don't know. Camouflage, maybe? Damnation, I have to do *something!*"

"I don't, apart from my matematics. Leabe me out of any idiotic schemes you may hatch."

"But if they catch us, we'll be killed!"

"I won't be," said Urushkidan smugly. "I am too baluable."

"You're a, uh, an accessory of ours."

"True, I did get carried away in te excitement. My hope was to aboid habing to waste my genius toiling for a mere engineering project. Tat hope has apparently been disappointed. Well, ten, te logical ting for me to do when te Jobians arribe is to go ahead and complete te dreary ting for tem, so tey will let me go home . . . wit proper payment for my serbices, I trust." The Martian paused. "As for you two, I will try to make it a condition tat your libes be spared. I am, after all, a noble person. I doubt you will eber be set free, but tink how many years you will habe, undistracted, to cultibate philosophical resignation."

Dyann tugged at Ray's sleeve. "Come on," she urged. "Let's hunt monsters."

"Waaah!" Goaded beyond endurance, the Earthman jumped on high — and, in Ganymedean gravity, cracked his pate on the overhead.

"Oh, poor darlin!" Dyann exclaimed, and folded him in an embrace that would have done credit to a bear.

"Let me go!" he raged. "Somebody here better think past the next minute!"

"You really must work on security," Urushkidan advised him. "Consider tings from te aspect of eternity. You are only a lower animal. Your fate is of no importance."

"You conceited octopus!"

"Temper, temper," Urushkidan wagged a flexible finger at the man. "Let me remind you why you should heed me. If your reasoning powers are so weak tat you cannot demonstrate *a priori* tat Martians are always right—by definition —ten remember te facts. Martians are beautiful. Martians habe a benerable cibilization. Eben physically, we are superior; I can libe under Eart conditions, but I dare you to try staying alibe under Mars conditions. I double-dog dare you."

"Martians," gritted Ray, "didn't come to Earth. Earthmen came to Mars."

"Of course. We had no reason to bisit you, but you had ebery reason to make pilgrimages to us, hoping tat a little beauty and wisdom would rub off on you. Enough. I am going aft to carry on my research and do not want to be disturbed, except tat when you get te galley going, you may bring me a bite to eat. I can ingest your kind of food, you know. I cannot, howeber, positibely cannot abide te taste of asparagus or truffles. Do not prepare me any dish wit asparagus or truffles." Urushkidan started off along the deck.

"You know, Ray," said Dyann, "I have been thinkin, and you are right. Now is not the time to hunt monsters. Let's make love."

"Oh, God!" the human groaned. "If I could get away from you two lunatics, you'd see me exceed the speed of light doing it."

He stiffened where he stood.

"Yes?" asked Dyann.

"Lord, Lord, Lord," he whispered. "That's the answer."

"Yes, tat's right, talk no louder tan tat while I am tinking," Urushkidan said from the after door.

"The drive, the faster-than-light drive—" Ray broke into a war-dance around the cramped compartment, bounding from chairs to aisle and back. "We've got all kinds of scientific supplies and equipment, we've got the Solar System's top authority on the subject, I'm an engineer, everybody knows that the basic effects have been shown in the laboratory and a real drive is just a matter of development—We'll do it ourselves!"

"Not so loud, I told you," Urushkidan grumbled. He passed by the door and slammed it behind him.

"Dyann, Dyann," Ray warbled, "we're going home."

Her eyes filled with tears. "Do you vant to leave me already?" she asked. "Do you not like me?"

"No, no, no, I want to save our lives, our freedom, that's all. Come on, let's go aft and take inventory. I'll need you to move the heavy stuff around."

Dyann shook her head. "No," she pouted. "If you don't care for me, vy should I help you?"

"Judas priest," Ray groaned. "Look, I love you, I adore you, I worship at your feet. Now will you give me a hand?"

Dyann brightened but insisted, "Prove it."

Ray kissed her. She seized him and responded enthusiastically.

"Yeow!" he screamed. "You're about to break my ribs! Leggo!" As she did: "Uh, we'll discuss this some other time, when we've less urgent business."

"Love," said Dyann, "has gotten to be very urgent business for me. Come here."

After a while Urushkidan opened the door. "If you two don't stop tose noises—" he began indignantly. His gaze went to the aisle. "Oh," he said. "Oh." He closed the door again.

Later, an aroma of coffee drew him back to the forward cabin. A disheveled Ray Tallantyre was busy at the little food preparation unit while Dyann sat polishing her sword and humming to herself.

"Well, hi," said the man with evident relief. "I guess we can get started. First, suppose I ask a few questions, to refresh and expand my knowledge of how this drive of yours works."

"It is not a dribe and it does not work," Urushkidan replied. "What I habe created is a structure of pure matematics. Besides, it is beyond te full comprehension of anybody but myself. Gibe me some coffee."

"You must have followed the experiments, though, and learned a good bit more along those lines from the Jovians who've been trying to build a usable device."

"Oh, yes, no doubt I could design something if I wanted to. I don't want to. My current interests are too cosmic." Urushkidan accepted a cup and slurped.

"Look," Ray argued, "if the Jovians catch us, they'll force you to do it for them. And afterward they'll overrun Mars along with the other planets. Logistics will no longer be a problem for them, you see, nor will there be any defense against their missiles."

"Tat would be unfortunate, I admit. Neberteless, it would be downright tragic if my present train of tought were interrupted, as it would be if I gabe your project my full attention, which I would habe to do if it were to habe any chance of success. Te Jobians can afford to employ me on a part-time basis. Let tem conquer te Solar System. In a tousand years tey will be a footnote in te history books. My accomplishments will be remembered while te uniberse endures."

Dyann hefted her sword. "You will do vat he says," she growled.

"You dare not harm me," Urushkidan gibed; "it would leabe you stranded for te Jobians to take rebenge upon."

He finished his coffee. "Where is te tobacco?" he asked. "I habe used my own up."

"Jovians don't smoke," Ray informed him with

savage satisfaction. "They consider it a degenerate habit."

"What?" The Martian's howl rattled the pot on the hotplate. "No tobacco aboard?"

"None. And I daresay your supply back in Wotanopolis has been confiscated and destroyed. That puts the nearest cigar store somewhere in the Asteroid Belt."

"Oh, no! How can I tink without my pipe? Te new cosmology ruined by tobacco shortage—" Urushkidan needed bare seconds to reach his decision. "Berry well. Tere is no help for it. If te nearest tobacco is millions of kilometers away, we must build te faster-tan-light engine at once.

"Also," he added thoughtfully, "if te Jobians did conquer te Solar System, tey might well prohibit tobacco on ebery world. Yes, you habe conbinced me, yours is a bital cause."

Ray made no attempt to use the Martian's equations in detail or to find elegant solutions of any. He merely wanted to compute the parameters of something that would work, and he proceeded with slashing approximations that brought screams of almost physical anguish from the other being.

He did, however, recognize the basic nature of Urushkidan's achievement, a final correlation of general relativity and wave mechanics whose formulation had certain surprising consequences.

Relativity deals with matter and energy, including potentials, which move at definite velocities that cannot exceed that of light. In contrast, wave mechanics treats the particle as a psi function which is only probably where it is. In the latter theory, point-to-point transitions are not speeds but shifts in the node of a complex wave. Urushkidan had abolished the contradiction by bringing in his own immensely generalized and refined concept of information as a condition of the plenum rather than as a physical quantity subject to physical limitations. It then turned out that the phase velocity of matter waves—which, unlike the group velocity, can move at any speed—could actually carry information, so that the most probable position of a particle went from region to region with no restrictions on the time derivatives.

The trick was to establish such conditions in reality that the theoretical possibility was realized.

"As I understand it," Ray had said, early on, "the proper configuration of quark interchanges will set up a field of space-strain. A spacecraft will react against the entire mass of the universe, won't even need rockets. In fact, we have here the key to a lot of other things as well, like gravity control. Right?"

"Wrong," answered Urushkidan.

"Well, we'll build it anyhow," Ray said.

His ambition was not as crazy as it might seem —not quite. The theory was in existence and considerable laboratory work had been done. Despite his scorn for empirical science, Urushkidan's mind had stored away the data about these and was perfectly capable of seeing what direction research should take next. Moreover, he was in fact the sole person with a complete grasp of his concepts; no physicist had, as yet, comprehended every aspect of them. Given motivation, he flung the full power of his intellect against the problem of practical application. Ray Tallantyre was actually quite a good engineer where it came to producing hardware. That hardware was not really complex, either, any more than a transistor or a tunnel diode is complex; the subtlety lies in the physical principles employed. In the present case, what was required was, basically, power, which the spacecraft had, and circuits with certain resonances, which could be constructed out of available materials. The result would not be neat, but in a slapdash fashion it ought to work.

Just the same, no R & D undertaking ever went smoothly, and this one labored under special difficulties. On a typical occasion—

"We'll want our secondary generator over here, I think, attached to this bench," Ray said. "Tote it for me, will you, Dyann?"

"All ve've done is vork, vork, vork," she sulked. "I vant to hunt monsters."

"Bring it, you lummox!"

Dyann glared but stooped above the massive machine and, between Ganymedean weight and Varannian muscles, staggered across the deck with it. Meanwhile Ray was checking electrical properties on an oscilloscope. Urushkidan was solving a differential equation while grumbling about heat and humidity and fanning himself with his ears. Elsewhere lay strewn a chaos of parts and tools.

"Damn!" the man exclaimed. "I hoped—but no, this piece of copper tube isn't right either. I need a resistance with so-and-so many ohms and such-and-such a capacitance, and nothing around seems to be modifiable for it."

"Specify your values," Urushkidan said.

Ray pawed through the litter around him, selected another object, and put it in his test circuit.

"No, this won't do." He cast it across the room; it clanged against a bulkhead. "Look, if we can't find something, this project is stopped cold."

Having put down the generator, Dyann went forward. She returned with the boat's one and only frying pan. "Vill this maybe be right?" she asked innocently.

"Huh? Get out of my way!" Ray screamed.

"Okay," she answered, offended. "I go hunt monsters."

You know—passed through the man's head; and: *What's to lose?* He clipped the pan into the circuit. Its properties registered as nearly what he required. *If I cut the handle off*—Excited, he began to do that.

"Are you mad?" protested Urushkidan.

"Well, I don't like the idea of living off cold beans any better than you do," Ray retorted, "but consider the alternative." He rechecked the emasculated frying pan. "Ye-e-s, given a few adjustments elsewhere, this'll serve." Viciously: "Starward the course of human empire."

"Martian empire," Urushkidan corrected, "unless we decide it is beneat our dignity."

"It'll be Jovian empire if we don't escape. Okay, bulgebrain, what comes next?"

"How should I know? I habe not finished here. How do you expect me to tink in tis foul, tick air, wit no tobacco?"

Dyann clumped in from the forward cabin, attired in a spacesuit whose adjustability she strained to the limit. Its faceplate was still open. Her right hand clutched the rifle she had taken, her left her sword. "I saw monsters out there," she announced happily. "I am goin to hunt them."

"Oh, sure, sure," muttered Ray without really

hearing. His attention was on a calculator. "Urushkidan, could you hurry it up a bit with that equation of yours? I really do need to know the exact resonant wave form before I can proceed." He glanced up. The Martian was trying to fill his pipe from the shreds and dottle in an ashtray. "Hey! Get busy!"

"Won't," said Urushkidan.

"By Heaven, you animated bagpipe, if you don't give me some decent cooperation for a change, I'll —I'll—"

"Up your rectifier."

The sound of an airlock valve closing snatched Ray out of his preoccupation. "Dyann?" he called. "Dyann. . . . Hey, she really is going outside."

"Apparently tere are monsters indeed," Urushkidan said.

Ray sprang into the forward cabin and peered through the nearest of its viewports. His heart stumbled. "Yes, a pair of grannydragons," he exclaimed. "Must've sensed our heat output—they could crack this hull wide open—"

"I will proceed wit te calculation," Urushkidan said uneasily.

—Dyann leaped from lock to ground. In the weird light and thin shriek of wind, the beasts seemed unreal. An Earthling would have compared them to long-legged crocodiles, ten meters from spiky tailtip to shovel jaws. "Thank you, Ormun," she said in her native language, aimed the rifle, and fired.

A dragon bellowed. In this atmosphere, the sound reached her as a squeak. The beast charged. She stood her ground and kept shooting.

A blow knocked her asprawl and sent the firearm from her grasp. She had forgotten the second dragon. Its tail whacked anew, and Dyann tumbled skyward. As she hit the rocks, both animals rushed her.

"*Haa-hai!*" she yelled, bounced to her feet, and sprang. She still had her sword, secured to her wrist by a loop of leather. Up she went, over the nearest head, and struck downward. Green ichor spurted forth. It froze immediately.

Dyann landed, got her back against a huge meteorite, and braced herself. The unhurt monster arrived, mouth agape. She hewed with a force that sang through her whole body. The terrible head flew off its neck. She barely jumped free of its still clashing teeth. The decapitated carcass staggered about, blundered against the companion animal, and started fighting.

Dyann circled warily around. The headless dragon collapsed after a while. The other turned about, noticed once more the heat-radiant boat, and lumbered in that direction. It had to be diverted. Dyann scrambled up on top of the meteorite, poised, and sprang. She landed astride the beast's neck.

It hooted and bucked. She tried to cut its head off also, but couldn't get a proper swing to her blade where she was. The injuries she inflicted must have done something to what passed for a nervous system, because the monster started galloping around in a wide circle. The violence of the motion was such that she dared not try to jump off, she could merely hang on.

Well-nigh an hour passed before the creature stopped, exhausted. Dyann slid to the ground, whirled her sword on high, and did away with this beast also. "Ho-ha!" she yelled joyously, retrieved her rifle, and skipped back to the boat.

—"Oh, Dyann, Dyann," Ray half sobbed when she was inside and her spacesuit off. "I thought sure you'd be killed—"

"It was grand fun," she laughed. "Now let's make love."

"Huh?"

She felt of her backside and winced. "Me on top."

Ray retreated nervously. Urushkidan, standing in the entrance to the lab section, snickered and shut the door.

The Ganymedean day drew to a close. Stars brightened in a darkened sky, save where Jupiter stood at half phase low to the south, mighty in his Joseph's coat of belts and zones. Weary, begrimed, and triumphant, Ray stepped back from his last job of adjustment. His gaze traveled fondly over the haywired mess that filled much of the forward cabin, all of the after cabin, and, via electrical conduits through the rad wall, most of the engine room.

"Done, I hope, I hope," he crooned. "My friends, we've opened a way to the universe."

Dyann nuzzled him. "You are too clever, my little darlin," she breathed. That rather spoiled the occasion for him. He'd grown fond of her—if nothing else, she was a magnificent companion, once she'd learned that there were limits to his strength as well as his available time—but she could not simper very successfully.

"I fear," said Urushkidan, "tat tis minor achiebement of mine will eclipse my true significance in te popular mind. Oh, well." He shrugged with his whole panoply of tentacles. "I can always use te money."

"Um-m-m, yeah, I haven't had a chance to think about that angle," Ray realized. "I'm safe enough from Vanbrugh—you don't bring a man to court who's prevented a war and given Earth the galaxy —but by gosh, there's also a fortune in this gadget."

"Yes, I will pay you a reasonable fee for helping me patent it," Urushkidan said.

Ray started. "Huh?"

"I would also like your opinion on wheter to charge an exorbitant royalty or rely on a high bolume of sales at a lower price. You are better fitted to deal wit such crass matters."

"Wait one flinkin' minute," Ray snarled. "I had a share in this development too, you know."

Urushkidan uttered a nasty laugh. "Ah, but can you describe te specifications?"

"Uh—uh—" Ray stared at the jungle of apparatus and gulped. He'd had no time to keep systematic notes, and he lacked the Martian's photographic memory. By Einstein, he'd built the damned thing but he had no proper idea whatsoever of how!

"You couldn't have done it without me," he argued.

"Nor could an ancient farmer on Eart habe done witout his mules. Did he consider paying tem a salary on tat account?"

"But . . . you've already got more money than you know what to do with, you bloated capitalist. I happen to know you invested both your Nobel Prizes in mortgages and then foreclosed."

"And why not? Genius is neber properly rewarded unless it rewards itself. Speaking of tat, I habe had no fresh tobacco for an obscene stretch of days. Take us to te nearest cigar store."

"Yes," Dyann said with unwonted timidity, "it might be a good idea if ve tested vether this enyine vorks, no?"

"All right!" Ray shouted in fury. "Sit down. Secure yourselves." He did likewise in the pilot's chair. His fingers moved across the breadboarded control panel of the star drive. "Here goes nothing."

"Nothin," said Dyann after a silence, "is correct."

"Judas on a stick," Ray groaned. "What's the matter now?" He unharnessed and went to stare at the layout. Meters registered, indicators glowed, electrorotors hummed, exactly as they were supposed to; but the boat sat stolidly where she was.

"I told you not to use tose approximations," Urushkidan said.

Ray began to fiddle with settings. "I might have known this," he muttered bitterly. "I'll bet the first piece of flint that the first ape-man chipped didn't work right either."

Urushkidan shredded a piece of paper into the bowl of his pipe, to see if he could smoke it.

"Iukh-ia-ua!" Dyann called. "Is that a rocket flare?"

"Oh, no!" Ray hastened forward and stared. Against the night sky arced a long trail of flame. And another, and another—

"They've found us," he choked.

"Well," said Dyann, not uncheerfully, "ve tried hard, and ve will go down fightin, and that vill get us admission to the Hall of Skulls." She reached out her arms. "Have ve got time first to make love?"

Urushkidan stroked his nose musingly. "Tallantyre," he said, "I habe an idea tat te trouble lies in te square-wabe generator. If we doubled te boltage across it—"

High in dusky heaven, the Jovian craft braked with a fury of jet-fires, swung about, and started their descent. Beneath them, vegetation crumbled to ash and ice exploded into vapor. An earthquake shudder grew and grew.

The boat's comset chimed. She was being signalled. Numbly, Ray switched on the transceiver. The lean hard features of Colonel Roshevsky-Feldkamp sprang into the screen.

"Uh . . . hello," Ray said.

"You will surrender yourselves immediately," the Jovian told him.

"We will? I mean . . . if we do, can we have safe conduct back to Earth?"

"Certainly not. But perhaps you will be allowed to live."

"About tat square-wabe generator—" Urushkidan saw that Ray wasn't listening, sighed, unstrapped himself, and crawled aft.

The first of the newcome craft sizzled to a landing. She was long and dark; guns reached from turrets like serpent heads. In the screen, Roshevsky-Feldkamp's image thrust forward till Ray had an idiotic desire to punch it. "You will surrender without resistance," the colonel said. "If not, you will suffer corporal punishment after your capture. Prolonged corporal punishment."

"Urushkidan vill die before he gives up," Dyann vowed.

"I will do noting of te sort," said the Martian. He had come to the machine he wanted. Experimentally, he twisted a knob.

The boat lifted off the ground.

"Well, well," Urushkidan murmured. "My intuition was correct."

"Stop!" Roshevsky-Feldkamp roared. "You must not do that!"

The boat rose higher. His lips tightened. "Missile them," he ordered.

Ray scrambled back to the pilot's seat, flung himself down, and slammed the main drive switch hard over.

He felt no acceleration. Instead, he drifted weightless while Jupiter whizzed past the viewports.

The engine throbbed, the hull shivered—wasted energy, but what could you expect from an experimental model? Stars blazed in his sight. Struck by a thought, he cast a terrified glance at certain meters. Relief left him weak. Even surface flyers in the Jovian System were, necessarily, equipped with superb magnetohydrodynamic radiation screens. Those of this boat were operating well. Whatever else happened, he wouldn't fry.

The stars began to change color, going blue forward and red aft. Was he traveling so fast already?

"Vat planet is that?" Dyann pointed at a pale gray globe.

"I think—" Ray stared behind him. "I think it was Neptune."

The stars appeared to be changing position. They crawled away from bow and stern till they formed a kind of rainbow around the waist of the boat. Elsewhere was an utter black. *Optical aberration*, he understood. *And I'm seeing by Dopplered radio waves and X-rays. What happens when we pass the speed of light itself? No, we must have already—is this what it feels like, then?* The starbow of science fiction song and story pinched out into invisibility; he flew through total blindness. *If only we'd figured out some kind of speedometer.*

"Glorious, glorious!" chortled Urushkidan, rubbing his tentacles together as if he were foreclosing on yet another mortgage. "My teory is confirmed. Not tat it needs confirmation, but now eben te Eartlings must needs admit that I am always right. And how tey will habe to pay!"

Dyann's laughter rolled Homeric through the hull. "Ha, ve are free!" she bawled. "All the vorlds are ours to raid. Oh, vat fun it is to ride in a vunforce boat and slay!"

Ray reassembled his wits. They'd better slow down and turn around while they could still identify Sol. He made himself secure in his seat, studied the gauges, calculated what was necessary, set the controls, and pushed the master switch.

Nothing happened. The vessel kept on going.

"Hey!" the man wailed. "Who! . . . Urushkidan what's wrong? I can't stop accelerating!"

"Of course not,' the Martian told him. "You must apply an exact counterfunction. Use te omega-wabe generator."

"Omega wave? What the hell is that?"

"Why, I told you—"

"You did not."

Ray and Urushkidan stared at each other. "It seems," the Martian said at length, "tat tere has been a certain failure of communication between us."

Weightlessness complicated everything. By the time that a braking system had been improvised, nobody knew where the boat had gotten to.

This was after a rather grim week. The travelers floated in the cabin and stared out at skies which, no matter how splendid, seemed totally foreign. Silence pressed inward with a might that would have been more impressive were it not contending against odors of old cooking and unwashed bodies.

"The trouble is my fault," Dyann said contritely. "If I had brought Ormun, she vould have looked after us."

"Let's hope she takes care of the Solar System," Ray said. "The Jovians aren't fools. When we left Ganymede, jetless, it must've been obvious we'd built the drive. They'll want to take action before we can give it to Earth."

"First," Urushkidan pointed out, "we habe to find Eart."

"It should be possible," Ray said. His tone lacked conviction. "We can't have gone completely out of our general part of the galaxy. Could those foggy patches yonder be the Magellanic Clouds? If they are, and if we can relate several bright stars to them—Rigel, for instance—we should be able to estimate roughly where we've come to."

"Bery well," Urushkidan replied, "which is Rigel?"

Ray held his peace.

"Maybe ve can find somevun who knows," Dyann suggested.

Ray imagined landing on a planet and asking a three-headed citizen, "Pardon me, could you tell me the way to Sol?" Whereupon the alien would answer, "Sorry, I'm a stranger here myself."

Never being intended for proper space trips, the boat carried no navigational or astronomical tables. Since she had passed close to Neptune, or whatever globe that was, she had presumably been more or less in the ecliptic plane. Therefore some of the zodiacal constellations, those from which she had moved away, ought to be recognizable, though doubtless distorted. Ordinarily an untrained eye might have been unable to identify any pattern, so numerous are the stars visible in space. However, after a week without cleaning, the ports here were greasy and grimy enough to dim the light as much as Earth's atmosphere does.

Nevertheless Ray was baffled. "If I'd been a Boy Scout," he lamented, "I might know the skies. As is, all I can pick out are Orion and the Big Dipper, and I've no idea how they lie with respect to the zodiac or anything else.' He gave Urushkidan an accusing glance. "You're the great astrophysicist. Can't you tell one star from another?"

"Certainly not," replied the Martian. "No astrophysicist eber looks at te stars if he çan help it."

"Oh, you vant to find the con — con — star-pictures?" Dyann asked.

"Yes, we have to," Ray explained. "Familiar ones that we can steer by. You're quite a girl in your way, honey, but I do wish you were more of an intellectual."

"Vy, of course I know the heavens," she assured him. "How could I ever find my vay around, huntin or raidin, othervise? And they are not very different in the Solar System. I learned your pictures for fun, vile I was on Earth." She floated around the chamber from port to port, peering and muttering. "Haa-ai, yes, yonder are Kunatha the Qveen and Skalk the Consort . . . not much chanyed except—" she chuckled coarsely— "it is even more clear to see here than at home that they are begettin the Heir. You Earthlins take a section right out of the middle betveen those two and make a figure you call ... m-m-m ... ah, yes, Virgo."

"And you can tell us how the rest are arranged, and steer us till they have the right configurations?" Ray exclaimed. "Dyann, I love you!"

"Then let's get home fast," she beamed. "I vant to be on a planet." During the outward flight she had been discomfited at discovering the erotic importance of gravity.

"Control your optimism, Tallantyre," Urushkidan said dourly. "Trying to nabigate by eyeball alone, wit only a barbarian's information to go on, we may perhaps find te general galactic region we want, but tereafter we could cast about at random until our food is gone and we starbe to deat."

"Oh, I know the constellations close," Dyann said, "and I know how to take stellar measurements. It vill not be hard to make a few simple instruments, like for measurin angles accurately, that I can use."

"*You?*" the Martian screeched. "How in Nebukadashtabu can you have learned such tings?"

"Every noble in Kathantuma does, for to practice the—vat do you call it?—astroloyee. It is needful for plannin battles and ven to sow grain and marriage dates and everythin."

"Do you mean to say you are an ... an ... an astrologer?"

"Of course. I thought you vere too, but it seems you Solarians are more backvard than I supposed. Vould you like me to cast your horoscope?"

"Well," said Ray helplessly, "I guess it's up to you to pilot us back, Dyann."

"Sure," she laughed. "Anchors aveigh!"

Urushkidan retched. "Brought home by an astrologer. Te ignominy of it all."

Somehow Ray got his shipmates herded into seats, the vessel aimed according to Dyann's instructions, and the drive started. Given the modifications they had made, they could accelerate the whole distance and then stop almost instantly. The passage should not be long.

Except, of course, for the time-consuming nuisance of frequent halts en route to take navigational sights. Ray pondered this in the next couple of days, while he constructed the instruments Dyann required. That task was comparatively simple, demanding precise workmanship but no original thought to speak of. His engineering talent had free play; if nothing else, the problem took his attention from the zero-gee pigpen into which he was crammed.

Starlight was still around. It was merely Dopplered out of visible wavelengths and aberrated out of its proper direction. Both these effects were functions of the boat's speed—if "speed" was a permissible word in this case, which Urushkidan would noisily deny—and that in turn depended in a mathematically simple fashion on drive-pulse frequency and time. The main computer aboard, which controlled most systems, could easily add to its chores a program for reversing optical changes. There were several television pickups and receivers in the hold; normally, explorers on a Jovian moon would use them to observe a locale from a distance, but they could be adapted. . . .

After a pair of days more, Ray had installed in the forward cabin a gadget as uncouth to behold as the star drive itself, but which showed, on a

large screen, ambient space undistorted. It was
adjustable for any direction. Playing with it,
Dyann found a group of stars which made her
smile. "See," she said, "now Avalla is takin shape.
That is the Victorious Warrior Returnin Vith Captive Man Slung Across Her Saddlebow."

"No," said Ray, "that's Ursa Major. You Kathantumans have a wild imagination."

Seated in the pilot's chair—for she had soon
mastered the controls of the star drive, as crude as
they were—Dyann continued swinging the
scanner around the heavens. Abruptly the screen
blazed. Had radiance not been stopped down, the
watchers might have been blinded. As was, they
saw a vast, incandescent globe from which flames
seethed millions of kilometers—"A blue giant
sun," Urushkidan whispered. For once he was
awed.

Dyann's eyes sparkled. "Let's play tag with it,"
she said, and applied a sidewise vector. "Yippee!"

"Hey!" the Earthling yelped. "Stop!"

They whizzed among the flames, dodging, while
Dyann roared out a battle chant. Urushkidan huddled in his chair, squinched his eyes shut, and
muttered, "I am being serene. I am being serene."
Ray tried to recollect his childhood prayers.

The star fell behind. "Okay, ve continue," Dyann
said. "Vasn't that fun? Ray, darlin, after this
trouble is over, ve vill take a cruise through the
galaxy, yust the two of us."

Time passed. The heavens majestically altered
their aspect. The conquerors of the light-years
floated about, gazed forth at magnificence, and
ate cold beans.

"Ve are in the yeneral sector ve seek," Dyann

said. "I have been thinkin. First ve go to Varann."

"Your native planet?" asked Urushkidan. "Ridiculous! We are returning directly to Uttu."

"Ve may need help in the Solar System," she argued. "Ve have been gone for two or three veeks. Much can have happened, most of it not good."

"But . . . but what help do you expect to get from a bunch of . . . Centaurians?" Ray spluttered. "It isn't practical."

Dyann grinned. "How vill you stop me, sveetheart?"

He considered the muscles which stirred beneath her tawny skin. "Oh, well," he said, "I always wanted to see Varann anyway."

For a few hours the amazon kept busy with instruments and pilot board. Then, astoundingly to Ray, she found her goal. Waxing in the screen were two yellowish suns very much like Sol. Out of the stellar background, a telescope identified a dim red dwarf at a greater distance. Nowhere else in this part of space did such a trio exist.

"Home, oh, home," Dyann murmured almost tearfully.

"Not quite," Ray reminded her with a certain slight malice. "How are you going to find your planet?"

"Vell . . . vell, uh—" She scratched her ruddy head.

He took pity and thought aloud for her benefit. "Planets are in the plane of the two main stars. They'd have to be. If we put ourselves in that plane, at a point where Varann's sun, Alpha A, appears to be the right size, and swing in a circle of that radius, we should come pretty close. It has a good-sized moon, doesn't it, and its color is greenish-blue? Yes, we ought not to have trouble."

"You are so clever," Dyann sighed. "It is sexy. Yust you vait till ve have landed."

At a modest fraction of the speed of light, a mere few thousand kilometers per second, the boat paced out her path. Before long, Dyann was jubilating, "There ve are! Look ahead! Home! After all these years, home!"

"I would still like to know what we are supposed to do when we get tere," Urushkidan snorted.

"I told Ray vat," Dyann retorted. "You suit yourself."

The man said nothing, being preoccupied. Terminal maneuvers were necessarily his responsibility. They took his entire flying skill and then some. He could use the cosmic drive to shed a velocity which would else have caused his craft to explode on striking atmosphere. However, he could not thereafter use the conventional jets; they were never meant for thick air or strong gravity. Thus he must also come down on the new system, which was incredibly precarious when he didn't have a universeful of room for error around him. He must make a descent which was largely aerodynamic, in a boat hijacked from a moon where aerodynamics was a farce. Probably he would never have succeeded, were it not for experience he'd gained when he spent part of his legacy on rakish sports flyers.

Wind boomed outside. The sky turned from black and starry to blue and cloud-wreathed. Weight dragged at bodies. The hull bucked and shuddered. Far below, landscape emerged. Ray had directed his approach by what he and Dyann remembered of maps—

"Kathantuma!" she shouted. "My own, my native land! See, I know her, yonder mountain, old

Hastan herself. Yes, and that town, Mayta. Ve're here!''

When Ray had thumped the boat down onto the ground and his teeth had stopped rattling, he admitted to himself that this was pretty country. Around him waved rows of white-tasseled grain, wildflowers strewn among them in small brave splashes of color. Beyond the field he glimpsed a thatch-roofed rustic cottage and outbuildings, surrounded by trees whose foliage shone green-gold. In the opposite direction gleamed a river, crossed by a stone bridge which led to Mayta. The town seemed an overgrown village, timber houses snuggled about the granite walls of a castle whose turrets bore lacy spires from which banners flew. Elsewhere thereabouts, the land was devoted to pasture and woodlots, whose verdancy turned blue with distance till it faded into the snow-crowned heights which guarded this valley.

"Home," Dyann exulted. She unharnessed, rose, and stretched sinew by sinew, like a great cat. "And yust feel, darlin, ve got a decent up and down again."

"Uh—yeah." Ray had less pleasure. Fifty percent more pull than on Earth. . . . Urushkidan groaned and collapsed over his own seat like so much molasses.

"Come on out for some fresh air," Dyann said, "and ve vill find us a nice soft patch of turf."

She started to operate the airlock. He prevented her barely in time, and opened the valves the merest crack. Atmospheric pressure outside was considerably in excess of that within. No sense in getting a sinus headache; let the buildup be gradual. "Keep chewing and swallowing," he advised as the inward draught began to shrill.

"Vat? Vell, if you say so." Dyann reached for a hunk of cheese.

When at length they could go forth, it was into a freshness of cool breezes and the manifold scents of growing things, into trillings and chirpings from winged creatures that darted beneath sun-brilliant clouds, into air whose richness made every lungful heady as wine, so that aches and exhaustion vanished. "A-a-ah," Ray breathed. "You were right to make us stop here, sweetheart. What we need most after what we've been through is unspoiled nature, peace and quiet and—"

An arrow hummed past his ear and rang like a gong off the boat.

"Yowp!" Ray dived into the grain. Another arrow zipped where he had been. Dyann stood fast. After a moment, he ventured to raise himself, behind her back, and see what was happening.

From the rustic cottage, half a dozen women ran: a squat and scarred older one, and five tall and youthful who must be her daughters. They hadn't stopped to armor themselves with more than helmets and shields, but they did brandish swords and axes. The archer among them slung bow on shoulder as her companions closed in, and drew a dirk. Several men watched nervously from the farmyard.

"*Ho-hai, saa, saa!*" whooped Dyann. She herself was in full battle gear, that being the only clothing she had brought along. Her blade hissed free of its sheath. The matriarch charged. Dyann's blow was stopped by her shield, and her ax clanged grazingly off the newcomer's helmet. Dyann staggered. Her weapon fell from her grasp. The rest came to ring her in.

Dyann recovered. A karate-like kick to the elbow disarmed Mother. At once Dyann seized her by the waist, raised her on high, and threw her. Two of the girls went down beneath that mass. While they were trying to disentangle themselves, Dyann got under the guard of the next nearest and grappled.

Centaurian hospitality! flashed through Ray's mind.

A backhanded blow sent him over. Dazed, he looked up to see a daughter looming above. She smacked her lips, picked him up, and laid him across her shoulder. A sister tugged at him—by the hair—and said something which might have meant, "Now don't be greedy, dear; we go shares, remember?" They didn't seem worried about the rest, who were busy with Dyann and would obviously soon overcome her.

A trumpet blare and a thunder of hoofs interrupted. From the castle had come galloping a squad of armored ladies. Their mounts were the size and general shape of Percheron horses, though horned, hairless, and green. They halted at the fight and started to wield clubbed lances with fine impartiality. Combat broke up in a sullen fashion. From his upside-down position, Ray saw that none of the gashed and bruised femininity had suffered grave wounds. Yet that didn't seem to have been for lack of trying.

The guttural, barking language of Kathantuma resounded. A rider, perhaps the chief, pointed a mailed hand at Ray's captor and snapped an order. The girl protested, was overruled, and tossed him pettishly to the ground.

When he recovered full awareness, his head was on Dyann's knees and she was stroking him. "Poor little man," she murmured. "Ve play too rough for you, ha?"

"What . . . was that . . . all about?"

"Oh, this family say they vas mad because ve landed in their grainfield. That's a lie. They could have demanded compensation. I'm sure they really hoped to seize our boat and claim it as plunder. Luckily, the royal cavalry got here in time to stop them. Since ve are still alive, ve can file charges of assault if ve choose, because this is not a legal duellin ground. I think I vill, to teach a lesson. There must be law and order, you know."

"Yes," whispered Ray, "I know."

Two days later—Varannian days, a bit shorter than Terrestrial—Dyann gave a speech. She and her traveling companions were on a platform by the main gate of the castle, at the edge of the market square. She stood; they sat in leather chairs, along with Queen Hiltagar, the Mistress of Arms, the Keeper of the Stables, and similar dignitaries. Pikes of troopers and lances of mounted ladies hedged the muddy plaza, to maintain a degree of decorum among the two or three hundred who filled it. These were the free yeowomen of the surrounding district, whose approval of any important action was necessary because they would constitute the backbone of the army. In coarse, colorful tunics, body paint, and massive jewelry, they kept flourishing their weapons and beating their shields. To judge by Dyann's gratified expression, that counted as applause. Here and there circulated public entertainers, scantily-clad men with flowers twined into their hair and beards, who strummed harps, sang softly, and watched the proceedings out of liquid, timid eyes.

Ray wasn't sure what went on, nor did he care very much. A combination of heavy weight, heavier meals, reaction to the rigors of his journey, and Dyann's demands kept him chronically sleepy. This evening, a lot of the potent local wine had been added. He could barely focus on the crowd. Beside him, Urushkidan snored, Martian style, which sounds like firecrackers in an echo chamber.

Dyann ended her harangue at last. Both cheers and jeers lifted deafeningly. Long-winded arguments followed, which tended to degenerate into fist fights, until Ray himself dozed off.

He was shaken awake when sunset turned heaven sulfurous above the roofs, and gaped blearily around. The assembly was dispersing, most people headed for the taverns which comprised a large part of Mayta. Stiff and sore, he lurched to his feet. Dyann was more fresh and rosy than he felt he should be asked to tolerate.

"It has been decided," she rejoiced. "Ve have agreement. Now ve must call other meetins throughout the realm, but there is no doubt they vill follow this lead. Already ve can send envoys to Almarro and Kurin, for negotiatin alliance. How soon can a fleet leave, Ray?"

"Leave?" he bleated. "For where?"

"Vy, for Yupiter. To attack the Yovians. Veren't you listenin?"

"Huh?"

"No, I forgot, you don't know our language. Vell, don't trouble your pretty little head about such things. Come on back to the castle, and ve vill make love before dinner."

"But," stammered Ray, "but, but, but."

How do you equip a host of barbarians, still in the early Iron Age, to cross four and a third light-years of space for purposes of waging war on a nation armed to its nuclear-powered teeth?

A preliminary question, perhaps, is: Do you want to?

Ray did not, but found that he had scant choice in the matter. Affectionately but firmly, Dyann made him understand that men kept in their place and behaved as they were bidden.

She did go so far as to explain her reasoning. Centaurians were not stupid, or even crazy. What they were—on this continent of Varann, at least—was warlike. While in the Solar System she had almost automatically, but shrewdly, paid close heed to the military-political situation. Afterward she had plugged the capabilities of the cosmic drive into her assessment. Most of the Jovian naval strength was deployed widely through space. If the escape from Ganymede had, indeed, made the Confederation decide to lean hard on the Union while the balance of power remained in its favor, that ought to leave the giant planet quite thinly guarded, sufficient to intercept conventional attackers but not any who came in faster than light. A raid in force should, if nothing else, result in the capture of Wotanopolis. No matter how austere by Terrestrial standards, that city was incredibly rich in Varannian terms. The raiders could complete their business and get home free, loaded with loot, covered with glory, and well supplied with captives. (As for the latter, there was hope of ransom, or possibly more hope of keeping them permanently as harem inmates. The polyandrous customs of this country worked hardship on many women.) While Earth might disown the action as piracy, it would doubtless not take punitive measures; everybody on the planet would be too relieved when an alarmed Confederation pulled its forces back to the Jovian moons.

Thus the calculation. Numerous ladies, Dyann foremost, recognized that it might prove disastrously wrong and the expedition end up as a cloud of incandescent gas or something like that. The idea didn't worry them much. If they fell audaciously, they would revel forever among the gods; and their names would ring in epic poetry while the world endured.

Failing to convince her otherwise, Ray sought out Urushkidan. The Martian, after an abortive attempt to steal the spaceboat and sneak off by himself, had been given a room high in a tower. Having adjusted a bit to the gravity, he sat amidst trophies of the hunt and covered a sheet of parchment with equations. *This place*, thought Ray, *has squids in the belfry.*

He poured forth his tale of woe. The Martian was indifferent. "What of it?" he said. "Tey may conceivably succeed, in which case we will doubtless be granted a bessel to trabel home in. If tey fail, ten it cannot be a matter of bery much time before te faster-tan-light engine is debeloped independently in te Solar System and somebody arribes here who can take us back."

"You don't understand," Ray informed him. "These buccaneers count on us as experts. They're bringing us along."

"Oh. Oh-oh! Tat is different. We better habe suitable armament." The Martian riffled through his papers. "Let me see. I tink equations 549 tro'

627 indicate—yes, here we are. It is possible to
project te same type of dribing field as we use for
transport in a beam which imparts a desired
pseudobelocity bector to an extraneous object.
Also . . . look here. Differentiation of tis equation
shows tat it would be equally simple to break
intranuclear bonds by trowing a selected type of
particle into te state, and none oter Te nucleus
would ten separate, wit a net energy release re-
gardless of where it lies on te binding curbe because of te altered potentials."

Ray regarded him in awe. "You," he breathed,
"have just invented the tractor beam, the pressor
beam, the disintegrator, and the all-fuel atomic
generator."

"I habe? Is tere money in tem?"

The man went to work.

Headquartered hereabouts, the three expeditions from Sol had each left behind a considerable
amount of supplies, equipment, and operating
manuals. The idea had been to accumulate enough
material for the establishment of a permanent scientific base—an idea that faster-than-light travel
had now made obsolete. Most of this gear was
stored in the local temple, where annual sacrifices
were made to the digital computer. It took an involved theological argument to get it released. The
point that Ormun must be rescued was conceded
to be a good one, but not until the high priestess
held an earnest private discussion with Dyann,
and was hospitalized for a while thereafter, did
the stuff become available.

Meanwhile Ray had been working on design
and, with native assistants, some of whom knew a
little English or Spanish, getting a team organized.

Urushkidan's new principles proved almost dismayingly easy to apply. Everything that wasn't in the depot, native smiths could hammer out, once given the specs. Atomic engines came forth capable of burning anything whatsoever. After consulting the gods, Queen Hiltagar decreed that the fuel be coal. Nobles vied for the honorable job of stokers.

The engines not only drove ships, but powered weapons such as Urushkidan had made possible. It proved necessary for Ray to call on the Martian for more — radiation screens, artificial gravity (after experiment showed that too many Kathantumans got sick in free fall and barfed), faster-than-light communicators, et cetera. These developments might well have taken years, except that the Martian grew sufficiently exasperated at the interruptions that he tossed off a calculus by which the appropriate circuits could be designed in hours.

Given this much, the spacecraft proper could be built to quite low standards. They were mere hulks of hardwood, slapped together by carpenters in a matter of weeks, varnished and greased for air tightness. Since the crossing would be made in a few hours, air renewal systems weren't required; it sufficed to have tanks of compressed gas, with leakage to prevent a buildup of excess carbon dioxide. Ray gave most of his attention to features like locks and viewports. Those had better not blow out! Still more did he concentrate on the drive circuits. They must be reliable during a trip to Sol and back, with an ample safety margin, but soon thereafter, they must fail. Not wishing the Centaurians ill, despite everything, he gave warning that this would happen, and was

glad when it was accepted. Everybody knew that
wire gave way after prolonged use, and here these
ships were festooned with wires. The prospect of
an amazon fleet batting about in the galaxy where-
soever it pleased had not been one that he could
cheerfully contemplate.

Meanwhile the amazons themselves poured in,
ten times as many as the thirty-odd hulls could
hold, riding and hiking from the uttermost ends of
Kathantuma and its neighbor queendoms to be in
on the most gorgeous piece of banditry ever
dreamed of. Only Dyann cared much about
Ormun, who was just her personal joss, and only
Ray gave a damn about Jupiter as a menace to
Earth. However, the man was surprised at how
quickly the chosen volunteers formed themselves
into disciplined crews and how readily the officers
of these developed the needful skills. It occurred
to him at length that their way of life selected for
alertness, adaptability, and—yes, though he hated
to admit it—intelligence.

Three hectic months after his arrival on Varann,
the fleet departed. After his labors, followed by
Dyann's idea of a celebration, he used most of the
travel time to catch a nap.

Enormous in the forward ports, banded with
hues of cloud and storm that could have
swallowed lesser worlds whole, diademmed with
stars, Jupiter swelled to vision. Ray's heart
bumped, his palms were cold and wet, his tongue
dry. Somehow he pushed his way through a throng
of armored women. Dyann sat at the controls of
the flagship, her gaze intent upon the giant ahead.

"Listen," he pleaded amidst the racket of eager
contralto voices, "let me at least call Earth and

find out what's been happening. You need to know
yourself."

"Okay, okay," she said. "But be qvick."

He settled himself before the comscreen and
fiddled with knobs. Last year, the notion of virtually instantaneous talk across nearly a billion kilometers would have been sheer fantasy. He,
though, was using a phase wave with unlimited
speed to beam radio photons. It released them at a
distance from Earth, which he had figured out on
his pocket calculator, such that their front would
reach a relay satellite with enough microwattage
to be detected, amplified, and bucked on. The
phone number attached to the signal was that of
the Union's central public relations office. It was
the only official one he knew where he could be
sure to get a response without running a gantlet of
secretaries.

The satellite beamed that reply back in the
direction which its instruments had registered—
with due allowance for planetary motions, of
course. The Urushkidan-Tallantyre standing wave
acquired the photons and passed them on. It also
happened to acquire a commercial for Chef
Quimby's Extra-Oleaginous Oleomargarine; and,
when Ray received the information officer, that
person resembled something seen through several
meters of rippled water. At any rate, her image
did. He hadn't had a chance to work the bugs out
of his circuits.

"Who is calling, please?" she asked through an
obbligato of *"Friends, in these perilous times, how
better to keep up your strength for the cause of
civilization than by a large, nutritious serving—"*

"This is Raymond Tallantyre, calling from the
vicinity of Jupiter. I've just returned from Alpha

Centauri on a spacecraft traveling faster than light."

"—deliciously vitaminized—"

"Sir," the Union spokesman said, "this is no time to be frivolous."

"—it's yum-yum GOOD—"

"Listen," Ray cried, "I want to give the technology to the Union. Stand by to record."

On the far side of Dyann, Urushkidan slithered to attention. "Hey!" he piped. "I neber said I'd gibe away—"

"Your behavior is in very poor taste," said the official, and switched off.

Presently Ray regained the wit to find a newcast. That wasn't hard; there were a lot of newcasts these days. He gathered that Jupiter had declared war "to assert racial rights long and cruelly denied." Three weeks ago, the Jovians had won a major naval engagement off Mars. They were not yet proceeding against Earth, but threatened to do it unless they got an armistice on terms which amounted to surrender. Without that, they would "regretfully take appropriate measures" against a planet whose defenses had become feeble indeed.

"Oh, gosh," said Ray.

"An armada like tat will stretch capabilities," Urushkidan opined. "Te Union has ships and bases elsewhere. It can cut Jobian supply lines—"

"Not if the Jovian strategy is to make a dash inward, put missile carriers in orbit, and pound poor old Earth into radioactive rubbish," the human mourned. "Meanwhile, those grunt-brains yonder won't believe I've got what's needed to save them."

"Would you beliebe tat, from a phone call?"

"Well . . . I guess not. . . . But damnation, this is

different!"

"I see a moon disc ahead," Dyann interrupted,
"and it looks like Ganymede. Out of the vay, you
two. Ve're clearin for action."

The flagship, which had been a peaceful laboratory boat, came in through atmosphere with a
whoop and a holler. After casting about for a while
above desolation, she found the dome of Wotanopolis and stopped at hover. The rest of the fleet,
still less agile, followed more leisurely.

Lacking spacesuits, the crew could not disembark and break out the battering rams, as had
been proposed back on Varann. After studying the
situation, Dyann proceeded to the main freight
terminal. There she cut loose with her disintegrator beam. The ship-sized airlock disappeared
in blue fire and flowing lava. Air streamed forth,
ghost-white as water vapor froze. Even a hole so
large would take hours to reduce pressure danger-
ously within a volume as great as that of the city.
Dyann sailed on through, into a receiving chamber
which was almost deserted now in wartime. She
set down near the entrance, unharnessed, and
leaped to her feet. "Everybody out!" she yelled in
English, and added a Kathantuman exhortation.
Her warriors bawled approval.

With fingers that shook, Ray buckled on helmet
and cuirass and drew sword. Meanwhile, the rest
of the barbarian fleet came in through the gap and
clunked to rest, some on top of others. When all
were inside, Urushkidan carried out his part of the
mission by deliberately melting the entry hole
shut, to conserve atmosphere. He would stay
behind, also, ready to open a passage for retreat.
How lucky can one being get? thought Ray, as a

swarm of warriors shoved him through the lock.

"Hoo, hah!" Dyann's sword shrieked on high. Her cohort poured after, whooping and bounding. The companion ships disgorged more. The abrupt change of pressure didn't seem to have given an ear ache to anybody except Ray. The racket of metal and girlish voices made that nearly unendurable. He had no choice but to be swept along in the rush.

Through the resonant reaches of the chamber— up a long staircase, five steps at a time—out over a plaza above, in clangor and clamor—

A machine gun raved. Ray bellywhopped onto the flooring before he had identified the noise. A couple of Varannians tumbled, struck, though they couldn't be too badly wounded to judge from the swiftness with which they rolled out of the line of fire. Across the square, he saw the gun itself, where a corridor debouched. Several men in gray uniform crouched behind it. Whatever garrison the city possessed was reacting efficiently. Ray tried to dig a burrow.

He needn't have bothered. With lightning reflexes, under a weight that to them was gossamer, the invaders had already escaped further bullets, leaping sideways or straight up. Spears, darts, flung axes replied. An instant later, the Centaurians arrived in person. Ray experienced an actual moment of sympathy for the Jovians. None of them happened to get killed either, but they were in poor shape.

An enemy squad emerged from the adjacent corridor. Their rapid-fire rifles could have inflicted fearful damage on the crowded amazons —except that one lady, who knew something about such things, picked up the .50-caliber machine gun and operated it rather like a pistol. The squad scampered back out of sight.

"Hai-ai!" the horde shouted, with additions. Ray, who had acquired a smattering of Kathantuman, might have blushed at these had time allowed. As was, he was again borne off on the tide of assault.

He saw little of what followed. In this warren of hallways and apartments, combat became almost entirely hand-to-hand. That was just what suited the Varannians, and what Dyann had counted on.

He did glimpse her in action when she rounded a corner and found a hostile platoon. She sprang, swung her feet ahead of her while she flew, and knocked the wind out of two men. As she landed on them, her sword howled in an arc which left two or three more disabled. One who stood farther off tossed a grenade at her. She snatched it and threw it back. He managed to catch and return it, but was barely able to duck before she flung it again and it blew in a door behind him. While this game went on, Dyann rendered a foeman unconscious by a swordblow to his helmet, broke the nose of another with the pommel of her weapon, and kneed a third. then several more Centaurians joined in.

The gang of them went on. They had nothing left to do here. Ray dodged among their victims, past the door which the grenade had obligingly opened, into the apartment beyond. Maybe he could hide under a bed.

A hoarse shout sent him spinning around. Two members of the platoon had recovered enough to stagger in pursuit of him. He would have cried, "Hail, Wilder!" and explained what a peaceful citizen he was. Unfortunately, he too wore barbarian helmet and cuirass.

Before he could raise his hands, a Jovian had lifted rifle and fired. The shot missed. Though the range as close, the man was shaken. Also, in his time on Varann Ray had inevitably developed some strength and quickness. He didn't exactly dodge the bullet, but he flinched fast. His wild sword-swing connected. The Jovian sank to the floor and got busy staunching a bad cut.

His companion charged, with a clubbed rifle that was perhaps empty. Ray turned to meet him and tripped on his own scabbard. He clattered to the floor and the enemy tripped over him. Ray climbed onto the fellow's back, removed his helmet, and beat his head up and down till he lay semi-conscious.

I've got to find someplace safe, Ray thought frantically. *Back to the ships, maybe?* He scuttled from the apartment, overleaped the human wreckage outside, and made haste.

Not far beyond, he came to an intersection. A tommy gun blast from the left nearly touched him. "No-o-o," he whimpered, and hit the deck once more.

A boot in his ribs gained his attention. "Get up!" he heard.

He reeled to obey. What he saw was like a physical blow. Elegantly black-clad men, the famous elite guard of the Leader, accompanied Martin Wilder himself. Beside the dictator stood none less than Colonel Roshevsky-Feldkamp—*in charge of local defense?* Ray wondered, and tried to stretch his arms higher.

"Tallantyre!" His old opponent glared at him for a time which took on characteristics of eternity. "So you are responsible."

"No, I'm not, so help me, no," Ray chattered.

"Who else could have brought these savages here?" The officer cuffed the Earthling; head wobbled on neck. "If it weren't for your hostage value, I'd shoot you immediately. But I had better defer that pleasure. March!"

The detachment proceeded wherever it was bound. That chanced to be down a mercantile corridor, on which shops fronted. Smashed glass and gutted displays showed that the Centaurians were already collecting souvenirs.

Wilder condescended to address the prisoner: "Never think that this criminal assault of yours has truly penetrated any part of us. We may have to retire temporarily from our capital, but already help has been summoned and is on its way, the entire navy bound here on a sacred mission of vengeance."

Will the Centaurians stop their looting in time to get clear of that? Ray thought in terror. *Somehow I doubt it.*

"I beg your pardon, glorious sir," interjected Roshevsky-Feldkamp, "but we really must make haste, before the invaders discover the emergency hangar we are bound for."

"No, no, that would never do," agreed the Leader.

"You must get aloft, glorious sir, to take charge of the counterattack."

"Yes, yes. I will strike a new medal. The Defense of the Racial Homeland Medal."

"You remember, of course, glorious sir, that we must not simply destroy the pirate spacecraft," Roshevsky-Feldkamp said. "We must capture them for examination. Afterward, the universe is ours."

"Hoo-hah!" rang between the walls. From a side

passage staggered a band of Centaurians, weighted down with armloads of assorted loot. The guardsmen sprang into formation and brought their rifles up.

Something like an atomic bomb hit them from the rear. Ray learned afterward that Dyann Korlas and Queen Hiltagar had, between them, evolved a tactical doctrine that employed scouts to keep track of important hostile units and decoys to distract these.

What he witnessed at the time seemed utter confusion. A kind of maelstrom flung him against a wall and kept him busy dodging edged metal. He did glimpse Dyann herself as she waded into the thick of the fight, hewing, striking, kicking, a veritable incarnation of that Will to Conquer which the Symmetrists preached. Her companions wrought equal havoc. Ray took a minor part in the action. A guardsman reeled near him, tommy gun gripped, seeking a clear shot that wouldn't kill comrades. The Earthling plucked his sidearm from its holster and shot him—in the left buttock, because of recoil, but that sufficed.

Dyann saw. "Oh, how cute!" she caroled while she broke yet another head.

Combat soon ended. Most of the Jovians had simply been knocked galley west, and yielded with dazed meekness. Ray spied Wilder and Roshevsky-Feldkamp being prodded off by a squat, one-eyed, grizzled amazon with a silly smirk on her lips. They were doubtless destined for her harem—their decorations may have struck her fancy—and he couldn't think of two people he'd rather have it happen to.

Only . . . the whole enemy fleet could be arriving any minute—

What Ray did not know until later was that Urushkidan had prudently taken the original spaceboat outside and was using her beams to disintegrate those vessels and their missiles as they descended. Meanwhile he hummed an old Martian work song. There are times when even a philosopher must take measures.

Official banquets on Earth are notoriously dull. This one was no exception. That the war was over, that the Confederated Satellites would become the Jovian Republic and a respectable member of the World Union, that the stars were attainable: all seemed to call forth more long and dismal platitudes than ever.

Ray Tallantyre admitted to himself that the food and drink had been fine. However, there had been such a lot of both. He would have fallen asleep under the speeches had his shoes not pinched him. Thus he heard with surprise the president of his university describe what a remarkable student he had been. As a matter of fact, he'd damn near gotten expelled.

On his right, Urushkidan, crammed into a tuxedo tailored for his species, puffed a pipe and made calculations on the tablecloth. Left of the man, Dyann Korlas, her bronze braids wound about a plundered tiara, was stunning in a low-cut formal gown. The dagger at her waist was to set a new fashion. True, some confusion had arisen when she placed Ormun the Terrible at her plate and insisted that grace be said to the idol. Nevertheless—

"—unique scientific genius, whom his alma mater is pleased to honor with a doctorate of law—"

Dyann leaned close to whisper in Ray's ear: "Ven vill this end?"

"God knows," he answered as softly, "but I don't believe He's on the program."

"Ve have really had no time together since the campaign, have ve? Too many people, everyvun vantin us to do sometin or other. Vat are your plans for ven you got a chance to be yourself?"

"Well, first I want to try and patent the cosmic drive before Urushkidan does. Afterward . . . I dunno."

"It vas fun vile it lasted, our romp, vasn't it?" Her smile held wistfulness. "Me, I must soon go back to Varann. I vant to do somethin vorthvile vith my life, like find a backvard area and carve me out a throne. You, though—Ray, you are too fine and beautiful for such rough vork. You belon here, in the bright lights and glamour, not amon a bunch of unruly vomen vere you can get hurt."

"Right," he said.

"I vill alvays remember you." Her hand dropped warm across his wrist. "Maybe someday ven ve are old, ve can meet again and bore the young people with brags about our great days."

She glanced around. "But for now, darlin, if only ve could get avay from here by ourselves. I know a good bar not far off. It has rooms upstairs, too."

"Hm-m-m," he murmured. The prospect attracted. When she wasn't being a warrior, she was very female. "This calls for tactics. If we could sort of slump down in our chairs bit by bit, acting tired—which ought not to surprise anybody that notices—till we've gradually sunk out of sight, then we could crawl under the table and slip out that service door yonder . . . ."

As he did, Ray heard Urushkidan, called upon for a speech, begin a detailed exposition of his latest theory.

THE SOLDIER FROM THE STARS

It was early morning, local time, when I felt the plane tilt forward and start the long swoop down. I stirred uncomfortably, stretching stiffened muscles and blinking open sandy eyelids. You don't sleep well when you are burdened with such knowledge as ours.

Not that I had much responsibility. I was only a guard for Samuels and Langford; throughout the whole business, I was little except an observer. But maybe I had a chance to observe more than anyone else, which is why I am writing this for those who will come after us.

There were a good dozen others crowded into the plane, Secret Service men and brawny soldiers with loaded rifles between their knees. But they were an empty gesture, and we all knew it. Taruz of Thashtivar had said sardonically that the envoys might have one guard apiece if it would make them happier. That was me.

Samuels moved in the seat next to mine. The clear pale dawnlight came through a window and touched his hair with a white halo. His face looked old and gray, not like the famous statesman and American plenipotentiary he was supposed to be. But then, we all felt small on that cold morning.

He tried to smile. "Hello, Hillyer," he said to me. "Have a good night's rest?"

"Hardly, sir. Just dozing."

"I wish I could have done as much," Samuels sighed. "Oh, well."

Dr. Langford pushed his nose against the window. "I always did want to see the Azores," he remarked. "But I never thought it would be under such circumstances."

He looked more human, less chilled and bloodless, than the rest of us. His keen eagle features were curved into a humorless grin, and the grizzled bush of hair as disordered as ever.

You may have heard of Dr. Langford, the physicist who was led through cybernetics into biology, neurology, psychology, and more understanding of history than most professors in that field. He was the best suited man in the country to act as Samuels' scientific advisor, though I wondered what good that would be.

I caught a glimpse of the island lifting before us, and then the plane was jouncing to a halt on the hastily enlarged airfield. Beyond its shacks I could see the little tile-roofed town, and a steep rise of land toward a sallow sky. There are only a few thousand people on Flores.

Our guard got out ahead of us, the soldiers forming a wary ring about the door while the Secret Service men conferred with the Portuguese officials.

Langford chuckled. "Stupid sort of thing," he declared. "If Taruz wished to wipe us out, those boys wouldn't make any more difference than putting two extra flies under a descending swatter."

"There are the Russians," answered Samuels wearily. "They might try, even though this is neutral ground." He took off his glasses and rubbed his eyes. "I wouldn't trust anyone in this place where you can buy power over all the earth. I'm not even sure that I could be trusted."

We came out into a cool salt wind and the flustered presence of a small Portuguese colonel. I looked around the field. Several other big planes were sitting at one end. I noticed British and French insignia and the Red Star, and moved a furtive hand to the comforting drag of the gun beneath my armpit. Even as we stood there, receiving voluble greetings in a highly individual English, another speck grew in the sky, circled, and rolled to a landing. Egyptian!

The eagles gather, I thought.

"Eef you hentlemen weel to break your fast weeth me, please," said the colonel. "Deescussions are not to be for a many hours yet."

We followed him off the field. A rickety official car took us to a house which may have been commandeered for the occasion, where a very decent breakfast was served—none of the usual Continental *cafe complait* this time.

I didn't have much appetite, but stowed away a sizeable amount, not knowing when the energy might be needed. There was little talk, and it shied clear of the reason we were here. Langford alone came close to the truth when he asked: "How many nations will be represented?"

"Twenty-three," said the colonel. "A beeg congress, eh, what?"

"Of course," said Langford, "bidders will be working together—"

"Hentlemen, please!" The colonel looked distressed. "Eet ees altogether far from my province."

That was a joke, but I suppose he had his orders. In offering Taruz the island site, Portugal had gone to extreme lengths to emphasize her neutrality. She would not be in the bidding—where would the money come from?—and she would not permit conferences between delegates outside the Taruz' stronghold.

I went into the garden afterward with Samuels and Langford. The envoy was nervously chewing on a dead stogie, and the scientist was littering the ground with cigarette stubs; his own hands were yellow from nicotine. Being that rare animal, a non-smoker, I concentrated on keeping an eye out for assassins, but I couldn't avoid hearing their conversation.

"Are you sure the British won't throw in with us?" asked Langford.

"Not at first, anyway," said Samuels. "Sir Wilfred represents the entire Commonwealth, you know; that's no small financial backing, what with the Canadian dollar being worth more than ours and all. It'd be quite a feather in his cap, and an answer to all the people yelling about American domination if he got Taruz' services exclusively for Her Majesty."

Samuels shrugged. "Frankly, I'd just as soon he did. We have nothing to fear from the British, and it'd be a huge saving to us if they paid Taruz. But of course, you know what our own nationalists would scream." He added soberly: "The important thing is to keep Russia from getting those units."

"I don't like it," said Langford. "Read your history and see what happened to all the world powers once they started hiring mercenaries."

"What choice have we?" shrugged Samuels. "It so happens that these mercenaries can lick any army on Earth."

"I still wish they'd stayed away," said Langford.

"I don't know. All right, so we pay them an enormous sum; but then we're safe forever—for many years, at least. We can relax the militarization which is ruining our whole tradition; we won't have to fear our cities being destroyed, we won't have to listen to those who'd strangle the Bill of Rights in a paranoid spy hunt—no, if Taruz can be trusted, and I think he can, this may be the greatest thing that ever happened to humanity."

"It's conventional to say that a certain Jewish carpenter was more important than any soldier before or since," answered Langford tartly. "I'm not a religious man, but there's truth in conventions."

After that, the talk declined. There was nothing they could say, after all. And Samuels was right, I thought; what choice did we have?

I went over the incredible background of the last three months. The giant ships soaring majestically around the world, hovering above every capital, swamping local radios with a broadcast in seven major languages.

"*We are the free companions of Thashtivar, General Taruz commanding, and we seek employment*—" The arrogant invitation to us to do our worst, and the explosion of everything from BB guns to hydrogen bombs leaving those shining metal forms untouched, the failure of poison gas and radioactive dust and airborne virus.

I was thinking too of the three demonstrations, spotted around the world and open to all who cared to see. In one a good-sized uninhabited island had vanished in flame while all Earth's seismographs trembled, in another our guns and engines had simply quit operating, and in a third men and animals had fallen unconscious before some invisible force in a radius of miles and lain so for hours.

It was a science as far beyond ours as ours is beyond the bow and arrow, a science which crossed the space between the stars, and it was at the disposal of the highest bidder for any defensive or offensive use he had in mind.

They must have studied us for a long time, hovering out in space or descending secretly; the perfection of their knowledge about us showed that the very study methods transcended anything we could imagine. Taruz' announcement had even revealed considerable financial shrewdness. He would only consider payment in dollars, pounds sterling, or Swiss francs, the rate of exchange not to be the official one but that prevailing in Tangier—one of the few really free money markets. He and his men must be allowed to spend their pay in any way they saw fit; no sale would be forced, but the contracting government might not forbid it.

"Why not the UN?" Langford's question was one which had been asked many times, in anguish, by all men who loved their race. "He could have gone to the UN, offered them—"

"Offered them what?" asked Samuels. "The UN has no army, and who would vote to pay him to set up one? He's not interested in teaching us his own science—probably a good idea, considering how uncivilized we are. He's a soldier, with his soldiering to see."

"I know." Langford's face was grim. "I'm only saying what I wish he had done. But I don't suppose we could expect any other planet to hold a race of saints. They have as much right to be greedy and callous and short-sighted as we."

"What puzzles me," said Samuels, "is why there are such mercenaries at all between the stars. I should think a culture that far along would have outgrown—"

"I can only guess," said Langford, "but I think there is no Galactic Union or Empire or whatever —no reason for one. A whole planet at that level of technology would be self-sufficient, little or no cause to trade; distances are too great, and the various races too alien to each other, to need or want a central government.

"But disputes may arise—relatively minor things, not worth risking an entire world for; so their petty wars are fought by hired soldiers, safely out in interstellar space. Insofar as comparison is possible, I imagine Taruz' culture is rather like that of the Italian city-states during the Renaissance.

"And because of temporary peace or something, he's out of work, so he came to this barbaric fringe of the Galaxy for any job he could pick up. With his earnings, he can buy portable wealth to take back home and exchange for his own kind of money."

The slow hours passed.

II

Our little colonel took us up to the hill. It was a jouncy ride over a road that seemed to be one long rut; at the top we could look across a metallic curve of ocean to the edge of the world. But we were more interested in the Thashtivarian camp.

The six great spaceships towered enormously above us, blinding bright in the sun. They clustered near the center of a circle formed by small, squat structures which I heard humming as we approached: generators for the protective force-field, I imagined. Within, there were two long, featureless buildings like outsize Quonset huts.

At each generator, a soldier lounged, holding a slim-barreled object that must be a gun. The free companions didn't bother with standing at attention, but there was alertness in their eyes. Overhead hovered a smaller craft, on guard.

"I think—" Langford rubbed his chin. "I think control of gravity, some means of artificially warping space and creating a gravitational field as desired, would explain both their ships and their defenses. The force screen is a potential barrier. Then they can also damp electrical and chemical reactions, perhaps by use of the same principle—A lot of good that does us! We haven't the faintest idea about gravity control."

Portuguese soldiers formed a wider ring near the base of the hill, and were escorting the envoys to the camp entrance. They'd enforce neutraility if they had to shoot all of us. Officially, of course, Portugal was in NATO, but that uneasy alliance had virtually collapsed, like everything else.

Other men were getting out of their cars. I recognized Sir Wilfred Martin of Britain, and Andre

Lafarge of France, and Yakov Dmitrovich of the Soviet Union. The rest were strange to me, though I knew that some king-sized wheels were here today. My eyes were more on the Thrashtivarians.

There weren't more than a few thousand of them. That fact had pretty well calmed most fears that they were out to conquer Earth. They could have whipped all our armies in the field, but the sheer task of administration would have been too much for that small number.

I noticed that they were about half female— natural enough, on the long lonely voyages they made, and a woman could handle one of their weapons as easily as a man. No children, and they all looked young, though probably they had some longevity system. A handsome race, startlingly human-like. The main difference was in the straight deep-blue hair, the pointed chin slanting down from high cheekbones, the oblique light eyes, and the yellow skin—not any of the brownish tints of Mongoloid humans, but a dully glowing gold.

They wore tight-fitting pants, soft shoes, loose tunics under metal breastplates, ridged helmets, and short cloaks, all in colorful hues. When they spoke, it was in a throaty purring language. All of them looked hard, toughened down to the very guts.

We were a muttering, unhappy throng as we stood at the invisible gate. A Thrashtivarian officer approached us and bowed very slightly.

"*Bon jour, messieurs,*" he said in excellent French. It had been announced that that language would be used at the parley. My year at the Sorbonne was one reason I was chosen for this trip. "Please come with me."

He led us into one of the huts. It was a single hall, bare save for long soft benches and a row of guards. There were no windows, but the material itself seemed to give off light and the air stayed fresh. At the farther end, facing the benches, was a dais with a kind of throne on it.

We were courteously shown our places, the delegates of the great powers at the front. There was a miserable time in which we shuffled portfolios and avoided each other's eyes. Then a door opened itself at the end of the hall and General Taruz came in.

He was tall and broad-shouldered, walking with a litheness that came near insolence. He was very plainly dressed apart from the seven-pointed gold star on his cuirass. His face was long and lean and straight-boned, the eyes pale blue, the lips thin. It was the coldest face I have every seen.

He sat down on the throne and crossed his legs, smiling a trifle. The stillness that followed hurt my eardrums.

"Good day, gentlemen," he said at last. "I trust you have had a pleasant journey. Not to waste any more of your valuable time, let us get down to business at once."

Taruz made a bridge of his fingers. "I will repeat my terms to make sure they are understood. The Free Company offers its services for ten years to the nation making the highest bid. Payment may be made in not more than three annual installments. At the end of ten years, the contracting nation has the option of renewing for another ten at the same price, subject to adjustments in case its currency has depreciated meanwhile. If it does not take up the option, the rest may bid again. I do not think we will be on Earth for more than twenty years.

"Our services consist of defending whatever sites you choose and assisting in any wars you may wage. We will not try to make policy for you; our part is but to serve in these capacities, though I may offer advice to be accepted or rejected as you desire. We will do our best, within the limitations imposed by our numbers and powers; however, I retain command of my forces and all orders to them will go through me.

"I believe that is the substance of the formal contract we will make. Are there any questions?"

"Yes!" A Pole stood up. He was clearly frightened, I knew that he was a cat's paw for his Russian bosses, but he spat out what he had to ask. "How do we know you will keep your word?"

For a moment, I think we all expected annihilation. Then Taruz smiled wider, completely unruffled. "A natural question, sir. I cannot give you references, since the nearest planet of my civilization is a good thousand light-years away, but I assure you that the Thashtivarian Company has always given satisfaction and that we never violate a contract. I am afraid you will just have to take my word. If you are suspicious, you need not bid today."

The Pole sat down, gulping in a dry throat.

"Now, gentlemen, what am I offered?" Taruz lounged back, not trying to excite us like a human auctioneer. He knew he had us strung close to breaking already.

There was another silence. Then Sir Wilfred got slowly up. "On behalf of Her Majesty's government and the British Commonwealth of Nations," he said, "I beg of you, sir, not to set men against each other in this fashion. The Union Nations—"

Taruz frowned. For a wild instant, I thought of drawing my gun and killing him. But it would do no good, no good at all; in fact, he was probably shielded.

Sir Wilfred saw he was beaten and turned gray. "Very well, sir," he said. "One hundred million pounds."

Samuels whistled. But actually, I thought, it was a ridiculously low offer. Two hundred eighty million dollars—no, less than that in Tangier—you couldn't fight even a battle for that sum nowadays.

Andre Lafarge rose, shakily. "One hundred and fifty billion francs!" he cried.

"In the accepted currencies, please," said Taruz.

"That is . . . I will say 500 million dollars . . . m'sieur." He had to swallow hard to get his pride down.

"This is a capitalist plot!" exclaimed Dmitrovich. "Your very methods are those of the degraded money-grubbing warmonger."

"Have you a bid to make, or a lecture?" asked Taruz coldly.

"Three hundred billion Swiss francs!" At least Dmitrovich wouldn't use that foul word "dollars." I made it about 750 megabucks.

A dark man in uniform got up. "From Egypt," whispered Samuels to me, "on behalf of the Arab League—"

I needn't go through the next couple of hours. They were a nightmare, with distorted faces and gibbering voices and the destiny of our world tumbling like a football around the chamber; over the whole mess hovered the chill smile of Taruz, an image of Satan.

The lesser nations were soon squeezed out. France stayed longer than I had expected; her government must have made the desperate decision to declare all her money freely convertible. Through it all, Samuels didn't say a word. He was a good poker player.

When Russia, throwing in with the other Iron Curtain countries, offered some four hundred billion dollars, I knew the crisis was on us.

Samuels got up. "My country," he drawled—odd how calm he was, all of a sudden—"bids four hundred billion, one hundred million dollars!"

Wow! The taxpayers weren't going to like that at all. But what price freedom?

Dmitrovich snarled, and raised us a hundred million dollars.

Samuels caught the eye of Sir Wilfred, who nodded imperceptibly. His next bid was on behalf of both us and the Commonwealth: five hundred billion.

Dmitrovich, white and sweating: that much, plus a hundred million more.

The Italians joined their previous bid to ours.

Dmitrovich cursed. I didn't blame him. Six hundred billion!

Langford leaned over to me. "Here's where we separate the men from the boys," he whispered. But his own face was wet.

Samuels offered six and a half.

"This is encirclement!" gasped Dmitrovich. "The aggressors are leaguing against the peace-loving peoples of the world!" He turned around and faced us all. "I warn you, the Soviet Union and the people's democratic republics consider this clear proof of aggressive intent."

"Do you bid, sir?" asked Taruz.

"I . . . do. Yes. Two and one-half trillion Swiss francs," said Dmitrovich.

That made over six hundred billion dollars. The Soviets would have to make their own currency convertible . . . no, wait! With Taruz' help, they could overrun the world and pay him from its loot.

Samuels realized as much, I could see. His hands trembled. "Seven billion dollars!"

Eight, nine, ten—how long would it go on?

France joined us. So did the other Western nations, one by one. *Yeah,* I thought, *the Swiss and the Swedes and everybody else who stayed away were playing it real smart.*

I was watching Dmitrovich closely now. After fifteen billion, he seemed to reach some kind of decision. More likely, his government's instructions had decided something for him. He raised us nearly fifty billion right away. He kept on raising that much, each time around.

Samuels turned white. I didn't get it at first, but Langford explained it to me. "They've given up hope of outbidding us. Now they're just staying in to raise the price we must pay."

At five trillion dollars, that price looked ruinous.

And if we dropped out, the Soviets still had their aim of world conquest to pay for them. I wondered if we might not be driven to such a course ourselves. Or was their this much money in the world?

"Ten trillion dollars!"

That ended it. Dmitrovich gathered his portfolio, nodded curtly, and stalked out with his satellites.

I don't remember very well just what happened next. I have a confused impression of people milling about, and talking, and being afraid.

Taruz was conferring with Samuels, and I caught a fragment of what he said: "—I hope you will be satisfied, sir. This conference has been an admirable example of diplomacy, not so? Open covenants openly arrived at—"

I thought his sense of humor rather fiendish, but maybe we deserved it.

What I do remember is Langford drawing me aside. He was very pale, and spoke fast. "We'd better get going," he said. "We'd better start for home right away. This means war."

He was right. We were still in mid-Atlantic, escorted by one of the Thashtivarian ships, when our radio brought the news that the Russians had H-bombed America.

III

We passed over what had been Washington. There wasn't much to see through the dust and smoke which still roiled miles high. The suburban rim was a tangle of shards, and beyond it there was fire.

Samuels bowed his head and wept.

We landed in Richmond, and a platoon of Marines surrounded us at once. The radio code had told us that what remained of our government was holed up here. I recalled that this city had been the capital of the Confederacy—if Taruz knew, how he must be grinning!

His ships were already there, posted in the sky above us, and I gathered that a force-field would be switched on over the town at the first alarm.

As we drove to meet the President, I saw that the streets were almost empty, except for a few wrecked cars and sprawled corpses which no one had yet had time to clean up. The spectacle, and the smashed windows and scarred walls, told me what a murderous stampede had run through the town the day before.

People had fled, blind and wild with fear, and those who remained were now huddled behind locked doors. There was likely to be starvation before long, because it would be impossible to restore essential services to a whole country gone lunatic.

A guard at the door of our new capitol tried to keep me out. I flashed my badge at him in the best movie manner, and shoved him aside. Nobody had told me to quit watching Samuels and Langford. He let me by, which shouldn't have happened; but something in his eyes showed me how stunned he was. I felt an inward emptiness myself, and I hadn't lived through the last several hours here.

There was a long, time-mellowed conference room, and in it sat the leaders of the nation. The President had had the foresight to leave Washington with the Cabinet and chief staff officers as soon as he got word Taruz was on our side. Most of Congress must have gone up—*in hot air,* said a ghastly imp within me—and such as had also left didn't know where we were. The rabble-rousers were good riddance, I thought, and the rest might seem superfluous with the whole country necessarily under martial law. But there had been fine and honest men among them who would be sorely missed.

It was to Taruz that my eyes went first. He sat imperturbably beside the President, and in all the desolation around us his wild alien form looked only natural. There was a world map spread out in front of him.

The President nodded at us. "Good day, gentlemen," he said tonelessly. "I hope you're not too tired to get right down to work. We need every brian we have."

"What's the situation?" asked Langford.

Samuels had collapsed into a heap on one of the chairs, staring at nothing, but the scientist was inhumanly composed.

"Well, the Soviets have struck," said the President. "Obviously they hope to overcome us, throw us into complete confusion, before we can get organized enough to make much of General Taruz' help. Washington, New York, Philadelphia, Seattle, San Francisco, Detroit—they're gone. So is our strategic counterforce."

As he moved his head, I saw how deep the lines in his face had become, almost overnight. "Clearly, they hope to bottle us up by wrecking our main seaports and industrial centers," he went on. "They're rolling in Europe and Korea. We've sent raids against Vladivostok and certain bases in the Urals, but don't yet know if they've succeeded."

"Why not Moscow?" snapped someone, a Cabinet secretary. "Blow those devils to hell, like they—Oh, God." He buried his face in his hands; later I found out that his family was gone with Washington.

"Surely you don't think their headquarters are still in Moscow," said the Chief of Staff. "I don't know where the Politburo is now."

"I think that information might be obtained," said Taruz quietly. His English was as good as his French.

"Eh?" We all wheeled about to look at him.

"Of course," he nodded. "Small one-man scout-boats, flying low with invisibility screens and telepathic receptors. I need only know approximately where they are to find them within . . . two weeks at the most. After that, one bomb—" He shrugged.

"That," said the President slowly, "kind of changes the picture."

"For what?" The Secretary of Labor leaned over the table and shook his fists at Taruz. "Why did you come here? Why did you want your, your blood money—from anyone who had it? You murdering devil, none of this would have happened if—"

"That's enough!" snapped the President. "We're faced with a fact. It's too late for recriminations." But he didn't apologize to Taruz.

The soldier took it in good part. "This war will be won," Taruz said. "It may take a little time, since my company is not large, but it can be won. However, there is the question of terms. You will note in the contract that the Free Companions do not have to act until the first payment has been made."

"Payment!" screamed the Secretary of Labor. "At a time like this you talk of payment—!"

The President nodded at two MP's, who led the weeping man out. Then he sighed.

"I understand your position, General," he said. "You owe us nothing, except in terms of a morality which seems to be unknown to you. But there are practical difficulties. The offices of the Treasury Department are gone—"

"You will write me a check for three point three trillion dollars," said Taruz coldly. "I shall have to ask that my quartermaster general be given powers in your Treasury Department to assure that the check is made good and that inflation does not rob us of full value."

"But—" The President shut up. It was appalling, to give the right to levy taxes away to a creature from space, with all the police powers implied, but Taruz had us and he knew it. There could be no argument now.

"Yes," said the President. "Please send your . . . man . . . to confer with our Secretary."

"Internal reorganization will also be necessary," declared Taruz. "There is no point in taxing and controlling prices if the taxpayers, merchants, and consumers cannot be located. I will appoint a couple of men to work with your officials."

The President lifted his head. "These concessions are only for the duration of the emergency," he stated.

"Of course," said Taruz smoothly. "And now shall we turn to the military problem?"

The next few weeks were a fever-dream. Like most people, I guarded my sanity by not reading many of the confused dispatches which came from all over our smoking globe, but simply concentrated on my work. That was with Langford at half a dozen cities, getting tracker shells into production.

We had given up on long-range missiles—the Thashtivarian ships handled such jobs better—but our armies in the field needed artillery missiles which could home on the target.

Officially I was still Langford's bodyguard; in practice, as soon as he found I had a degree in physics (which had given me a certain specialized usefulness in the Secret Service), he drafted me to be his assistant. Our job was trouble-shooting in both the organizational and technical lines.

Still, I did follow the broad development of the

struggle—more so than most; because Samuels had arranged for Langford to be kept abreast of even confidential information, which he passed on to me. During that frightful summer, I knew that Army units stationed within the country had managed to restore a degree of order. There were more raids on us, but the bombs exploded harmlessly against Thashtivarian force screens, and only unimportant, unprotected Atlanta went to hell—by mistake, I imagine.

With Thashtivarian help, the Communists were soon bounced out of Korea and Japan. The Nationalist Chinese assault from Formosa to the mainland was also successful because a spaceship accompanied their army. Energy beams methodically melted the tracks of the trans-Siberian railway, thus cutting the Soviets off from their own eastern territory.

A frew raids on the gigantic prison camps, weapons dropped to the convicts, and we had the Siberian Commune set up and fighting with us. We let the Vietminh overrun Indo-China, and then isolated them for future reference.

In Europe, our forces were driven back to the Pyrenees and the English Channel, but there they stayed. It was bitter fighting. A few spaceships roved about, annihilating Russian forces wherever they could be found. But even such immense power was spread so thin that our men bore the brunt of the war.

Within one month, the head of the Soviet monster had been cut off. Taruz' scouts hunted down and killed the leaders, and located all the factories and military bases for his ships to destroy. But there were still millions of armed men, living off the country and fighting with a desperation that would have been called heroic if they had been ours. Even with Thashtivarian help, it would be a long haul.

"There was quite a conference in Richmond about strategy," remarked Langford one night. We were in a dingy hotel room overlooking Pittsburgh. The city was dimmed out, merely to conserve power, and it made the red glow of the great mills seem malignant in the sky. "The President was for negotiating terms with the scattered Red armies, but Taruz was for forcing them all to surrender unconditionally. He finally won his point."

"How?" I asked. I sprawled on the bed, too bone-weary to look at his drawn face. It seemed like forever since I had had a good night's sleep.

"By pointing out that his company wasn't going to be on Earth indefinitely, and that we had better make damn sure of a final peace while we still have this much strength." Langford pulled off a shoe, and it dropped to the floor with a hollow sound. "I suppose he's right. He always seems to be right. But I don't like it, somehow."

"Just why do you rate all this top-secret information?" I inquired.

"Samuels pulled for me. He said he wanted a . . . an impartial observer. What's happening is too big to be grasped by any human mind, and most of our leaders are too busy with immediate problems to think beyond them. He thought maybe I could spot the significant trends and warn him of them."

"Have you?"

"I don't know. If I just had to sit and think. But I've got my own immediate job to do. There's something, call it a hunch, I don't know, but I have an idea that somehow we're sacrificing our long-range interests for expediency."

"What else can we do?"

"Search me." He shrugged skinny shoulders and climbed into bed. "History tells us that no good comes of hiring mercenaries, but you know what Shaw said: 'The only thing we learn from history is that we learn nothing from history."

After a while I got to sleep.

IV

World War Three did not end; it fizzled out, bit by bit, through the next two years. In the first winter, it was plain that Soviet Rusia had been smashed; but ridding the world of Communism was a long and bloody business. It was men with flamethrowers crawling through Indo-Chinese jungles, it was a bayonet charge up Yugoslavian hills, it was an artillery spotter dying to let his unit know where one tank was.

Taruz' forces were only of limited value in this small-scale war which spotted the world like pox. He could destroy or immobilize a regiment, but against guerrillas he could offer little except protection for the American base.

Martial law was lifted here at home on the first New Year's Day, and a specially chosen Congress met the day after. They were not a pretty sight; you couldn't expect them to be, after what the nation had gone through. Public contempt for their wrangling while millions of Americans starved did much to undermine our tradition of constitutional government.

Nobody said a word against the Thashtivarians, in spite of what they cost us. They were the heroes of the day. Wherever one of their haughty golden-skinned men appeared, a crowd would gather to cheer. A rage for their type of dress swept through the land, and women took to tinting their complexions amber and dying their hair blue. The aliens were always correct and reserved among Americans, even when they visited our night clubs where they were pretty lavish spenders.

I saw a less pleasant side of them in Russia, when Langford and I took a trip there in the late winter to study conditions. It was in Podolsk, near Moscow. There was muddy snow in the streets, and a raw wet wind melted it off the roofs, drip, drip, drip, like tears. A spaceship had landed and the Thashtivarians were out after loot. I smelled smoke in the air, and saw dead men in the gutters.

A soldier went by with an armful of tapestries and icons from some church; another was wrenching a gold ring from the finger of an old woman who cried and huddled into her long black dress. Maybe it had been her wedding ring. A third alien was leading a nice-looking girl off, she had a bruise on her cheek and followed him mechanically. Our races were enough alike for such attraction, though there could not be issue from it. I felt sick.

Still, such incidents were rare, and in accordance with the Thashtivarians' customs. Underneath all their technology, they were barbarians, like German tribesmen armed with Roman weapons. And they did not operate slave camps, nor exterminate whole populations, nor kill more helpless civilians than they had to. Our nation, the first to use atomic bombs and jellied gasoline, should not cast the first stone.

By the end of that year, things had settled down in the Americas. Europe and Asia were still chaos, but mile by mile peace and order were being restored. American boys were drafted and sent out, and many did not come back. But at home the work of reconstruction went on steadily and a hectic, rather unhealthy gaiety flourished where it could.

There wasn't much spending, though; Taruz' rigidly enforced economic program saw to that. People went about in sleazy clothes and waited in long queues for cigarettes and meat. They grumbled about the ferocious taxes, but at least there was no further inflation.

The Big Strike that fall raised a hullaballoo. It started with the coal miners, who saw all their painfully made gains swallowed in taxes, demanding higher pay, but it spread like a grass fire. For a week the country was almost paralyzed. Then the President declared martial law again and called out the Army. Soldiers whose comrades were dying for lack of supplies were not sympathetic to the strikers.

Langford told me that Taruz had gotten the President to do it, and mumbled something ominous about precedents.

For a while it looked like civil war. There was, indeed, open rioting here and there. But the President made a series of television appeals, and the Thashtivarians used their catalepsy beams, and the whole business caved in. Workers were sullen, but they went back to their jobs. Martial law was not lifted, but Congress continued to sit.

Shortly thereafter, Taruz himself, who had always remained in the background, appeared on a well-known news commentator's show. I watched it closely. He was a fine actor. He had dropped his usual arrogance, and said he was only serving his own people, whose interests were the same as ours. A plain and truthful statement of what his army meant to us in terms of safety, a few "human interest" remarks about his kiddies at home, a hint or two about the wonders to be expected when his influence got us in on Galactic civilization and commerce—and he had America in his hand.

There was one offhand saying of his which got Langford started on another round of worries. In proof of his own far-sighted humanitarianism, Taruz explained that he was investing most of his company's pay in large American corporations doing vital reconstruction work.

The money wasn't being taken out of the world, it was staying right here in the good old U.S.A. Why, you needed only to look at the next new building or the next big rubble-clearing bulldozer to see the benefits you were getting from it.

"The big industrialists will love him for that," said Langford wryly, "especially since all his money is tax free. That's written into the contract, you know. Fine point. And the people are conditioned to follow the businessmen's lead. Also, I happen to know that he's hired the three biggest public-relations outfits in the country to put himself over."

"Well, what of it?" I said. "It serves his own interests, sure, he makes a whopping profit, but it serves us too. Suppose he simply used the money to buy our machinery and oil and whatnot, and shipped it out into space. Where'd we be then? As it is, we get the use of the stuff."

"And he gets the control of it," said Langford. "Money is power, especially in so rigidly frozen an economy as ours now is."

"General Motors or General Taruz—does it

matter who owns title to the machines?" I persisted. "It's not you or me or Joe Smith in either case."

"There's a hell of a big difference," said Langford. "But never mind. The pattern is beginning to emerge, but so far I don't see just what to do about it."

The United Nations met in Stockholm about Christmas time, and went into an interminable debate over revising the charter. I think even the delegates knew by then that the UN had become a pious mummery. Without universal disarmament and an international army to enforce peace, it could only handle secondary matters.

The smaller countries were eager for such an arrangement, and the United States, the only remaining world power, could have brought it about with one word. Samuels stumped hard for the idea prior to the meeting, but then he died—heart attack—and the man we did send was as stiff-necked as the Russians had ever been. Even had Samuels lived, there would probably have been no difference.

America was in no mood to surrender her authority. You heard a lot of talk about not being able to trust any foreign country because sooner or later, it would turn on you. We had paid a bitter price for dominion, and would not sell it for peanuts.

What we did do was make the new Russian Republic disarm and renounce war—something tried in Japan after World War Two. The newly liberated countries and Europe were too hungry and enfeebled to matter.

About that time, I was able to quit working for the government, something I'd wanted for a long time. The old atmosphere of witch hunting before the war had been bad enough. But because I'd liked my work and believed in its importance I'd kept my mouth shut and stayed in. But now the new tight-lipped, puritanical notion that we alone could save civilization was just too much.

Langford retired too, to accept a professorship at M.I.T., without giving up all his connections in Richmond. I got a position with an electronics firm in Boston, so we still saw a lot of each other. The next year I got married and began to settle down into the not uncomfortable creeping-up of middle age.

In the third year, the last Communist army surrendered, but there was no celebration because war was not yet ended. Order had to be restored to lands running wild with a dozen fanatic new creeds, whipped on by hunger and despair. We were fighting Neonihilists in the Balkans and Whiteslayers in Africa and Christomoslems in Southwest Asia. Taruz was a big help, but I wondered if it would ever end.

At least, I was free to wonder.

V

Langford glanced up from his newspaper as I came into his home. "Hello, there," he said. "Seen the latest?"

"The new war?" I asked, for the struggle between Portugal and South Africa had just begun, when the semi-fascist government of the latter tried to take over Portuguese Angola.

"No. The editorial. 'Any war, anywhere, may become another world conflagration. It is past time that we, for our own safety, laid down the law to nations which seem to know no law."

"That's an old idea," I said, easing myself into a chair.

"Yes, but this is a conservative and influential paper. The idea is beginning to spread."

I sighed. "What's so bad about it? A *Pax Americana* may not be the sort of thing I dreamed of once, but it's better than nothing."

"But what will we gain? Safety at the price of mounting guard on the entire planet . . . read your Roman history."

"Rome could have lasted if it had been a little smarter," I said. "Suppose they'd conquered Germany, Arabia, and southern Russia while they were in their heyday. That was where all their enemies eventually came from. The Empire might be with us yet."

"Yes," said Langford. "I'm afraid that something similar is about to happen. I never did like the Romans."

The natives of Angola, who knew very well what would happen to them under South African rule, rallied behind Portugal and licked the hell out of the invaders. Then India came in on Portugal's side, alleging mistreatment of Indian minorities—true enough, but an old excuse. They just wanted territory, Goa as the price of help and chunks of Africa as loot. This inspired uprisings in Spanish Morocco. One thing led to another, and Spain marched on Portugal.

Being more closely tied to the latter, we got involved, and from our Liberian bases soon quelled the Falangists. Then we proceeded to write the peace without consulting either Portugal or India. Such was our national temper at the time. Can you blame us after all we had suffered?

Taruz accepted the third installment of his pay and continued to serve us. Economic controls remained in effect, to keep inflation from depreciating his money, but things looked up a bit for the average taxpayer. You began to see some new cars and some clothes that were not shoddy. Langford showed me certain reports: Taruz was not only operating shrewdly as a major stockholder in established corporations, he was founding his own.

"But isn't that against the antitrust laws?" I asked.

"If so, nobody is prosecuting," answered Langford. "Nobody is saying a word. We're too dependent on him by now."

He nodded grimly, and left me.

I noticed sentiment for the *Pax Americana* growing day by day. It seemed the only logical course to insure that we would not again be laid in ashes. Right now we were invincible; best to consolidate that position while we could.

There would be a new President this year. The incumbent party selected James, a previously obscure man—dynamic type, good speaker, good record as governor and senator, but nothing spectacular.

"Smoke-filled back rooms, eh?" I asked Langford. "How did he get picked? There were more obvious candidates."

"Money will do a lot," said Langford, "and I don't mean crude bribery—I mean influence, lobbying, publicity. Taruz has money."

"You mean this is . . . Taruz' man?"

"Of course. Why not? The Thashtivarians have a vested interest in us. It's up to them to preserve it. Not that James is their puppet; he just agrees with

them on important issues, and thinks along pre-
dictable lines. That's all which is necessary."

I voted against James, mostly because Langford
had disquieted me. But I was in the minority.

"I think," said Langford the night of the election, "it's time for me to stop croaking doom and
start doing something."

"What?" I asked. "You claim Taruz is putting us
in his pocket, and maybe you're right, but how do
you make the average man see it?"

"I write a book," said Langford. "I give the facts
and figures. They're all available, nothing is class-
ified. It's just that no one else has waded through
that mess of data and seen its meaning. I'll have
SEC reports to show how much he owns and how
much more he controls, the Congressional Record
to show laws that are being ignored and new laws
passed in his favor, and lobbyist registry to show
how many hired agents he has, the assembled
news releases and white papers to show how bit
by bit he's gotten virtual command of the military—"

"Oh, yes. A few thousand people will actually
read the book, and they'll get alarmed and convince the rest."

"You could—get into trouble," I said.

"It might be fun," he grinned. "It just might be."

Having reached a decision, Langford looked
happier and healthier than I'd seen him for a long
time. "The Thashtivarians *can't* conquer us. There
aren't enough of them, as was pointed out long
ago. So simple a thing as a world-wide sit-down
strike could get rid of them, merely by making
Earth unprofitable."

He got a year's leave of absence from the Institute and went down to Richmond to gather his

facts. I had to stay where I was.

The year passed, beginning with sporadic war over the world but material conditions rapidly improving at home. Some of the most irritating government controls were lifted, which made people think we were getting somewhere.

Taruz appeared again on TV and remarked that he thought we were far enough ahead now to start thinking about raising wages. Within a month, a bill permitting that had become law. In the general excitement and cheering, few of us seemed to notice that Taruz, the alien, the hired soldier, had in effect told us what we could do.

The news from abroad remained bad. China and India didn't like us, and said so. They formed an alliance. Some sharp questions were being asked in the British House of Commons, and Argentina was getting downright insulting. A lot of talk arouse abroad about allying against a United States whose hand was increasing heavy.

That it was. We had to have bases, and we had to requisition supplies, and all too often we had to dictate internal policy. There was no help for it, if we were to survive in an ugly world. But our satellites and protectorates didn't like it. I think only the fear of Taruz prevented a general war against us.

That fear was breaking down, though. It was being pointed out that the Thashtivarians couldn't be everywhere at once, that the destruction of the thinly spread American forces would leave them virtually without an employer and ready to bargain, that—et cetera, et cetera, et cetera. Only later did it occur to me how much of that talk must have been started by Taruz' own pawns.

In September, hell broke lose again. An H-bomb

rubbed out most of Chicago. Its force screens had been turned off long ago in the confidence that there would be no more raids. The blame was laid on the Sino-Indian alliance. They denied it, and to this day I'm not sure if they might not have told the truth. But two million dead Americans left us in no mood to listen. We went into all-out war again.

My factory shifted back to military production, and I worked pretty hard for two years. Protection was given to all our major cities, or course, and the civilian population was organized in a quasi-military manner, so things went smoothly and efficiently at home. The Thashtivarians labored hard for our side, and the Alliance surrendered in a few months. The war dragged on because by that time nobody in this country argued against the *Pax* idea, and it had to be stuffed down the rebellious throat of an unwilling planet.

It was. In two years, no country on Earth but us had any armed forces except local police. Every government was our puppet, and our garrisons and inspectors were everywhere. We still called our proconsuls "Ambassadors in chief" and our occupying armies "protective alliances."

But nobody was fooled or intended to be fooled. This could not be worked by democratic means, so a Constitutional amendment went through which virtually scrapped the Constitution. Congress retained certain powers, but the balance was now with the executive.

I waited for the secret police and the marching uniforms, but they didn't come. There was still a wide latitude of free speech, provided you didn't criticize the fundamentals or the top leaders. There were comparatively few political arrests, and little if any brutality in such cases.

As dictatorships go, this was a gentle one. And it showed considerable statesmanship in many ways, such as the international currency reforms, increased freedom of travel, and work to rehabilitate the devastated parts of the world.

It wasn't Utopia, but I wondered if it might not be better than we deserved.

VI

Langford had been called back to government service during the war—Intelligence this time—and for a while after, so I didn't see him for nearly three years. Then he came back to resume his professorship, and I went around to welcome him home.

We sat by the fire, with no other lights, sipping a good red wine and speaking slowly. The flames glowed, and danced, and whispered at us in thin dry voices; shadows moved huge in the corners, here and there lifting from an old picture or a dark massive piece of furniture. Outside, a winter wind muttered at the door. It was good, and snug, and very human.

"Did you see much of Taruz during the war?" I asked.

"Yes," said Langford. The red light wove across his hawk face with an oddly gentle effect. "Sometimes we worked together pretty closely. He knew what I thought, but didn't care as long as my actions remained loyal—in fact, I think he rather likes me. He's not such a bad sort. Not a fiend at all; just a smart adventurer."

"I suppose your book will never be written, though," I said.

"Hardly." Langford's laugh was small and sad. "Not because it's forbidden, but because it's too late. The Thashtivarians could not have conquered Earth, but—*divide and rule!*—they got us to conquer it for them."

"And now they own us, who own the world," I murmured.

"Not that simple. It's more accurate to say that they hold the reins. You'll see a gradual change in the next decade or so, shifting more and more of the power over to them, but it won't be obtrusive. Taruz is too clever for that."

"And what will he do with us?"

"Rule us. What else? I don't believe he's power-mad. I think he and his immediate successors will be rather easy-going and tolerant. What reason would they have to be otherwise? Ruling Earth is a profitable business. It means big estates and luxurious homes and lots of human servants and general high living—not ideological tyranny of the Hitler-Stalin sort."

He added after a moment: "Another shipload of Thashtivarian immigrants arrived last week. There must be a million of them here by now. But there won't ever be any great number, because they'll be the aristocracy, and an aristocracy must be kept small."

"You don't sound as bitter about it as you once did," I said.

"What's the use of being bitter about an accomplished fact? As a scientist, I've learned to live with facts. And to get moral about it, Taruz is no more than mankind had coming. A united world could have laughed at him. A peaceful world would never have hired him."

"The real situation was different," I protested.

"You can't condemn your whole race just because Taruz arrived at an unlucky moment."

"True enough. But even with that setup, the free world could have stayed free. We might have averted war altogether by making it clear in advance that if we hired Taruz our only orders to him would be to get the hell off Earth.

"Or maybe we should have turned his services over to one of the small, neutral but democratic nations. Or if all this sounds too unrealistic, we had a chance to unite all our race at the Stockholm meeting. World government, a *human* world army, and Taruz would have been superfluous. He wouldn't even have tried to take over then, knowing it would never pay.

"But we had to be clever, and realistic. We had to look out for Number One. *Si monumentum requiris, circumspice!*" Langford laughed harshly.

"Can't we do something, even now?" I wondered.

"No, we can't. Who's interested? Ask yourself, Hillyer. You have a family, a good job, a nice home, security and a chance for advancement. Does the fact that someday you'll be saying 'sir' to every Thashtivarian warrant throwing all that away to die on the barricades?"

I shook my head.

"It could be worse," went on Langford. "Taruz played his cards ruthlessly. His poker chips were human lives in the millions, but now that he's here to stay we'll get *some* benefits. No more war, which means a gigantic economic surplus of which man will get at least part; maybe, eventually, no more poverty. Perhaps we can learn a lot of their science, especially when they start getting lazy and training human technicians to man their machines for them. We lost our freedom because we couldn't get together as a race. Now the unity is forced on us, and it will last."

"But we *have* lost our freedom," I said. "The decisions may be wiser from now on, but they'll be made for us. Enter that on the debit side."

"Quite so. That's a face we'll have to live with for centuries."

Langford stared into the fire, and a little smile played about his mouth. "It's an old pattern of history. Rome, Roman Britain—the hired soldiers were called in to help and ended by taking over. But there's another part of the pattern too. Conquerors are culturally assimilated, like the Normans in England; or they decay and can be overthrown at last, like the Hyksos in Egypt. Mankind can wait for one thing or another to happen. Our many-greats grandchildren will be united *and* free. It's up to us to start laying the foundation for them. *Right now.*"

He drained his glass and set it down.

THE WORD TO SPACE

" '—begat Manod, who reigned over the People for 99 years. And in his day lawlessness went abroad in the land, wherefore the Quaternary One smote the People with ordseem (Apparently a disease—Tr.) and they were sore afflicted. And the preacher Jilbmish called a great prayer meeting. And when the People were assembled he cried unto them: Woe betide you, for you have transgressed against the righteous command of the Secondary and Tertiary Ones, namely, you have begrudged the Sacrifice and you have failed to beat drums (? — Tr.) at the rising of Nomo, even as your fathers were commanded; wherefore this evil is come upon you.' Sheemish xiv, 6.

"Brethren beyond the stars, let us ponder this next together. For well you know from our previous messages that ignorance of the Way, even in its least detail, is not an excuse in the sight of the

Ones. 'Carry Our Way unto the ends of creation, that ye may save from the Eternal Hunger all created beings doomed by their own unwittingness.' Chubu iv, 2. Now the most elementary exegesis of the words of Jilbmish clearly demonstrated—"

Father James Moriarty, S.J., sighed and laid down the typescript. Undoubtedly the project team of linguists, cryptographers, anthropologists, theologians and radio engineers was producing translations as accurate as anyone would ever be able to. At least until the barriers of space were somehow overleaped and men actually met the aliens, face to face on their own planet. Which wasn't going to happen in the foreseeable future.

Father Moriarty had been assured that the different English styles corresponded to a demonstrable variation in the original language. If he insisted on absolute scholarship, he could consult the Primary Version, in which the logical and mathematical arguments for every possible English rendering of every alien symbol were set forth. By now the Primary Version filled a whole library, each huge volume threshing out the significance of a few hundred words.

Fortunately, such minute precision wasn't necessary for Father Moriarty's purpose. He couldn't have understood the arguments anyhow. His own science was geology. So he accepted the edited translation of the messages from Mu Cassiopeiae.

"Only why," he asked himself as he stuffed his pipe, "must they use that horrible dialect?" He touched a lighter to the charred bowl and added, "Pseudo-King James," with a bare touch of friendly malice.

A cluster of buildings appeared below. Despite

lawns and gardens, the big central structure and
its outlying houses looked forlorn, as if dumped
there in the little valley among summer-green Virginia hills. Even the radio telescope and mast had
a forsaken air about them. Everything was neatly
maintained, but small and old-fashioned. Also,
Moriarty thought, a good deal of the ghost town
impression must be subjective, since he knew
what an orphan Ozma was.

The autopilot beeped and said: "You are approaching an area where overhead flight is prohib-
ited. The vehicle will take a course around it."

"Oh, shut up," said Moriarty. "Ever since you
machines got voices, you've been insufferable."
He punched the LAND button. The autopilot requested permission from the autocontrol tower
and got a beam. The gravicar slanted downward to
the parking lot. When it had rolled to a stop, the
priest got out.

He stood for a moment stretching his muscles
and enjoying the sunlight. The flight had been
long, several hours from Loyola University of Los
Angeles; this old jalopy could barely keep minimum legal speed in the traffic lanes. Good to be
here at last—yes, and to see real greenwood on the
hills, after all those years in California. The air
was very still. Then, a liquid note and another . . . a
mocking bird?

To keep himself from becoming maudlin, he
threw back his head and looked toward the great
webwork of the radio telescope. Beyond those
meshes, the sky was a deep gentle blue. Though
Project Ozma had been going on since before he
was born—for a century and a third, in fact, so
that its originators were one in the history books
with Aristotle and Einstein—he found it emotion-

ally impossible to reconcile such a sky with the cold black gap of space beyond, twenty-five light-years to that sun whose second planet was talking with Earth.

"Talking at Earth, I should say," he tried to smile. Perhaps after dark, when the stars were out, this would all seem less eldritch. Formerly Ozma had been in the background of his life, something one read about and made the appropriate marveling noises over, like the Jupiter expedition or the longevity process or the Egyptian-Israeli Entente, a thing with no immediate effects on the everyday. But this hour he was here, his application accepted, an actual part of it!

He suppressed his excitement and focused on a large middle-aged man in rumpled blue tunic and slacks who was nearing him. The priest, tall and stooped and prematurely balding, walked forward. "Dr. Strand, I presume from your television interviews? This is an honor. I didn't expect the director himself to meet me."

Strand's handshake was lackadaisical and his expression unamiable. "What the hell else is there for me to do?" Embarrassed: "Uh, beg your pardon, Father."

"Quite all right. I admit, like any specialist, I wish outsiders wouldn't use technical terms so loosely, but that's a minor annoyance." Moriarty felt his own shyness fading. He remembered he was here for excellent reasons. He took a fresh drag on his pipe. "Your settlement looks peaceful," he remarked.

"Dead, you mean." Strand shrugged. "The normal condition of the project. There are just half a dozen people around at the moment."

"No more? I should have thought—"

"Look, we only use the radio telescope these days to sweep the sky in the hydrogen band for signals from other stars. That operation's been almost completely automated. Only needs a couple of maintenance men, and I myself check the tapes. Then there's my secretary, who's got the biggest sinecure in the country, and two care-takers for the buildings and grounds. Frankly, I wonder why you came here." Strand essayed a rather stiff smile. "Glad to see you, of course. Showing you around will at least break the mono-tony. But I don't know what you can accomplish that you couldn't do in your own office back at your college."

"I take it the translators don't work here?"

"No. Why should they? They've better facilities in Charlottesville. I suppose you know the University of Virginia is now handling that side of the project. I used to run over there every week with a new batch of tapes, but lately a big receiver right on campus has been turned over to us. The space station bucks the Cassiopeian transmissions directly there, and also takes outgoing messages. Our own radio mast is quite idle."

They began to walk. "By the way," he asked Strand, "where are you staying?"

"Nowhere, yet. I thought one of your dormi-tories—"

"M-m-m-m . . . nobody uses them any more." Strand looked reluctant. "You can talk to Joe about it, but personally I'd advise you get a room in some nearby town. Commuting's easy enough." He seemed to wrestle with himself before polite-ness overcame hostility. "How about a cup of coffee in my office? You must be tired from your trip."

Moriarty felt like a young bloodhound, released in a barnyard full of the most fascinating new smells and then suddenly called to heel. But he couldn't well refuse the offer. Besides, it might give him an opening to broach his real purpose in coming. "Thank you, that's very kind."

As they crossed the grounds, he added, "So you still haven't gotten any other extraterrestrial signals?"

"No, of course not. We wouldn't keep that secret! Hope's growing dim, too. Even in the southern hemisphere, Ozma's pretty well checked out most of the likely stars within range of our instruments. I suspect that until we get much more powerful equipment, Akron is the only extra-solar planet we'll ever be in touch with. And we won't be granted such equipment till we can show some worthwhile results with Akron. Talk about your vicious circles!"

Moriarty's smile turned wry. "You know," he said, "I've often suspected one of your problems in getting funds for this work has been the unfortunate coincidence that Mu Cassiopeiae II happens to be called Akron in its own principal language. With the star's astronomical name containing, from the English viewpoint, such a wanton aggregate of vowels, it was inevitable the people would nickname it Ohio."

"Spare me," groaned Strand. "The jokes about messages from Akron, Ohio were dead and rotten before either of us was born."

"I was just thinking that those jokes themselves may have been an unconscious reason for starving Ozma. Who could take a planet named Akron very seriously?"

Strand shrugged again. "Could be. The project's

had nothing but trouble, ever since those cursed signals were first detected." He gave Moriarty a sharp sidewise glance. The unspoken thought went between them: *I'm afraid you're going to be still another plague on our house. A Jesuit couldn't transfer himself casually; his superiors would have to approve, at the very least. And after that, why did Washington okay your application? I know a Catholic President would be more than ordinarily ready to listen to whatever fisheating notion you came up with. But damn and blast, I've got work to do!*

They entered the main building and went through a gloomy foyer to a hall lined with locked doors. "Even so," said Moriarty, in delayed answer, "this was once a major enterprise." Coming in from brilliant daylight, he found the emptiness all the more depressing.

"Once," the director conceded wearily. "When the original Project Ozma first picked up signals from Ohi—from Mu Cassiopeiae—way back in the 1980's. Oh, they made headlines all over the world then! That was when this got set up as an independent Federal operation."

"I know," said Moriarty. To drive off the sadness from them both, he chuckled. "I've read about the old hassles. Every branch of government wanted Ozma. The Navy much resented losing it, but what with the State Department insisting this was their line of work, while the Department of the Interior argued that since the construction would be on public land— But that was before the taxpayers realized the truth. I mean, what a long, tedious, expensive process it would be, establishing communication with a nonhuman race twenty-five light-years away."

Strand opened a door. Beyond was an anteroom in which a small Nisei sat at a desk. He bounced up as Strand said, "Father Moriarty, meet my secretary, Philibert Okamura."

"An honor, Father," said the little man. "A great honor. I've been so happy you were coming. I read your classic work on the theory of planetary cores. Though I admit the mathematics got beyond me in places."

Strand raised his brows. "Oh? I knew you were a geologist, Father, but I hadn't quite understood—"

Moriarty looked at his shoes. He didn't enjoy personal attention. "That paper is nothing," he mumbled. "Just playing with equations. The Solar System doesn't have a great enough variety of planetary types for most of my conclusions to be checked. So it's only a trifling monograph."

"I wouldn't call a hundred pages of matrix algebra trifling," said Okamura. He smiled at his chief, as proudly as if he had invented the newcomer. "Math runs in his family, Dr. Strand. The Moriartys have been scientists for more than two hundred years. You are descended, aren't you, from the author of *The Dynamics of an Asteroid*?"

Since that particular ancestor was not one he cared to be reminded of, the priest said hastily, "You'll sympathize, then, with my special interest in Ozma. When you released those data about the size and density of Akron, a few years ago—really, I was tempted to think God had offered us the exact case we needed to verify Theorem 8-B in my paper. Not to mention all the other details, which must be radically different from the Solar System—"

"And the biology, biochemistry, zoology, botany, anthropology, history, sociology . . . and who knows how far ahead of us they may be in some technologies? Sure. Those hopes were expressed before I was born," snapped Strand. "But what have we actually learned so far? One language. A few details of dress and appearance. An occasional datum of physical science, like that geological information you spoke of. In more than a hundred years, that's all!" He broke off. "Anything in the mail today?"

"Two dollars from a lady in Columbus, Nebraska, in memory of her sweet little Pekingese dog Chan Chu," said Okamura.

"I suppose you've heard, Father, Project Ozma is accepting private contributions," said Strand bitterly. "Anything to stretch our funds. You wouldn't believe the dodges they find in Washington to pare down the money we get. Not that the total official appropriation ever amounts to much."

"I should think," said Moriary, "there would be a rich source of income in donations from those weird religions which have grown up in response to the preachments from Akron."

Strand's eyes bugged. "*You'd* take *their* money?"

"Why not? Better than having them spend it on proselytization."

"But as long as the only messages are that garbled gospel—"

"Additional idiocies won't make any difference. The people who've adopted the Akronite faith (or, rather, one of the dozen distorted versions) will simply modify their beliefs as more sermons pour in. You don't make total chaos worse by stirring the pot a bit more."

"Hm-m-m." Strand rubbed his chin and stared at the ceiling. Then, reluctantly; "No. We couldn't. Too many other churches would holler about favoritism. In fact, the inspiration we're giving those nut cults is one reason our project is in danger of being terminated altogether."

Okamura began with diffidence, "I heard Bishop Ryan's speech last month."

"Bishop Ryan's opinions are his own," said Moriarty. "In spite of what non-Catholics think, the Church is not a monolithic dictatorship, even in matters of faith. Unlike Bishop Ryan, I assure you the Society of Jesus would reckon it a catastrophe if communication with Akron were stopped."

"Even when all we get is religious discussion?" asked Okamura.

"Religious ranting, you mean," said Strand sourly.

Moriary grimaced. "Correct word, that. I was reading the latest translation you've released, on my way here. No sign of any improvement, is there?"

"Nope," Okamura said. "As of twenty-five years ago, at least, Akron's still governed by a fanatical theocracy out to convert the universe." He sighed. "I imagine you know the history of Ozma's contact with them? For the first seventy-five years or so, everything went smoothly. Slow and unspectacular, so that the public got bored with the whole idea, but progress was being made in understanding their language. And then—when they figured we'd learned it well enough—they started sending doctrine. Nothing but doctrine, ever since. Every message of theirs a sermon, or a text from one of their holy books followed by an analysis that my Jewish friends tell me makes the medieval rabbis look like romantic poets. Oh, once in a great while somebody slips in a few scientific data, like that geological stuff which got you so interested. I imagine their scientists are just as sick at the wasted opportunity as ours are. But with a bunch of Cotton Mathers in control, what can they do?"

"Yes, I know all that," said Moriarty. "It's a grim sort of religion. I daresay anyone who opposes its ministers is in danger of burning at the stake, or whatever the Akronite equivalent may be."

Okamura seemed so used to acting as dragoman for visitors who cared little and knew less about Ozma, that he reeled off another string of facts the priest already had by heart. "Communication has always been tough. After the project founders first detected the signals, fifty years must pass between our acknowledgment and their reply to that. Of course, they'd arranged it well. Their initial message ran three continuous months before repeating itself. In three months one can go all the way from 'two plus two equals four' to basic symbology and telling what band a sonic 'cast will be sent on if there's an answer. Earth's own transmission could be equally long and carefully thought out. Still, it was slow. You can't exactly have a conversation across twenty-five light-years. All you can do is become aware of each other's existence and then start transmitting more or less continuously, meanwhile interpreting the other fellow's own steady flow of graded data. But if it weren't for those damned fanatics, we'd know a lot more by now than we do.

"As it is, we can only infer a few things. The

theocracy must be planet-wide. Otherwise we'd be getting different messages from some other country on Akron. If they have interstellar radio equipment, they must also have weapons by which an ideological dictatorship could establish itself over a whole world, as Communism nearly did here in the last century. The structure of the language, as well as various other hints, proves the Akronites are mentally quite humanlike, however odd they look physically. We just had the bad luck to contact them at the exact point in their history when they were governed by this crusading religion."

Okamura stopped for breath, giving Strand a chance to grunt, "Ozma's characteristic bad luck. But instead of gassing about things we all know as well as we know the alphabet, suppose you get us some coffee."

"Oh. Sorry!" The secretary blushed and trotted out.

Strand led Moriarty on into the main office. It was a spacious room with a view of gardens, radioscope, and wooded hillside. Where the walls weren't lined with books, they were hung with pictures. The most conspicuous was a composite photograph of an Akronite, prepared from the crude television images which Ozma's private satellite station had recently become able to receive. The being gave an impression of height; and they had in fact reported themselves as standing ten *axuls* tall on the average, where an *axul* turned out to equal approximately one-point-on-one million cadmium red wavelengths. The gaunt body was hidden by robes. A Terrestrial request for a picture of nude anatomy had been rejected with Comstockian prudishness. But one could see the Akronite had three-toed feet and four-fingered hands. The crested head and long-nosed face were so unhuman they had nothing grotesque about them: rather, those features were dignified and intelligent. Hard to believe that someone who looked like this had written in dead seriousness:

The next word in the sentence from Aejae xliii, 3 which we are considering is 'ruchiruchin,' an archaic word concerning whose meaning there was formerly some dispute. Fortunately, the advocates of the erroneous theory that it means 'very similar' have now been exterminated and the glorious truth that it means 'quite similar' is firmly established."

But the human race had its share of such minds.

Besides this picture, there were photographs of a Martian landscape and Jupiter seen from space, and a stunning astronomical view of the Andromeda Galaxy. The books tended to be very old, including works by Oberth and Ley. Through a veil of pipe smoke, Moriarty studied Michael Strand's worn countenance. Yes, the man was a dreamer—of a most splendid dream, now dying in other Earthly souls. No other type could have kept going with such heroic stubbornness, through a lifetime of disappointments. But he might on that very account prove hard to deal with, when Moriarty's scheme was advanced. Best, perhaps, to lead up to it gradually. . . .

"Siddown." Strand waved at a chair and seated himself behind his desk. A breeze from the open window ruffled his gray hair. He took a cigaret from a box, struck it with a ferocious motion and drew heavily on the smoke. Moriarty lowered his own long body.

"I assume," said the priest, "that your beam-casts to Mu Cassiopeiae continue to be of factual data about ourselves."

"Sure. It's either that, or stop sending altogether. Every so often somebody gets the bright idea that we should ask them to cut out their infernal propaganda. But of course we don't. If they can't get the hint from our own messages, a direct request would probably offend them so much they'd quit transmitting anything."

"You're wise. I've had some acquaintance with religious monomaniacs." Moriarty tried to blow a smoke ring, but the air was too restless. "The information we send must help keep scientific curiosity alive on Akron. As witness those bootleg data we do sometimes get." He smiled an apology. "I hope I may think of myself as a member of your team, Dr. Strand?"

The other man's mouth drew into a harsh line. He leaned across the desk. "Let's be frank with each other," he said. "What are you actually here for?"

"Well," said Moriarty in his mildest voice, "those geological facts were what first snapped me to attention as regards Ozma."

"Come, now! You know very well that we won't be getting more than one quantitative datum a year, if we're lucky. And what we do get is released in the scientific journals. You don't have to join us to know everything we find out. You could have stayed at Loyola. Instead . . . there was pressure put on me. To be perfectly honest, I didn't want you, even on this temporary appointment of yours. But word came from the White House that you had, quote, 'the warmest Presidential recommendation.' What could I do?"

"I'm sorry. I never intended—"

"You're here for religious reasons, aren't you? The Catholic Church doesn't like this flood of alien propaganda."

"Do you?"

Strand blinked, taken aback. "Well . . . no," he said. "Certainly not. It's a repulsive religion. And the home-grown crank cults based on it are even worse. " He struck his desk with a knotted fist. "But as long as I'm director, we'll keep on publishing all we learn. I may not like the messages from Akron, or their effect on Earth, but I will not be party to suppressing them!"

Moriarty could not resist a sarcastic jab, though he set himself a small penance for it: "Then of course you'll wish to release the whole inside story of Project Ozma?"

"What?" Strand's expression turned blank. "There's never been anything secret about our work."

"No. Except the motivations behind some of the things done in the past. Which are obvious to anyone with a training in, ah, Jesuitry." Moriarty raised a hand, palm out. "Oh, please don't misunderstand. Your predecessors desired nothing except to keep Ozma alive, which is an entirely honorable desire. And yet, as long as we're alone, why not admit some of their methods were, shall I say, disingenuous?"

Strand reddened. "What're you getting at?"

"Well, just consider the history of this enterprise. After the first flush of enthusiasm had departed, when the government and the public saw what a long hard pull lay ahead. Even more so, after the sermons began to come and outright public hostility developed. There was a continual scramble for tax funds to keep Ozma going. And . .

I've looked into the old records of Congressional hearings. At first the director played on a national desire for scientific prestige. 'We mustn't let the Russians get ahead of us in this, too.' Then, when war broke out, the argument was that maybe we could get valuable technical information from Akron—a ludicrous argument, but enough Congressmen fell for it. After the war, with no foreign competition to worry about, the government almost killed Ozma again. But a calculatedly mawkish account of paraplegic veterans returning to work here was circulated, and the American Legion pulled your chestnuts out of the fire. When that stunt had been used to death, the Readjustment was in full swing, jobs were scarce, it was argued that Ozma created employment. Again, ridiculous, but it worked for a while. When conditions improved and Ozma was once more about to get the ax, one director retired and a Negro was appointed in his place. Ergo, no one dared vote against Ozma for fear of being called prejudiced. Et cetera, et cetera. The project has gone on like that for a hundred years."

"So what?" Strand's voice was sullen.

"So nothing. I don't say a word against shrewd politics." Moriarty's pipe had gone out. He made a production of relighting it, to stretch out the silence. At what he judged to be the critical instant, he drawled:

"I only suggest we continue in the same tradition."

Strand leaned back in his swivel chair. His glum hostility was dissolving into bewilderment. "What are you getting at? Look here, uh, Father, it's physically impossible for us to change the situation on Akron—"

"Oh?"

"What d' you mean?"

"We can send a reply to those sermons."

"What?" Strand almost went over backward.

"Other than scientific data, I mean."

"What the devil!" Strand sprang to his feet. His wrath returned, to blaze in face and eyes, to thicken his tones and lift one fist.

"I was afraid of this!" he exclaimed. "The minute I heard a priest was getting into the project, I expected this. You blind, bloody, queercollared imbecile! You and the President—you're no better than those characters on Akron—do you think I'll let my work be degraded to such ends? Trying to convert another planet—and to one particular sect? By everything I believe holy, I'll resign first! Yes, and tell the whole country what's going on!"

Moriarty was startled at the violence of the reaction he had gotten. But he had seen worse, on other occasions. He smoked quietly until a pause in the tirade gave him a chance to say:

"Yes, my modest proposal does have the President's okay. And yes, it will have to be kept confidential. But neither he nor I are about to dictate to you. Nor are we about to spend the tax money of Protestants, Jews, Buddhists, unbelievers . . . even Akronists . . . on propagating our own Faith."

Strand, furiously pacing, stopped dead. The blood went slowly out of his cheeks. He gaped.

"For that matter," said Moriarty, "the Roman Catholic Church is not interested in converting other planets."

"Huh?" choked Strand.

"The Vatican decided more than a hundred years ago, back when space travel was still a mere theory, that the mission of Our Lord was to Earth only, to the human race. Other intelligent species did not share the Fall and therefore do not require redemption. Or, if they are not in a state of grace—and the Akronites pretty clearly are not—then God will have made His own provision for them. I assure you, Dr. Strand, all I want is a free scientific and cultural exchange with Mu Cassiopeiae."

The director reseated himself, leaned elbows on desk and stared at the priest. He wet his lips before saying: "What do you think we should do, then?"

"Why, break up their theocracy. What else? There's no sin in that! My ecclesiastical superiors have approved my undertaking. They agree with me that the Akronist faith is so unreasonable it must be false, even for Akron. Its bad social effects on Earth confirm this opinion. Naturally, the political repercussions would be disastrous if an attempt to subvert Akronism were publicly made. So any such messages we transmit must be kept strictly confidential. I'm sure you can arrange that."

Strand picked his cigaret out of the ashtray where he had dropped it, looked at the butt in a stupefied fashion, ground it out and took a fresh one.

"Maybe I got you wrong," he said grudgingly. "But, uh, how do you propose to do this? Wouldn't you have to try converting them to some other belief?"

"Impossible," said Moriarty. "Let's suppose we did transmit our Bible, the Summa, and a few similar books. The theocracy would suppress them at once, and probably cut off all contact with us."

He grinned. "However," he said, "in both the good and the bad senses of the word, casuistry is considered a Jesuit specialty." He pulled the type-script he had been reading from his coat pocket. "I haven't had a chance to study this latest document as carefully as I have the earlier ones, but it follows the typical pattern. For example, one is required 'to beat drums at the rising of Nomo,' which I gather is the third planet of the Ohio System. Since we don't have any Nomo, being in fact the third planet of our system, it might off-hand seem as if we're damned. But the theocracy doesn't believe that, or it wouldn't bother with us. Instead, their theologians, studying the astronom-ical data we sent, have used pages and pages of hairsplitting logic to decide that for us Nomo is equivalent to Mars."

"What of it?" asked Strand; but his eyes were kindling.

"Certain questions occur to me," said Moriarty. "If I went up in a gravicar, I would see Mars rise sooner than would a person on the ground. None of the preachings we've received has explained which rising is to be considered official at a given longitude. A particularly devout worshipper now-adays could put an artificial satellite in such an orbit that Mars was always on its horizon. Then he could beat drums continuously, his whole life long. Would this gain him extra merit or would it not?"

"I don't see where that matters," said Strand.

"In itself, hardly. But it raises the whole ques-tion of the relative importance of ritual and faith. Which in turn leads to the question of faith versus works, one of the basic issues of the Reformation. As far as that goes, the schism between Catholic and Orthodox Churches in the early Middle Ages turned, in the last analysis, on one word in the Credo *filioque*. Does the Holy Ghost proceed from the Father and the Son or from the Father alone? You may think this is a trivial question, but to a person who really believes his religion it is not. Oceans of blood have been spilled because of that one word.

"Ah . . . returning to this sermon, though. I also wonder about the name 'Nomo.' The Akronite theologians conclude that in our case, Nomo means Mars. But this is based on the assumption that, by analogy with their own system, the next planet outward is meant. An assumption for which I can recall no justification in any of the scriptures they've sent us. Could it not be the next planet inward—Venus for us? But then their own 'Nomo' might originally have been Mu Cassiopeiae I, instead of III. In which case they've been damning themselves for centuries by celebrating the rising of the wrong planet!"

Strand pulled his jaw back up. "I take it, then," he said huskily, "you want to—"

"To send them some arguments much more elaborately reasoned than these examples, which I've simply made up on the spot," Moriarty answered. "I've studied the Akronist faith in detail . . . with two millennia of Christian disputation and haggling to guide me. I've prepared a little reply. It starts out fulsomely, thanking them for showing us the light and begging for further information on certain points which seem a trifle obscure. The rest of the message consists of quibbles, puzzles, and basic issues."

"And you really think—How long would this take to transmit?"

"Oh, I should imagine about one continuous month. Then from time to time, as they occur to us, we can send further inquiries."

Father James Moriarty leaned back, crossed his legs, and puffed benign blue clouds.

Okamura entered with three cups of coffee on a tray. Strand gulped. In an uneven voice he said, "Put 'em down and close the door, please. We've got work to do."

Epilogue

Moriarty was hoeing the cabbages behind the chapter house—which his superior had ordered as an exercise in humility—and speculating about the curious fossil beds recently discovered on Callisto—which his superior had not forbidden—when his wrist-phone buzzed. He detested the thing and wore it only because he was supposed to keep himself accessible. Some silly call was always interrupting his thoughts just when they got interesting. He delivered himself of an innocent but sonorous Latin phrase and pressed the ACCEPT button. "Yes?" he said.

"This is Phil Okamura." The tiny voice became unintelligible. Moriarty turned up the volume. Since he had passed the century mark his ears hadn't been so good; though praise God, the longevity treatment kept him otherwise sound. "—remember? The director of Project Ozma."

"Oh, yes." His heart thumped. "Of course I remember. How are you? We haven't met for . . . must be five years or more."

"Time sure passes. But I had to call you right away, Jim. Transmission from Akron resumed three hours ago."

"What?" Moriarty glanced at the sky. Beyond the clear blue, the stars and all God's handiwork! "What's their news?"

"Plenty. They explained that the reason we haven't received anything from them for a decade was that their equipment got wrecked in some of the fighting. But now things have quieted down. All those conflicting sects have been forced to reach a modus vivendi.

"Apparently the suggestions we sent, incidental to our first disruptive questions seventy-five years ago—and based on our own experience—were helpful: separation of church and state, and so on. Now the scientists are free to communicate with us, uncontrolled by anyone else. They're sure happy about that! The transition was painful, but three hundred years of stagnation on Akron have ended. They've got a huge backlog of data to give us. So if you want your geology straight off the tapes, you better hurry here. All the journals are going to be snowed under with our reports."

"*Deo gratias.* I'll ask my superior at once—I'm sure he'll let me—and catch the first robus headed your way." Father Moriarty switched off the phone and hobbled toward the house. After a moment he remembered he'd forgotten the hoe. Well, let somebody else pick the thing up. He had work to do!

A LITTLE KNOWLEDGE

They found the planet during the first Grand Survey. An expedition to it was organized very soon after the report appeared; for this looked like an impossibility.

It orbited its G9 sun at an average distance of some three astronomical units, thus receiving about one-eighteenth the radiation Earth gets. Under such a condition (and others, e.g., the magnetic field strength which was present) a subjovian ought to have formed; and indeed it had fifteen times the terrestrial mass. But—that mass was concentrated in a solid globe. The atmosphere was only half again as dense as on man's home, and breathable by him.

"Where 'ave h'all the H'atoms gone?" became the standing joke of the research team. Big worlds are supposed to keep enough of their primordial hydrogen and helium to completely dominate the chemistry. Paradox, as it was unofficially christened, did retain some of the latter gas, to a total of eight percent of its air. This posed certain technical problems which had to be solved before anyone dared land. However, land the men must; the puzzle they confronted was so delightfully baffling.

A nearly circular ocean basin suggested an answer which studies of its bottom seemed to confirm. Paradox had begun existence as a fairly standard specimen, complete with four moons. But the largest of these, probably a captured asteroid, had had an eccentric orbit. At last perturbation brought it into the upper atmosphere, which at that time extended beyond Roche's limit. Shock waves, repeated each time one of these everdeeper grazings was made, blew vast quantities of gas off into space: especially the lighter molecules. Breakup of the moon hastened this process and made it more violent, by presenting more solid surface. Thus at the final crash, most of those meteoroids fell as one body, to form that gigantic astrobleme. Perhaps metallic atoms, thermally ripped free of their ores and splashed as an incandescent fog across half the planet, locked onto the bulk of what hydrogen was left, if any was.

Be that as it may, Paradox now had only a mixture of what had hitherto been comparatively insignificant impurities, carbon dioxide, water vapor, methane, ammonia, and other materials. In short, except for a small amount of helium, it had become rather like the young Earth. It got less heat and light, but greenhouse effect kept most of its water liquid. Life evolved, went into the photosynthesis business, and turned the air into the oxynitrogen common on terrestrials.

The helium had certain interesting biological effects. These were not studied in detail. After all, with the hyperdrive opening endless wonders to them, spacefarers tended to choose the most obviously glamorous. Paradox lay a hundred parsecs from Sol. Thousands upon thousands of worlds were more easily reached; many were more pleasant and less dangerous to walk on. The expedition departed and had no successors.

First it called briefly at a neighboring star, on one of whose planets were intelligent beings that had developed a promising set of civilizations. But, again, quite a few such lay closer to home.

The era of scientific expansion was followed by the era of commercial aggrandizement. Merchant adventurers began to appear in the sector. They ignored Paradox, which had nothing to make a profit on, but investigated the inhabited globe in the nearby system. In the language dominant there at the time, it was called something like Trillia, which thus became its name in League Latin. The speakers of that language were undergoing their equivalent of the First Industrial Revolution, and eager to leap into the modern age.

Unfortunately, they had little to offer that was in demand elsewhere. And even in the spacious terms of the Polesotechnic League, they lived at the far end of a long haul. Their charming arts and crafts made Trillia marginally worth a visit, on those rare occasions when a trader was on such a route that the detour wasn't great. Besides, it was as well to keep an eye on the natives. Lacking the means to buy the important gadgets of Technic society, they had set about developing these for themselves.

Bryce Harker pushed through flowering vines which covered an otherwise doorless entrance. They rustled back into place behind him, smelling like allspice, trapping gold-yellow sunlight in their leaves. That light also slanted through ogive windows in a curving wall, to glow off the grain of the wooden floor. Furniture was sparse: a few stools, a low table bearing an intricately faceted piece of rock crystal. By Trillian standards the ceiling was high; but Harker, who was of average human size, must stoop.

Witweet bounced from an inner room, laid down the book of poems he had been reading, and piped, "Why, be welcome, dear boy—oo-oo-ooh!"

He looked down the muzzle of a blaster.

The man showed teeth. "Stay right where you are," he commanded. The vocalizer on his breast rendered the sounds he made into soprano cadenzas and arpeggios, the speech of Lenidel. It could do nothing about his vocabulary and grammar. His knowledge did include the fact that, by omitting all honorifics and circumlocutions without apology, he was uttering a deadly insult.

That was the effect he wanted—deadliness.

"My, my, my dear good friend from the revered Solar Commonweath," Witweet stammered, "is this a, a jest too subtle for a mere pilot like myself to comprehend? I will gladly laugh if you wish, and then we, we shall enjoy tea and cakes. I have genuine Lapsang Soochong tea from Earth, and have just found the most darling recipe for sweet cakes—"

"Quiet!" Harker rasped. His glance flickered to the windows. Outside, flower colors exploded beneath reddish tree trunks; small bright wings went fluttering past; The Waterfall That Rings

Like Glass Bells could be heard in the distance.
Annanna was akin to most cities of Lenidel, the
principal nation on Trillia, in being spread
through an immensity of forest and parkscape.
Nevertheless, Annanna had a couple of million
population, who kept busy. Three aircraft were
crossing heaven. At any moment, a pedestrian or
cyclist might come along The Pathway Of The
Beautiful Blossoms And The Bridge That Arches
Like A Note Of Music, and wonder why two
humans stood tense outside number 1337.

Witweet regarded the man's skinsuit and boots,
and pack on his shoulders, the tightly drawn sharp
features behind the weapon. Tears blurred the
blue of Witweet's great eyes. "I fear you are
engaged in some desperate undertaking which dis-
torts the natural goodness that, I feel certain, still
inheres," he quavered. "May I beg the honor of
being graciously let help you relieve whatever
your distress may be?"

Harker squinted back at the Trillian. *How much
do we really know about his breed, anyway?
Damned nonhuman thing—Though I never
resented his existence till now*—His pulse
knocked; his skin was wet and stank, his mouth
was dry and cottony-tasting.

Yet his prisoner looked altogether helpless. Witweet was an erect biped; but his tubby frame
reached to barely a meter, from the padded feet to
the big, scalloped ears. The two arms were broom-
stick thin, the four fingers on either hand suggested straws. The head was practically spherical,
bearing a pug muzzle, moist black nose, tiny
mouth, quivering whiskers, upward-slanting tufty
brows. That, the tail, and the fluffy silver-gray fur
which covered the whole skin, had made Olafsson

remark that the only danger to be expected from this face was that eventually their cuteness would become unendurable.

Witweet had nothing upon him except an ornately embroidered kimono and a sash tied in a pink bow. He surely owned no weapons, and probably wouldn't know what to do with any. The Trillians were omnivores, but did not seem to have gone through a hunting stage in their evolution. They had never fought wars, and personal violence was limited to an infrequent scuffle.

Still, Harker thought, *they've shown the guts to push into deep space. I daresay even an unarmed policeman—Courtesy Monitor—could use his vehicle against us, like by ramming.*

Hurry!

"Listen," he said. "Listen carefully. You've heard that most intelligent species have members who don't mind using brute force, outright killing, for other ends than self-defense. Haven't you?"

Witweet waved his tail in assent. "Truly I am baffled by that statement, concerning as it does races whose achievements are of incomparable magnificence. However, not only my poor mind, but those of our most eminent thinkers have been engaged in fruitless endeavors to—"

"Dog your hatch!" The vocalizer made meaningless noises and Harker realized he had shouted in Anglic. He went back to Lenidellian-equivalent. "I don't propose to waste time. My partners and I did not come here to trade as we announced. We came to get a Trillian spaceship. The project is important enough that we'll kill if we must. Make trouble, and I'll blast you to greasy ash. It won't bother me. And you aren't the only possible pilot we can work through, so don't imagine you can block us by sacrificing yourself. I admit you are our best prospect. Obey, cooperate fully, and you'll live. We'll have no reason to destroy you." He paused. "We may even send you home with a good piece of money. We'll be able to afford that."

The bottling of his fur might have made Witweet impressive to another Trillian. To Harker, he became a ball of fuzz in a kimono, an agitated tail and a sound of coloratura anguish. "But this is insanity . . . if I may say that to a respected guest . . . One of *our* awkward, lumbering, fragile, unreliable prototype ships—when you came in a vessel representing centuries of advancement—? Why, why, why, in the name of multiple sacredness, why?"

"I'll tell you later," the man said. "You're due for a routine supply trip to, uh, Gwinsai Base, starting tomorrow, right? You'll board this afternoon, to make final inspection and settle in. We're coming along. You'd be leaving in about an hour's time. Your things must already be packed. I didn't cultivate your friendship for nothing, you see! Now, walk slowly ahead of me, bring your luggage back here and open it so I can make sure what you've got. Then we're on our way."

Witweet stared into the blaster. A shudder went through him. His fur collapsed. Tail dragging, he turned toward the inner rooms.

Stocky Leo Dolgorov and ash-blond Einar Olafsson gusted simultaneous oaths of relief when their leader and his prisoner came out onto the path. "What took you that time?" the first demanded. "Were you having a nap?"

"Nah, he entered one of their bowing, scraping, and unction-smearing contests." Olafsson's grin held scant mirth.

"Trouble?" Harker asked.

"No-no . . . three, four passersby stopped to talk—
we told them the story and they went on," Dolgorov said. Harker nodded. He'd put a good deal
of thought into that excuse for his guards' standing around—that they were about to pay a social
call on Witweet but were waiting until the pilot's
special friend Harker had made him a gift. A lie
must be plausible, and the Trillian mind was not
human.

"We sure hung on the hook, though." Olafsson
started as a bicyclist came around a bend in the
path and fluted a string of complimentary greetings.

Dwarfed beneath the men, Witweet made reply.
No gun was pointed at him now, but one rested in
each of the holsters near his brain. (Harker and
companions had striven to convince everybody
that the bearing of arms was a peaceful but highly
symbolic custom in *their* part of Technic society,
that without their weapons they would feel more
indecent than a shaven Trillian.) As far as Harker's
wire-taut attention registered, Witweet's answer
was routine. But probably some forlornness crept
into the overtones, for the neighbor stopped.

"Do you feel quite radiantly well, dear boy?" he
asked.

"Indeed I do, honored Pwiddy, and thank you in
my prettiest thoughts for your ever-sweet consideration," the pilot replied. "I . . . well, these good
visitors from the starfaring culture of splendor
have been describing some of their experiences—
oh, I simply must relate them to you later, dear
boy!—and naturally, since I am about to embark
on another trip, I have been made pensive by this."

Hands, tails, whiskers gesticulated. *Meaning what?* wondered Harker in a chill; and clamping jaws together: *Well, you knew you'd have to take risks to win a kingdom.* "Forgive me, I pray you of your overflowing generosity, that I rush off after such curt words. But I have promises to keep, and considerable distances to go before I sleep."

"Understood." Pwiddy spent a mere five minutes bidding farewell all around before he pedaled off. Meanwhile several others passed by. However, since no well-mannered person would interrupt a conversation even to make salute, they created no problem.

"Let's go." It grated in Dolgorov's throat.

Behind the little witch-hatted house was a pergola wherein rested Witweet's personal flitter. It was large and flashy—large enough for three humans to squeeze into the back—which fact had become an element in Harker's plan. The car that the men had used during their stay on Trillia, they abandoned. It was unmistakably an off-planet vehicle.

"Get started!" Dolgorov cuffed at Witweet.

Olafsson caught his arm and snapped: "Control your emotions! Want to tear his head off?"

Hunched over the dashboard, Witweet squeezed his eyes shut and shivered till Harker prodded him. "Pull out of that funk," the man said.

"I . . . I beg your pardon. The brutality so appalled me—" Witweet flinched from their laughter. His fingers dripped levers and twisted knobs. Here was no steering by gestures in a light-field, let alone simply speaking an order to an autopilot. The overloaded flitter crawled skyward. Harker detected a flutter in its grav unit, but decided nothing was likely to fail before they reached the spaceport. And after that, nothing would matter except getting off this planet.

Not that it was a bad place, he reflected. Almost Earthlike in size, gravity, air, deliciously edible life forms—an Earth that no longer was and perhaps never had been, wide horizons and big skies, caressed by light and rain. Looking out, he saw woodlands in a thousand hues of green, meadows, river-gleam, an occasional dollhouse dwelling, grainfields ripening tawny and the soft gaudiness of a flower ranch. Ahead lifted The Mountain Which Presides Over Moonrise In Lenidel, a snowpeak pure as Fuji's. The sun, yellower than Sol, turned it and a few clouds into gold.

A gentle world for a gentle people. Too gentle. Too bad. For them.

Besides, after six months of it, three city-bred men were about ready to climb screaming out of their skulls. Harker drew forth a cigarette, inhaled it into lighting and filled his lungs with harshness. *I'd almost welcome a fight*, he thought savagely.

But none happened. Half a year of hard, patient study paid richly off. It helped that the Trillians were—well, you couldn't say lax about security, because the need for it had never occurred to them. Witweet radioed to the portmaster as he approached, was informed that everything looked okay, and took his flitter straight through an open cargo lock into a hold of the ship he was to pilot.

The port was like nothing in Technic civilization, unless on the remotest, least visited of outposts. After all, the Trillians had gone in a bare fifty years from propeller-driven aircraft to interstellar spaceships. Such concentration on research and development had necessarily been at the expense of production and exploitation. What few vessels they had were still mostly experimental. The scientific bases they had established on planets of next-door stars needed no more than three or four freighters for their maintenance.

Thus a couple of buildings, and a ground-control tower bounded a stretch of ferrocrete on a high, chilly plateau; and that was Trillia's spaceport. Two ships were in. One was being serviced, half its hull plates removed and furry shapes swarming over the emptiness within. The other, assigned to Witweet, stood on landing jacks at the far end of the field. Shaped like a fat torpedo, decorated in floral designs of pink and baby blue, it was as big as a Dromond-class hauler. Yet its payload was under a thousand tons. The primitive systems for drive, control, and life support took up that much room.

"I wish you a just too, too delightful voyage," said the portmaster's voice from the radio. "Would you honor me by accepting an invitation to dinner? My wife has, if I may boast, discovered remarkable culinary attributes of certain sea weeds brought back from Gwinsai; and for my part, dear boy, I would be so interested to hear your opinion of a new verse form with which I am currently experimenting."

"No . . . I thank you, no, impossible, I beg indulgence—" It was hard to tell whether the unevenness of Witweet's response came from terror or from the tobacco smoke that had kept him coughing. He almost flung his vehicle into the spaceship.

Clearance granted, *The Serenity of the Estimable Philosopher Ittypu* lifted into a dawn sky.

When Trillia was a dwindling cloud-marbled sapphire among the stars, Harker let out a breath. "We can relax now."

"Where?" Olafsson grumbled. The single cabin barely allowed three humans to crowd together. They'd have to take turns sleeping in the hall that ran aft to the engine room. And their voyage was going to be long. Top pseudovelocity under the snail-powered hyperdrive of his craft would be less than one light-year per day.

"Oh, we can admire the darling murals," Dolgorov fleered. He kicked an intricately painted bulkhead.

Witweet, crouched miserable at the control board, flinched. "I beg you, dear, kind sir, do not scuff the artwork," he said.

"Why should you care?" Dolgorov asked. "You won't be keeping this junkheap."

Witweet wrung his hands. "Defacement is still very wicked. Perhaps the consignee will appreciate my patterns? I spent *such* a time on them, trying to get every teensiest detail correct."

"Is that why your freighters have a single person aboard?" Olafsson laughed. "Always seemed reckless to me, not taking a backup pilot at least. But I suppose two Trillians would get into so fierce an argument about the interior decor that they'd each stalk off in an absolute snit."

"Why, no," said Witweet, a trifle calmer. "We keep personnel down to one because more are not really needed. Piloting between stars is automatic, and the crewbeing is trained in servicing functions. Should he suffer harm en route, the ship will put itself into orbit around the destination planet and can be boarded by others. An extra would thus uselessly occupy space which is often needed for passengers. I am surprised that you, sir, who have set a powerful intellect to prolonged consideration of our astronautical practices, should not have been aware—"

"I was, I was!" Olafsson threw up his hands as far as the overhead permitted. "Ask a rhetorical question and get an oratorical answer."

"May I, in turn, humbly request enlightenment as to your reason for . . . sequestering . . . a spacecraft ludicrously inadequate by every standard of your oh, so sophisticated society?"

"You may." Harker's spirits bubbled from relief of tension. They'd pulled it off. They really had. He sat down—the deck was padded and perfumed— and started a cigarette. Through his bones beat the throb of gravity drive: energy wasted by a clumsy system. The weight it made underfoot fluctuated slightly in a rhythm that felt wavelike.

"I suppose we may as well call ourselves criminals," he said; the Lenidellian word he must use had milder connotations. "There are people back home who wouldn't leave us alive if they knew who'd done certain things. But we never got rich off them. Now we will."

He had no need for recapitulating except the need to gloat: "You know we came to Trillia half a standard year ago, on a League ship that was paying a short visit to buy art. We had goods of our own to barter with, and announced we were going to settle down for a while and look into the possibility of establishing a permanent trading post with a regular shuttle service to some of the Technic planets. That's what the captain of the ship thought too. He advised us against it, said it couldn't pay and we'd simply be stuck on Trillia till the next League vessel chanced by, which wouldn't likely be for more than a year. But when we insisted, and gave him passage money, he shrugged," as did Harker.

"You have told me this," Witweet said. "I thrilled to the ecstasy of what I believed was your friendship."

"Well, I did enjoy your company," Harker smiled. "You're not a bad little osco. Mainly, though, we concentrated on you because we'd learned you qualified for our uses—a regular freighter pilot, a bachelor so we needn't fuss with a family, a chatterer who could be pumped for any information we wanted. Seems we gauged well."

"We better have," Dolgorov said gloomily. "Those trade goods cost us everything we could scratch together. I took a steady job for two years, and lived like a lama, to get my share."

"And now we'll be living like fakirs," said Olafsson. "But afterward—afterward!"

"Evidently your whole aim was to acquire a Trillian ship," Witweet said. "My bemusement at this endures."

"We don't actually want the ship as such, except for demonstration purposes," Harker said. "What we want is the plans, the design. Between the vessel itself, and the service manuals aboard, we have that in effect."

Witweet's ears quivered. "Do you mean to publish the data for scientific interest? Surely, to beings whose ancestors went on to better models centuries ago—if, indeed, they ever burdened themselves with something this crude—surely the interest is nil. Unless . . . you think any will pay to see, in order to enjoy mirth at the spectacle of our fumbling efforts?" He spread his arms. "Why, you could have bought complete specifications most cheaply; or, indeed, had you requested of me, I would have been bubbly-happy to obtain a set and make you a gift." On a note of timid hope: "Thus, you see, dear boy, drastic action is quite unnecessary. Let us return. I will state you remained aboard by mistake—"

Olafsson guffawed. Dolgorov said, "Not even your authorities can be that sloppy-thinking." Harker ground out his cigarette on the deck, which made the pilot wince, and explained at leisured length:

"We want this ship precisely because it's primitive. Your people weren't in the electronic era when the first human explorers contacted you. They, or some later visitors, brought you texts on physics. Then your bright lads had the theory of such things as gravity control and hyperdrive. But the engineering practice was something else again.

"You didn't have plans for a starship. When you finally got an opportunity to inquire, you found that the idealistic period of Technic civilization was over and you must deal with hardheaded entrepreneurs. And the price was set 'way beyond what your whole planet could hope to save in League currency. That was just the price for diagrams, not to speak of an actual vessel. I don't know if you are personally aware of the fact—it's no secret—but this is League policy. The member companies are bound by an agreement.

"They won't prevent anyone from entering space on his own. But take your case on Trillia. You had learned in a general way about, oh, transistors, for instance. But that did not set you up to manufacture them. An entire industrial complex is needed for that and for the million other nec-

essary items. To design and build one, with the inevitable mistakes en route, would take decades at
a minimum, and would involve regimenting your
entire species and living in poverty because every
bit of capital has to be reinvested. Well, you
Trillians were too sensible to pay that price. You'd
proceed more gradually. Yet at the same time,
your scientists, all your more adventurous types
were burning to get out into space.

"I agree your decision about that was intelligent
too. You saw you couldn't go directly from your
earliest hydrocarbon-fuelled engines to a modern
starship—to a completely integrated system of
thermonuclear powerplant, initiative-grade nav-
igation and engineering computers, full-cycle life
support, the whole works, using solid-state circuits, molecular-level and nuclear-level transitions, forcefields instead of moving parts—an *organism*, more energy than matter. No, you
wouldn't be able to build that for generations,
probably.

"But you could go ahead and develop huge,
clumsy, but workable fission-power units. You
could use vacuum tubes, glass rectifiers, kilometers of wire, to generate and regulate the necessary forces. You could store data on tape if not
in single molecules, retrieve with a cathode-ray
scanner if not with a quantum-field pulse,
compute with miniaturized gas-filled units that
react in microseconds if not with photon inter-
plays that take a nanosecond.

"You're like islanders who had nothing better
than canoes till someone happened by in a
nuclear-powered submarine. They couldn't copy
that, but they might invent a reciprocating steam
engine turning a screw—they might attach an air-

pipe so it could submerge—and it wouldn't impress the outsiders, but it would cross the ocean too, at its own pace; and it would overawe any neighboring tribes."

He stopped for breath.

"I see," Witweet murmured slowly. His tail switched back and forth. "You can sell our designs to sophonts in a proto-industrial stage of technological development. The idea comes from an excellent brain. But why could you not simply buy the plans for resale elsewhere?"

"The damned busybody League," Dolgorov spat.

"The fact is," Olafsson said, "spacecraft—of advanced type—have been sold to, ah, less advanced peoples in the past. Some of those weren't near industrialization, they were Iron Age barbarians, whose only thought was plundering and conquering. They could do that, given ships which are practically self-piloting, self-maintaining, self-everything. It's cost a good many lives and heavy material losses on border planets. But at least none of the barbarians have been able to duplicate the craft thus far. Hunt every pirate and warlord down, and that ends the problem. Or so the League hopes. It's banned any more such trades."

He cleared his throat. "I don't refer to races like the Trillians, who're obviously capable of reaching the stars by themselves and unlikely to be a menace when they do," he said. "You're free to buy anything you can pay for. The price of certain things is set astronomical mainly to keep you from beginning overnight to compete with the old-established outfits. They prefer a gradual phasing-in of newcomers, so they can adjust.

"But aggressive, warlike cultures, that'd not be interested in reaching a peaceful accommodation

—they're something else again. There's a total pro-
hibition on supplying their sort with anything that
might lead to them getting off their planets in less
than centuries. If League agents catch you at it,
they don't fool around with rehabilitation like a
regular government. They shoot you."

Harker grimaced. "I saw once on a telescreen
interview," he remarked, "Old Nick van Rijn said
he wouldn't shoot those kinds of offenders. He'd
hang them. A rope is reusable."

"And this ship *can* be copied," Witweet
breathed. "A low industrial technology, lower
than ours, could tool up to produce a modified
design, in a comparatively short time, if guided by
a few engineers from the core civilization."

"I trained as an engineer," Harker said. "Likewise Leo; and Einar spent several years on a
planet where one royal family has grandiose ambi-
tions."

"But the horror you would unleash!" wailed the
Trillian. He stared into their stoniness. "You
would never dare go home," he said.

"Don't want to anyway," Harker answered.
"Power, wealth, yes, and everything those will
buy—we'll have more than we can use up in our
lifetimes, at the court of the Militants. Fun, too."
He smiled. "A challenge, you know, to build a
space navy from zero. I expect to enjoy my work."

"Will not the, the, the Polesotechnic League . . .
take measures?"

"That's why we must operate as we have done.
They'd learn about a sale of plans, and then they
wouldn't stop till they'd found and suppressed our
project. But a non-Technic ship that never
reported in won't interest them. Our destination is
well outside their sphere of normal operations.

They needn't discover any hint of what's going on —till an interstellar empire too big for them to break is there. Meanwhile, as we gain resources, we'll have been modernizing our industry and fleet."

"It's all arranged," Olafsson said. "The day we show up in the land of the Militants, bringing the ship we described to them, we'll become princes."

"Kings, later," Dolgorov added. "Behave accordingly, you xeno. We don't need you much. I'd soon as not boot you through an airlock."

Witweet spent minutes just shuddering.

The Serenity, etc. moved on away from Trillia's golden sun. It had to reach a weaker gravitational field than a human craft would have needed, before its hyperdrive would function.

Harker spent part of that period being shown around, top to bottom and end to end. He'd toured a sister ship before, but hadn't dared ask for demonstrations as thorough as he now demanded. "I want to know this monstrosity we've got, inside out," he said while personally tearing down and rebuilding a cumbersome oxygen renewer. He could do this because most equipment was paired, against the expectation of eventual in-flight down time.

In a hold, among cases of supplies for the research team on Gwinsai, he was surprised to recognize a lean cylindroid, one hundred twenty centimeters long. "But here's a Solar-built courier!" he exclaimed.

Witweet made eager gestures of agreement. He'd been falling over himself to oblige his captors. "For messages in case of emergency, magnificent sir," he babbled. "A hyperdrive unit, an autopilot, a radio to call a journey's end till someone comes and retrieves the enclosed letter—"

"I know, I know. But why not build your own?"

"Well, if you will deign to reflect upon the matter, you will realize that anything we could build would be too slow and unreliable to afford very probable help. Especially since it is most unlikely that, at any given time, another spaceship would be ready to depart Trillia on the instant. Therefore this courier is set, as you can see if you wish to examine the program, to go a considerably greater distance—though nevertheless not taking long, your human constructions being superlatively fast—to the planet called, ah, Oasis . . . an Anglic word meaning a lovely, cool, refreshing haven, am I correct?"

Harker nodded impatiently. "Yes, one of the League companies does keep a small base there."

"We have arranged that they will send aid if requested. At a price, to be sure. However, for our poor economy, as ridiculous a hulk as this is still a heavy investment, worth insuring."

"I see. I didn't know you bought such gadgets— not that there'd be a pegged price on them; they don't matter any more than spices or medical equipment. Of course, I couldn't find out every detail in advance, especially not things you people take so for granted that you didn't think to mention them." On impulse, Harker patted the round head. "You know, Witweet, I guess I do like you. I will see you're rewarded for your help."

"Passage home will suffice," the Trillian said

quietly, "though I do not know how I can face my kinfolk after having been the instrument of death and ruin for millions of innocents."

"Then don't go home," Harker suggested. "We can't release you for years in any case, to blab our scheme and our coordinates. But we could smuggle in whatever and whoever you wanted, same as for ourselves."

The head rose beneath his palm as the slight form straightened. "Very well," Witweet declared.

That fast? jarred through Harker. *He is non-human, yes, but—*The wondering was dissipated by the continuing voice:

"Actually, dear boy, I must disabuse you. We did not buy our couriers, we salvaged them."

"What? Where?"

"Have you heard of a planet named, by its human discoverers, Paradox?"

Harker searched his memory. Before leaving Earth he had consulted every record he could find about his entire stellar neighborhood. Poorly known though it was to men, there had been a huge mass of data—suns, worlds. . . . "I think so," he said. "Big, isn't it? With, uh, a freaky atmosphere."

"Yes." Witweet spoke rapidly. "It gave the original impetus to Technic exploration of our vicinity. But later the men departed. In recent years, when we ourselves became able to pay visits, we found their abandoned camp. A great deal of gear had been left behind, presumably because it was designed for Paradox only and would be of no use elsewhere, hence not worth hauling back. Among these machines we came upon a few couriers. I suppose they had been overlooked. Your civilization can afford profligacy, if I may use that term in due respectfulness."

He crouched, as if expecting a blow. His eyes glittered in the gloom of the hold.

"Hm." Harker frowned. "I suppose by now you've stripped the place."

"Well, no." Witweet brushed nervously at his rising fur. "Like the men, we saw no use in, for example, tractors designed for a gravity of two-point-eight terrestrial. They can operate well and cheaply on Paradox, since their fuel is crude oil, of which an abundant supply exists near the campsite. But we already had electric-celled grav motors, however archaic they are by our standards. And we do not need weapons like those we found, presumably for protection against animals. We certainly have no intention of colonizing Paradox!"

"Hm." The human waved, as if to brush off the chattering voice. "Hm." He slouched off, hands in pockets, pondering.

In the time that followed, he consulted the navigator's bible. His reading knowledge of Lenidellian was fair. The entry for Paradox was as laconic as it would have been in a Technic reference; despite the limited range of their operations, the Trillians had already encountered too many worlds to allow flowery descriptions. Star type and coordinates, orbital elements, mass density, atmospheric composition, temperature ranges, and the usual rest were listed. There was no notation about habitability, but none was needed. The original explorers hadn't been poisoned or come down with disease; Trillian metabolism was similar to theirs.

The gravity field was not too strong for this ship to make landing and, later, ascent. Weather shouldn't pose any hazards, given reasonable care in choosing one's path; that was a weakly energized environment. Besides, the vessel was meant for planetfalls, and Witweet was a skilled pilot in his fashion. . . .

Harker discussed the idea with Olafsson and Dolgrorov. "It won't take but a few days," he said, "and we might pick up something really good. You know I've not been too happy about Militants' prospects of building an ample industrial base fast enough to suit us. Well, a few machines like this, simple things they can easily copy but designed by good engineers . . . could make a big difference."

"They're probably rustheaps," Dolgorov snorted. "That was long ago."

"No, durable alloys were available then," Olafsson said. "I like the notion intrinsically, Bryce. I don't like the thought of our tame xeno taking us down. He might crash us on purpose."

"That sniveling faggot?" Dolgorov gibed. He jerked his head backward to Witweet, who sat enormous-eyed in the pilot chair listening to a language he did not understand. "By accident, maybe, seeing how scared he is!"

"It's a risk we take at journey's end," Harker reminded them. "Not a real risk. The ship has some ingenious failsafes built in. Anyhow, I intend to stand over him the whole way down. If he does a single thing wrong, I'll kill him. The controls aren't made for me, but I can get us aloft again, and afterward we can re-rig."

Olafsson nodded. "Seems worth a try," he said. "What can we lose except a little time and sweat?"

Paradox rolled enormous in the viewscreen, a

darkling world, the sky-band along its sunrise horizon redder than Earth's, polar caps and winter snowfields gashed by the teeth of mountains, tropical forest and pampas a yellow-brown fading into raw deserts on one side and chopped off on another side by the furious surf of an ocean where three moons fought their tidal wars. The sun was distance-dwarfed, more dull in hue than Sol, nevertheless too bright to look near. Elsewhere, stars filled illimitable blackness.

It was very quiet aboard, save for the mutter of powerplant and ventilators, the breathing of men, their restless shuffling about in the cramped cabin. The air was blued and fouled by cigarette smoke; Witweet would have fled into the corridor, but they made him stay, clutching a perfume-dripping kerchief to his nose.

Harker straighted from the observation screen. Even at full magnification, the rudimentary electro-optical system gave little except blurriness. But he'd practiced on it, while orbiting a satellite, till he felt he could read those wavering traces.

"Campsite and machinery, all right," he said. "No details. Brush has covered everything. When were your people here last, Witweet?"

"Several years back," the Trillian wheezed. "Evidently vegetation grows apace. Do you agree on the safety of a landing?"

"Yes. We may snap a few branches, as well as flatten a lot of shrubs, but we'll back down slowly, the last hundred meters, and we'll keep the radar, sonar, and gravar sweeps going." Harker glanced at his men. "Next thing is to compute our descent pattern," he said. "But first I want to spell out again, point by point, exactly what each of us is to do under exactly what circumstances. I don't aim to take chances."

"Oh, no," Witweet squeaked. "I beg you, dear boy, I beg you the prettiest I can, please don't."

After the tension of transit, landing was an anti-climax. All at once the engine fell silent. A wind whistled around the hull. Viewscreens showed low, thick-boled trees; fronded brownish leaves; tawny undergrowths; shadowy glimpses of metal objects beneath vines and amidst tall, whipping stalks. The sun stood at late afternoon in a sky almost purple.

Witweet checked the indicators while Harker studied them over his head. "Air breathable, of course," the pilot said, "which frees us of the handicap of having to wear smelly old spacesuits. We should bleed it in gradually, since the pressure is greater than ours at present and we don't want earaches, do we? Temperature—" He shivered delicately. "Be certain you are wrapped up snug before you venture outside."

"You're venturing first," Harker informed him.

"What? Oo-ooh, my good, sweet, darling friend, no, please, no! It is *cold* out there, scarcely above freezing. And once on the ground, no gravity generator to help, why, weight will be tripled. What could I possibly, possibly do? No, let me stay inside, keep the home fires burning—I mean keep the thermostat at a cozy temperature—and, yes, I will make the nicest pot of tea—"

"If you don't stop fluttering and do what you're told, I'll tear your head off," Dolgorov said. "Guess what I'll use your skin for."

"Let's get cracking," Olafsson said. "I don't want to stay in this Helheim any longer than you."

They opened a hatch the least bit. While Para-

doxian air seeped in, they dressed as warmly as
might be, except for Harker. He intended to stand
by the controls for the first investigatory period.
The entering gases added a whine to the wind-
noise. Their helium content made speech and
other sounds higher pitched, not quite natural;
and this would have to be endured for the rest of
the journey, since the ship had insufficient reserve
tanks to flush out the new atmosphere. A breath of
cold got by the heaters, and a rank smell of alien
growth.

But you could get used to hearing funny, Harker
thought. And the native life might stink, but it was
harmless. You couldn't eat it and be nourished,
but neither could its germs live off your body. If
heavy weapons had been needed here, they were
far more likely against large, blundering herbi-
vores than against local tigers.

That didn't mean they couldn't be used in war.

Trembling, eyes squinched half-shut, tail
wrapped around his muzzle, the rest of him
bundled in four layers of kimono, Witweet crept
to the personnel lock. Its outer valve swung wide.
The gangway went down. Harker grinned to see
the dwarfish shape descend, step by step into the
sudden harsh hauling of the planet.

"Sure you can move around in that pull?" he
asked his companions.

"Sure," Dolgorov grunted. "An extra hundred-
fifty kilos? I can backpack more than that, and
then it's less well distributed."

"Stay cautious, though. Too damned easy to fall
and break bones."

"I'd worry more about the cardiovascular system," Olafsson said. "One can stand three gees a
while, but not for a very long while. Fluid begins

seeping out of the cell walls, the heart feels the strain too much—and we've no gravanol along as the first expedition must have had."

"We'll only be here a few days at most," Harker said, "with plenty of chances to rest inboard."

"Right," Olafsson agreed. "Forward!"

Gripping his blaster, he shuffled onto the gangway. Dolgorov followed. Below, Witweet huddled. Harker looked out at bleakness, felt the wind slap his face with chill, and was glad he could stay behind. Later he must take his turn outdoors, but for now he could enjoy warmth, decent weight—

The world reached up and grabbed him. Off balance, he fell to the deck. His left hand struck first, pain gushed, he saw the wrist and arm splinter. He screamed. The sound came weak as well as shrill, out of a breast laboring against thrice the heaviness it should have had. At the same time, the lights in the ship went out.

Witweet perched on a boulder. His back was straight in spite of the drag on him, which made his robes hang stiff as if carved on an idol of some minor god of justice. His tail, erect, blew jauntily in the bitter sunset wind; the colors of his garments were bold against murk that rose in the forest around the dead spacecraft.

He looked into the guns of three men, and into the terror that had taken them behind the eyes; and Witweet laughed.

"Put those toys away before you hurt yourselves," he said, using no circumlocutions or honorifics.

"You bastard, you swine, you filthy treacherous xeno, I'll kill you," Dolgorov groaned. "Slowly."

"First you must catch me," Witweet answered.

"By virtue of being small, I have a larger surface-to-volume ratio than you. My bones, my muscles, my veins and capillaries and cell membranes suffer less force per square centimeter than do yours. I can move faster than you, here. I can survive longer."

"You can't outrun a blaster bolt," Olafsson said.

"No. You can kill me with that—a quick, clean death which does not frighten me. Really, because we of Lenidel observe certain customs of courtesy, use certain turns of speech—because our males in particular are encouraged to develop esthetic interests, and compassion—does that mean we are cowardly or effeminate?" The Trillian clicked his tongue. "If you supposed so, you committed an elementary logical fallacy which our philosophers name the does-not-follow."

"Why shouldn't we kill you?"

"That is inadvisable. You see, your only hope is quick rescue by a League ship. The courier can operate here, being a solid-state device. It can reach Oasis and summon a vessel which, itself of similar construction, can also land on Paradox and take off again . . . in time. This would be impossible for a Trillian craft. Even if one were ready to leave, I doubt the Astronautical Senate would permit the pilot to risk descent.

"Well, rescuers will naturally ask questions. I cannot imagine any story which you three men, alone, might concoct that would stand up under the subsequent, inevitable investigation. On the other hand, I can explain to the League's agents that you were only coming along to look into trade possibilities and that we were trapped on Paradox by a faulty autopilot which threw us into a descent curve. I can do this in *detail*, which you could not if you killed me. They will return us all to Trillia, where there is no death penalty."

Witweet smoothed his wind-ruffled whiskers. "The alternative," he finished, "is to die where you are, in a most unpleasant fashion."

Harker's splinted arm gestured back the incoherent Dolgorov. He set an example by holstering his own gun. "I . . . guess we're outsmarted," he said, word by foul-tasting word. "But what happened? Why's the ship inoperable?"

"Helium in the atmosphere," Witweet explained calmly. "The monatomic helium molecule is ooh-how-small. It diffuses through almost every material. Vacuum tubes, glass rectifiers, electronic switches dependent on pure gases, any such device soon becomes poisoned. You, who were used to a technology that had long left this kind of thing behind, did not know the fact, and it did not occur to you as a possibility. We Trillians are, of course, rather acutely aware of the problem. I am the first who ever set foot on Paradox. You should have noted that my courier is a present-day model."

"I see," Olafsson mumbled.

"The sooner we get our message off, the better," Witweet said. "By the way, I assume you are not so foolish as to contemplate the piratical takeover of a vessel of the Polesotechnic League."

"Oh, no!" said they, including Dolgorov, and the other two blasters were sheathed.

"One thing, though," Harker said. A part of him wondered if the pain in him was responsible for his own abnormal self-possession. Counterirritant against dismay? Would he weep after it wore off? "You bargain for your life by promising to have ours spared. How do we know we want your terms? What'll they do to us on Trillia?"

"Entertain no fears," Witweet assured him. "We are not vindictive, as I have heard some species are; nor have we any officious concept of 'rehabilitation.' Wrongdoers are required to make amends to the fullest extent possible. You three have cost my people a valuable ship and whatever cargo cannot be salvaged. You must have technological knowledge to convey, of equal worth. The working conditions will not be intolerable. Probably you can make restitution and win release before you reach old age.

"Now, come, get busy. First we dispatch the courier, then we prepare what is necessary for our survival until rescue."

He hopped down from the rock, which none of them would have been able to do unscathed, and approached them through gathering cold twilight with the stride of a conqueror.